Feather and Claw

Susan Handley

Published by Sunningdale Books

A CIP catalogue record for this book is available from the British Library

For my grandmother, Ada Handley

One

The phone danced across the bedside table, its irritating buzz intruding on his dreamless slumber. He stirred and swiped the screen before pressing it to his ear.

'Hello?' he said, his voice still rough with sleep.

'It's me. They've hit again.'

He eased up onto an elbow and rubbed a hand over his face.

'Where?'

'Yanni's. In the Old Town.'

'Anyone hurt?'

'I don't know. I just got here.' He heard the caller mutter something in the background. 'No. No casualties. So, how long?'

He looked over to where she was sleeping. Her arms and legs hung loosely from her slight frame. Her blonde hair clung to her damp forehead. He thought about turning the air-con on. Bad idea, the noise would only wake her.

'I'll need fifteen, twenty minutes to sort things out here and another ten to get there.' He glanced over to the clock. 'I should be with you no later than half-past.' He hung up and sat motionless, letting the meaning of this latest news sink in.

Once again, the hunters had become the hunted.

Two

Barely a ripple disturbed the reflection of the sun and cloud-free sky in the clear blue water of the pool.

'God it's hot,' Cat said.

It was hot. Much hotter than the holiday brochures had predicted for Cyprus in May and almost certainly too hot for skin that hadn't seen the light of day for over six months.

Amy mumbled her agreement, not bothering to raise her head from the sunbed.

Cat flopped back, closed her eyes and let her slim, well-toned body soften, ready to give herself over to the sun and silence. She let out a long breath. A whole week with nothing more demanding than the latest bestseller and God, did she need the break. Work had been so busy recently, all late nights and early mornings.

Sensing a shadow cast over her, she opened her eyes and gave a start on seeing the barman standing over her. She noticed the crepe soles of his black shoes, which accounted for his silent approach.

He set down two glasses onto the white plastic table next to her sunbed.

'Your drinks, ladies.'

Amy stirred and reached for an ice-cold lager. A trail of condensation ran down its side.

'Thank you, Andreas.' She flashed him a smile.

Cat noticed the name badge pinned on his shirt.

'Parakalo,' he said, giving a polite nod.

Amy stared at the retreating figure of the slim-hipped barman, as he walked away.

'I don't know what he said but it sounded good.'

'I think he said you're welcome, but I doubt he meant it literally,' Cat said.

'You're the one who said you needed a bit of sun, sea and—'

'Sleep! I definitely didn't say anything about sex.'

'You won't be able to squirrel yourself away forever.'

Cat closed her eyes, savouring the sunshine on her face.

'I can't believe only this morning we were in a cold and rainy Gatwick.'

'That's the benefit of getting a flight out at stupid o'clock. I told you we'd get a couple of hours in by the pool. And nice try but changing the subject won't wash. This holiday's the perfect opportunity to have a bit of fun.'

'Mike's side of the bed isn't even cold yet. And besides, after the way he treated me I'm in no hurry.'

'Forget him. You just need to move on.'

'Easier said than done. I keep finding his stuff all around the house. Maybe when there are no more reminders of Mike and all the scars have healed, then I'll give you a run for your money.'

Suddenly reminded of the events leading up to her and Mike's split, Cat put a hand to where the wound was still healing, the scar tissue pink and sensitive. A sigh escaped her. She sat up and looked around. Only a handful of loungers were occupied, a few more were reserved with strategically placed towels and books, but the majority lay empty.

'It's so quiet here.'

But she spoke too soon as squeals of laughter carried through the still air, coming from the direction of the children's paddling pool. Cat looked over and spotted a young girl splashing about in the shallow water, shoulders streaked white with high factor sunscreen. Just then, another noise—a loud juddering, scraping

3

sound—drowned out the little girl's giggles. On the other side of the pool, a young man in long trousers and a t-shirt bearing the hotel's logo was struggling to manoeuvre a wooden lounger into a narrow gap alongside a run of sunbeds. Cat let her gaze slide to the neighbouring sunbeds, where three women lay, looking like a trio of life-size Barbie dolls, with flawlessly tanned size-zero bodies and sun-kissed blonde hair tousled to perfection, despite the wilting heat.

The scraping sounds stopped and Cat looked back at the red-faced attendant as he mopped his brow. Out of the shade, a man in a pastel yellow Pringle shirt and patterned shorts, more fitting for a round of golf than a dip in the pool, stepped forward. Small and stocky, he had deep olive skin and a full head of black hair, in spite of his advancing years. He pulled out a thick roll of cash from his pocket and peeled off a couple of notes, pushing them into the hand of the sweating attendant. With the hired-help dispensed with, the man sat on the edge of the sunbed and lifted his sandal-clad feet to lie under a large umbrella, safely screened from the sun.

Cat smiled. With the quiet restored, at last she could relax.

'Are you sure I don't need any more concealer?' Amy asked, dabbing her nose with a powder compact as they walked, her inflamed skin glowing cherry red.

They'd stayed by the pool until dusk, only leaving after the sun had disappeared below the rooftops, taking with it the last of the day's heat.

'It's fine. Just leave it. You'll only make it worse.' Cat looked at her watch and upped her pace. 'We're late.'

'We're not late.'

'It said nibbles and fizz were being served between seven and half-past. It's nearly twenty to eight.'

'I'm sure they'll still be going around, topping up glasses. You know what it's like, nobody ever turns up on time.'

Only it was clear as soon as they walked into the bar, everyone had turned up on time. Every seat was taken and there was no sign of anyone serving the promised pre-dinner champagne and canapés.

'It is busy, isn't it?' Amy said, scanning the room. 'Quick, over there...' She set off, rushing to claim a couple of bar stools just as they were being vacated. In one smooth movement she lifted herself up and leaned forward over the counter, immediately attracting the attention of Andreas, the barman who had served their drinks earlier.

Amy ordered a couple of beers then turned in her seat.

'Hey, nice look.' She nodded towards the door where a woman sporting a Ferrari-red jumpsuit was standing.

Cat recognised her as one of the three blondes from the pool.

The woman took a slow look around and then sauntered, hips swinging, towards a gap at the bar a little further along from Cat and Amy. Closer up, Cat could see the cracks in the veneer. Despite the woman's Botox-boosted brow, peroxide pony tail and the petite frame of a lady who doesn't do lunch—or breakfast or dinner for that matter—it was clear she was no twenty-something. Not even a thirty-something.

Cat felt an elbow jog her arm.

'Looks like Christmas has come early,' Amy said. 'I must have been a very good girl.'

She followed Amy's gaze, towards the door. A tall man with skin the colour of honey and thick black hair that broke into gentle waves at the nape of his neck was scanning the room. He started towards them and joined the blonde in the red outfit.

'Better luck next time,' Cat said.

She reached for her drink and turned back just as the old man from the pool arrived; still wearing Pringle, only this time the

5

colour of strawberry milkshake. He walked towards the bar and raised a hand, clicking his fingers to attract the attention of Andreas. He came to stand next to the blonde woman, who barely acknowledged his arrival, and pressed his hand against her back, his fat fingers splayed wide across her shoulder blades. After a moment, the hand slowly slid down, coming to a stop in the small of her back.

Amy looked back at Cat and twitched her eyebrows, eyes twinkling.

'I may be in luck after all.'

At eight o'clock the waiting staff started to usher guests through to the dining room. The tables and chairs were laid out in a horseshoe. Cat stifled a groan at the prospect of an evening of stilted conversation with some complete stranger seated next to her. A young waitress approached. After asking for their room number she consulted a typed seating list and escorted them to the top of the arc of tables.

'Fantastic,' Amy said. 'We're right in the middle of things.'

Cat took her seat, between Amy and an empty chair, and kept an anxious watch as the other guests entered. All the while Amy recounted stories of previous communal dining experiences.

Andreas was making his way around the room, taking drinks orders. He came over and offered them a large embossed menu.

'You wish to place an order?' he asked.

Amy reached for the menu but Cat was too distracted by the arrival of the old man in Pringle who took a seat a little further along from her. Then the three blondes from the pool joined him. Two of them were little more than teenagers. With their hair worn the same way and sporting the same fashionista outfits, Cat would have found it impossible to tell one girl from the other if it wasn't for a clear height difference.

Cat noticed one of the girls nudge the other. She mouthed something under her breath. A spiteful look pinched her otherwise pretty features.

'Cat!' Amy said loudly.

'Sorry.' Cat turned to Amy who offered her the wine menu.

'Do you want to look at the wine list?'

'I thought wine was included?'

Both she and Amy looked at Andreas.

'Yes, there is the house wine,' he said, 'but if you would like to order from our list, it is specially selected.'

'I'm happy with the house stuff,' Cat said.

'We're okay, thanks.' Amy pushed the menu back towards Andreas who moved on to the next group.

The room had steadily filled and most of the diners were now seated, though the chair next to Cat remained conspicuously empty. She watched as the last few stragglers arrived. Slowly a smile crossed her face.

'Hi. Ethan Garrett.' The tall man from the bar extended a hand. He was even better looking up-close and had smooth Californian drawl to go with his confident, yet gentle handshake.

'Hi. I'm Caitlin. Everyone calls me Cat.'

Cat felt Amy push against her and paused just long enough to be sure she was squirming in her seat before sliding back in her chair.

'Ethan, this is my friend, Amy.'

Amy leaned forward.

'Hi,' she said, offering an extended hand and a bird's eye view of her ample cleavage.

'This is an unusual set up,' Cat said, waving a finger to indicate the room's layout. 'Is it like this every night?'

'No. Tonight's like a gala night. There's entertainment later.'

'Sounds like fun,' Amy said.

'I guess,' he said. 'This is the first one I've been to.'

7

'Did you arrive today as well?' Cat asked.

Ethan opened his mouth to reply but paused when he heard the start of an argument breaking out behind him.

'Tony, just leave it!' snapped the older blonde woman.

Cat looked down the line of chairs and was surprised to see the man in Pringle staring back in her direction, his face screwed into an angry knot. The woman laid a restraining hand on his shoulder but he pushed her away, stood up and started for the door.

Moments later, one of the teenager girls approached Ethan. She bent down to talk to him.

'Daddy's still going on about it. Could you go and explain it again?' She spoke with a silky-smooth voice just loud enough for Cat to recognise that she too was American.

Ethan glanced towards the door, at the old man's retreating back, and frowned. He turned back to the teenager.

'There's no point Isabella. I'll do it tomorrow, when he's calmed down a bit.'

The teenager adopted a pained expression.

'Please?'

Ethan leaned forward in his seat to look down the row of diners, towards where the old man had been sitting.

'Jaclyn!' he called, attracting the attention of the older blonde.

She looked at him and shrugged, rolling her eyes, before resuming her conversation with the man to her right.

Ethan turned back to Isabella.

'If he's not listening to your mother, nothing I can do will make any difference.'

She blinked at him with big doe eyes.

Ethan sighed and shook his head; a small exasperated gesture. He turned and gave Cat and Amy a tight smile.

'Excuse me,' he said, rising from the table.

By the time Ethan reappeared, the food had arrived. In keeping with the themed night, dinner had turned out to be a Greek meze, made up of many little courses that kept coming and coming. Only after the meal was finished and the table was littered with empty plates, did they resume their conversation.

Ethan laid down his cutlery and turned to Cat.

'Well, that was delicious.' He pointed to the dishes scattered in front of her. 'You seem to have had something different to me.'

'It was the vegetarian meze. I don't eat meat.'

'Ah.'

Silence followed, marking the newness of their acquaintance, and then suddenly they both spoke at once. Ethan opened his hand, inviting Cat to speak.

'I was just going to ask how long you've been here,' she said.

'Just over three weeks.'

'Yet this is the first time you've done the Greek night?'

'Technically I'm not here on holiday, more of a business trip. We import speciality Mediterranean foods: artichokes, sun-dried tomatoes, aubergine, porcini, that sort of thing. Well I say we, Tony owns the company. I mainly deal with the logistics.'

'Tony?'

'The guy from earlier, you know...'

'Oh.' Cat looked across at the older man who had since returned to his seat following Ethan's intervention. She cast an eye over the rest of the party.

'Are you all here on business?'

Ethan followed Cat's gaze down the table.

'No. Only me and Tony, and his son, Michael, who's learning the ropes. Oh, and the fair-haired guy in the check shirt, that's David, Tony's lawyer. I guess you could say he's here on business. The women are just here for the sun and the shopping.'

Cat laughed.

'I hope there's not going to be a test later.'

9

Ethan laughed. He took a drink and then carefully set his glass back down on the table, providing a suitably long pause for Cat to get a better look at him.

'What can I say? Tony's a family kinda guy.'

Three

The waiting staff buzzed about, clearing away the remains of the dinner service. Cat passed over her empty coffee cup and refilled her wine glass. She was aware of a growing debate amongst the American group on her right. Ethan's voice could be heard, still calm but a little louder than before. He was responding to the older man, Tony, who was grumbling about something.

Cat turned towards Amy and was surprised to see her slouched in her seat.

'You alright?'

Amy rolled her head towards her, a bored expression on her face.

'Did you know, Cyprus is one of the best locations for watching the migration of birds from Africa to Europe? No? Excuse me while I yawn.'

Cat looked at her.

'What are you on about?'

Her friend shot a glance at the two empty seats on her left, where a long-haired, bearded man and a tiny oriental woman had been sitting.

'Mr and Mrs Beardy Dull. He's a birdwatcher and she's hardly said a word.' She dropped her voice to a whisper, 'I bet she doesn't speak English. Probably an internet bride.'

Cat laughed.

'Oh, come on. You were the one who was like, yeah, let's mix it up. You can't complain if you don't like who you get to mix it up with.'

She knew she'd won the argument when Amy responded by pulling a face.

'Wait, hold that look!' she said, pulling her phone from her bag.

Amy replied with a wide grin.

Cat was about to slip the phone back into her bag when Amy held out her hand.

'Here, let me take one of you.'

Just then the lights dimmed and the chatter faded. A row of spotlights illuminated the area at the front of the horseshoe of tables. Out of the shadows five men in traditional Greek dress filed onto the makeshift stage. The room was silent. A sixth man, similarly attired in a white robe ornately trimmed with red and gold, made straight for a bouzouki resting on a short stool. He picked up the long-necked guitar with a flourish, took a short bow and sat down, settling the instrument across his lap. Slowly he began to pluck out the familiar notes of Zorba the Greek.

The dancers hooked arms and started to cross the front of the room, kicking and twisting their feet. Without warning, Cat found herself transported to a different sun-kissed island, to a different time, one when she and Mike had been happy. The tempo picked up, growing more frantic by the second and Cat's thoughts jumped to more recent times, when infidelity and deceit had reared their ugly heads. Aware of her rising emotions she took a deep breath and banished all thoughts of her ex, forcing herself to enjoy the here and now.

After the formal display, the dancers moved amongst the guests, inviting them to try their hand at Greek dancing. Whether it was effects of the wine or the cheerful coaxing of the staff, almost all of the diners showed willing. Even Cat, if only for ten minutes, after which she excused herself, content just to watch.

'Had enough already?' Ethan asked, as she joined him at the side of the dance floor.

'Having a well-deserved rest.'

She wiped her fingers gently either side of her nose, conscious she might be doing a little more than glowing after her exertions.

'You're not tempted?' she said.

'Two left feet.' Ethan made a point of looking down at his shoes.

Cat laughed.

'Even if anyone noticed I don't think they'd care. Have you seen what's going on over there? I thought Amy was pretty manic but your boss is going for it big time.'

Simultaneously they looked over to the dance floor, to Tony, who did indeed appear to be giving it his all. Despite his unsteady state he was somehow managing to stay vertical. Only just though.

For a moment they stood in silence. When Cat turned back, she was surprised to see Ethan's brow set into a deep V.

He flashed her an anxious look and hurriedly put his whisky glass down on the table.

'I'm sorry. I'll only be a minute.'

She watched as he made for the back of the room, where Jaclyn was leaning against the wall, staring into space, only rousing when Ethan was almost upon her.

It was a short exchange. He talked and she nodded. Finally, she shrugged.

Ethan returned looking altogether more relaxed. He reached for his drink.

'Sorry about that.'

'That's alright,' Cat said. 'Everything okay?'

'Yeah, it's fine. I was worried about Tony. He's a diabetic. From the way he's behaving... well, I just wanted to make sure he'd taken his insulin shot after dinner. It's probably just the drink.' He cast a glance towards the dance floor. Cat noticed the dark circles under his eyes.

'Do you get any downtime while you're here or is it all business?' she asked.

'Actually, we signed the last deal today. I'm off to Cairo on Wednesday for a couple of days.'

'Cairo?' Cat said, wondering if she'd heard him correctly. 'As in Cairo, Egypt?'

'Yes. It's only an hour's flight from Paphos. It's one of the excursions run by the hotel.'

'I had no idea we were that close. Are you all going?'

'No. Just me and Michael.'

'Hey!' Amy bounced off the dance floor, her face all flushed. 'Why aren't you two dancing?'

'We were just chatting,' Cat said.

Amy shot her a look before leaning over and retrieving her glass from the table.

'What's wrong?' Cat asked.

'Nothing,' Amy said. She took a quick mouthful of her beer. 'What are we chatting about?' She directed her question to Ethan, all but turning her back on Cat.

Cat ignored the rebuff.

'We were talking about Cairo,' she said.

'Cairo?'

'I was just telling Cat, I'm off to Cairo for a couple of days on one of the hotel's excursions.'

'Ooh, that sounds like fun. Do you know if there are any spare places?' Amy said.

'Seriously? We've only got a week,' Cat said.

'But I've always wanted to visit Egypt,' Amy said, looking fleetingly at Cat before turning back to Ethan. 'Did you just book it at reception?'

But before he could reply, the sound of a woman's cry from the direction of the dance floor caused all three of them to turn and look.

'Hey! Watch what you're doing,' Tony shouted. The words oozed from his mouth like a man suffering the aftermath of the dentist's chair. He staggered sideways, revealing the diminutive frame of the birdwatcher's wife sitting awkwardly on the floor, shock registering on her face.

Amy let out a spontaneous laugh.

'Did he just knock that woman over?' she said.

Ethan rushed over, stopping to help the birdwatcher lift his wife to her feet. Cat could see him offering his apologies. Just then, Cat felt a hand brush her shoulder.

'Excuse me,' the lawyer, David Foulds, said as he skirted around her.

Tony stood in a small clearing, swaying unsteadily on his feet. He flung out a finger.

'Tomorrow. First thing,' he slurred. 'You'd better be right.'

But the gusto had gone out of him and David Foulds led him away without protest. Cat snatched the phrase 'something to eat' from the air as the two men walked past.

'I wonder what that was all about?' she said.

Amy shrugged and looked down at her empty glass.

'Another round?'

Cat drained the last of her beer and passed Amy her glass.

'I need the loo. I'll come and find you in the bar.'

Cat had to step around Isabella who was standing directly on the other side of the door to the ladies' toilets. Too caught up in her rapid-fire texting on a diamante encrusted mobile, she barely noticed Cat as she squeezed by, heading for the nearest unoccupied cubicle.

Seconds later, Cat heard the bathroom door open followed by the tip tap of heels crossing the tiled floor.

'Isabella, if your father catches you, you'll be in trouble,' came an American woman's voice.

'I was just checking for messages.'

15

'Sure you were.'

'I was. Anyway, Pops needs to loosen up a bit. It's just a bit of fun.'

'Save it lady. It's not me you need to explain to.'

'But Mom...'

Cat left the cubicle just as the teenager left the room, pulling the door to the corridor open with such force it crashed loudly into the wall. Cat made her way over to the hand basins where the glamorous blonde, Jaclyn, was touching up what already looked to be unblemished make-up. Again, Cat adjusted her estimation of the woman's age, figuring her to be nearer fifty than forty, but there was no denying it, she wore it well.

Cat gave a polite smile, feeling a little awkward at having overheard what was clearly intended to be a private conversation.

'Nineteen and she thinks she's invincible,' Jaclyn said, the scowl on her brow and purse of her lips rendering all of her beautifying efforts worthless.

She threw the tube of mascara back into her bag and walked out.

Cat made her way back to the bar, to where Amy was waiting, the two empty glasses still on the counter in front of her.

'Have they stopped serving?' She checked her watch. It wasn't even eleven.

'No, the barman's just taken some drinks through to the other room.'

When Andreas returned, they ordered a couple more beers. He was just pouring the bottled Budweiser into clean glasses when Jaclyn joined them.

'You've got the right idea, stick to the imported stuff. A double Chivas Regal, barman, when you're ready,' she said.

Amy reached for her drink.

'Cheers,' she said, nudging Cat's glass with her own. 'Here's to Cairo.'

Cat opened her mouth to speak but paused, distracted by the arrival of a seriously drunk-looking Tony. David Foulds steered him through the room, to an armchair tucked away in the corner. After seeing Tony comfortably settled, he started towards the bar. From behind her, Cat heard Jaclyn drag her glass of aged whisky over the counter. She approached David, stopping him in his tracks. They stepped close, heads bent in conversation. Shortly, Jaclyn nodded, then left the room, while David Foulds resumed his approach to the bar.

'Two scotch on the rocks. Room three-twelve,' he said to Andreas.

Cat watched the barman take hold of the Chivas Regal bottle without needing to be asked, despite the fact it was twice, if not three times, the price of the most popular branded whisky on offer. David Foulds stared blankly at the optics on the back wall. He roused as Andreas placed two glasses of caramel-coloured liquid in front of him. Walking away, Cat noticed his confident stride. The lawyer appeared a picture of health: tall, lean and muscular, with a full head of hair the colour of Bali sand. Unlike Tony, whose heavily lined skin had taken a swarthy, diseased appearance under the room's unflattering lights. He looked up as David approached and said something. David Foulds muttered something in reply and thrust a tumbler of whisky on to the table, turned and walked out, taking his own drink with him.

Cat turned back to face Amy, who was lazily swirling her beer around the glass.

'You alright?'

Amy looked up.

'Yeah. I was just thinking about this Cairo trip. It wouldn't hurt to see if they've got any spare places...?' She fixed Cat with a hopeful smile.

'I bet you get hardly any time there.'

17

'I thought you'd jump at the chance to see the pyramids and all that ancient stuff.'

'I would but I'd rather do it properly as part of a Nile cruise.'

'It'll be a laugh.'

'I thought you wanted to go for the sightseeing.'

It was an empty challenge. They both knew that Amy's motivation was more Californian than cultural. Her friend slouched back in her seat and adopted a hangdog expression designed to tug at the hardest of heart strings. But Cat was too tired to buy.

'Amy, if you want to go then go, but I don't want to. I'm sorry.'

Cat knew any respite would be short-lived. Amy was unlikely to give in easily, but at least it was off the table for now. She reached for her glass, finishing her drink in one easy mouthful.

'Bedtime I think,' she said and made a move to gather her things.

Across the room, Andreas came through the door, a tray of empty glasses in his hands. As he made his way to the bar Amy jumped out of her seat.

'Let's just have one more. We can go check out the action on the dance floor.'

Earlier in the evening the Greek dancing had been traded for a pop-up disco, DJ'd by a flamboyantly dressed Elvis wannabe, who was attempting to entice the hotel's clientele onto their feet with an eclectic mix of dance tracks.

Cat's shoulders slumped.

'Amy, I'm too tired.'

'Oh, come on. We're on holiday,' Amy urged.

Cat took in the hopeful expression on Amy's face, on top of which she couldn't help but feel a little guilty about Cairo.

'Go on then. One more but them I'm definitely going to bed. And you can forget the disco.'

Amy was at the bar, being served, when the shouting started. Cat looked over. Yet again it was the American, Tony. He had been joined by his son, Michael; lean, long-legged and blessed with a thick head of dark curly hair. It was difficult to tell whether he was older or younger than his sister, Isabella. Teenage girls always looked so much more mature than their years. There was another outburst from Tony and Michael stood hurriedly, causing his chair to tip over. Its wooden back clattered on the tiled floor. He picked it up then rushed out of the room, escaping the slurred shouts of his father.

Left to himself, Tony's words quickly dried up. Cat saw his eyes alight on the scotch, which glowed warmly, courtesy of a nearby table lamp. He reached over and picked it up and started to slowly swirl the liquid around the glass. Presently his hand stilled and his gaze drifted, seeming to focus on nothing in particular. Shortly, he roused himself and looked back at his drink. He knocked it back and reclined in his seat, a morose expression on his face.

For the next twenty minutes Cat and Amy mustered enough small talk to see them through to the end of their drinks. Blinking away the tiredness, Cat stifled a yawn.

'Come on, time to go,' she said.

This time her comment garnered no disagreement from Amy. She reached around for her handbag and jacket. Her hand felt the familiar fabric of her coat but the bag was gone. She twisted to look over the back of her seat. The fallen bag lay underneath her chair, its contents spilled across the floor.

'Oh great!'

She dropped to her knees and started to throw everything back into the bag. After returning what she thought was the last item, she took a last look around and spotted a tube of lip salve underneath a nearby table. She walked over to retrieve it and noticed they weren't alone.

'Amy, look...' She pointed to Tony, slumped in his seat, barely visible above the high sides of the chair.

'Ahh bless, he's nodded off,' Amy said. 'I'm not surprised, the way he was going for it. He's going to have one hell of a headache in the morning.'

On their way out, they stepped aside to let Andreas past. Amy set off behind him but Cat stalled.

'Amy, wait...'

Amy stopped and turned.

'What?'

'Do you think it's okay to leave him there like that? Ethan said he's a diabetic. Isn't too much alcohol dangerous for diabetics?' Even as she said it, she didn't like the sound of it.

Amy shrugged.

'Well I'm worried,' Cat said.

They made their way back to the bar where Cat leaned over the sleeping man.

'Sir, are you alright?'

When Tony didn't respond, Amy stepped forward and, taking a blunter approach, shook him violently by the shoulders.

'Hey mate, wake up. Are you okay?'

Cat stared at his chest, looking for the familiar rise and fall.

'I don't think he's breathing.'

She leaned in and placed her ear close to his face. But instead of the steady somnolent intake of breath and soft breeze of exhaled air there was nothing.

She placed two fingers on the right side of his throat and waited. After a couple of seconds, she moved them slightly, just a fraction of an inch.

'I can't feel any pulse.' She moved to the other side of his neck and repeated the exercise. She shook her head. 'Nothing.'

'Here, let me try,' Amy said.

They switched places.

Cat held her breath, half expecting the man to open his eyes and launch into a verbal assault, spurning their efforts. Only he didn't. There was no doubt about it. There would be no comeback. There was no pulse. He was definitely dead.

Four

He snatched up the phone.

'Another attack?' He was already out of bed and pulling on his jeans.

'No. Not this time,' the caller said flatly.

'What then?' He paused, one leg in and one leg out. 'What's happened?'

The sunlight streamed through the gaps in the curtains and illuminated the face of the clock on the bedside table. It was just after six.

'The old man's dead. A couple of guests found him in the bar around midnight last night.'

'What?' He sat down heavily on the bed.

'No obvious signs of foul play.'

'Seriously?'

'What can I say? That is how it looks.'

'After all this time.' He sounded tired. 'So, what now?'

A pause. He wasn't sure but he thought he detected a sigh.

'Keep your eyes and ears open. There's a chance it isn't what it seems. And, of course, there's still the possibility he wasn't working alone. Just make sure you don't attract any attention to yourself, otherwise it really will be over.'

Five

News of Tony's demise had spread quickly and the atmosphere at breakfast was subdued. For some, the excitement of the night had worn them out and they were lucky enough to sink into a dream-filled slumber from which they would awake refreshed and invigorated. Others, whose memories, pangs of guilt and feelings of regret had taken the place normally reserved for dreams, weren't so fortunate. As a detective in a murder investigation team, more used to dealing with death than most, Cat had slept well and could already feel the stresses of everyday life melting away. She fed two slices of bread into the commercial toaster and watched the comings and goings in the busy dining room while she waited.

The dead man's son, Michael, and lawyer, David, crossed the floor from the direction of the pool. Sporting wet hair and with damp towels thrown over their shoulders they chatted casually and seemed relaxed. Cat was immediately struck by the change in David Foulds. Lines that had previously traversed his brow and puckered the skin above his nose now seemed smoothed. He looked younger and well-rested.

The bread fell from the toaster with a clang and Cat looked down to find two barely-warm, hardly-brown slices lying in the rack. She picked them up and fed them back through.

'Good morning ma'am,' David Foulds said as he joined her at the toaster.

'Morning,' she said, a little surprised. He hadn't seemed the friendly type.

'David Foulds. A close friend of Tony Vostanis.' A perfectly manicured hand gripped hers and pumped enthusiastically.

He picked up a couple of pieces of pre-sliced wholegrain and threw them onto the horizontal rack.

'I understand you're one of the ladies who discovered poor Tony.'

'Yes.' She cast a glance over to the table where the rest of the American party were sitting. 'Please pass on my condolences to his family.'

'Thank you. I'll be happy to. It must have been a real shock.'

'Yes. We thought at first, he'd just fallen asleep.'

'So, he was, you know, gone, when you found him?'

'Yes.'

'No final words or anything like that?'

'No. Nothing. I'm sorry.'

He clamped his lips tight and gave a solemn shake of the head.

The sound of toast rattling out of the bottom of the machine caused them both to look down and before Cat could stop him, David Foulds had picked up her two perfectly golden slices, dropped them onto his plate and walked away. She let out a long sigh and turned back to wait for his two slices to appear, ready for a second grilling.

Twenty minutes later, Cat was pouring the last of the tea from the pot when a little girl hurtled past. Clumsy and uncoordinated, like most of her age, she tripped on nothing in particular and spilled onto the floor. Cat leaned out of her seat and lifted the child to her feet. Dressed in pink gingham, with her blonde braids brushed out, Cat recognised the youngster as the one playing in the pool the previous day.

'Bethany! What did I say about not running?' said a man who had rushed over and now bent to face the child. The little girl's bottom lip began to quiver. He looked her up and down before gently brushing away the tears from her welled-up eyes. 'I think you'll survive.' He stood up and turned to Cat. 'Thanks for picking her up.' A Londoner, probably West London, Cat guessed from his accent. The little girl clung onto her father's leg and mumbled something.

'I think that was a thank you.' He smiled and started to lead his daughter away but paused. 'I'm Phil, by the way.'

'I'm Caitlin. Everyone calls me Cat.' Noticing him glance over at the empty place setting opposite, she added, 'My friend's gone down to the pool to get a couple of sunbeds,' immediately cursing herself for feeling the need to explain why she was breakfasting alone.

'You should be alright. There's normally plenty to go around.'

'Why do you think I'm sitting here enjoying a leisurely breakfast?'

He gave her a warm smile. His hair was a little on the long side, straight and mouse-brown, but his glasses emphasised his eyes, which seemed so alert. He looked bookish, yet handsome in a very English sort of way.

'Well... enjoy the rest of your day,' he said, before shepherding the little girl to a nearby empty table.

Cat lifted her cup to her lips and took a drink. She grimaced. The tea was cold and overly stewed. She put the cup back on the table and reached for her sunglasses.

Amy was, as expected, lying on a sunbed with her head buried in the pages of an open book. Despite Phil's assurances, the pool area was already busy and Cat noticed at least half a dozen sunbeds reserved with towels laid out down their length, including her own.

'Good to see the Americans aren't letting something as mundane as a death in the family put them off their holiday,' Amy said as Cat sat down.

Looking across the pool Cat could see a row of six loungers perfectly aligned to the sun's angle. The shorter of the two teenage girls was lying flat on her front, soaking up the rays. Isabella, the dead man's daughter, was sitting cross-legged on the next lounger, with her slender frame on show, clearly comfortable in her own skin. She had her head bowed and was concentrating on something in her hand. Just then her thumb began to move swiftly over the surface of her mobile phone.

Cat switched her attention to the fourth female of the party and by a process of elimination figured her to be David Foulds's wife. She was a plain, middle-aged woman, so nondescript that she appeared to blend into the background. At that moment Foulds was a very fitting name as she had somehow managed to get herself tangled up in her kaftan as she lifted it over her head, the fabric getting caught in her ample proportions. In sharp contrast to her husband's and daughter's lithe sun-kissed limbs, she had orange-peel skin that looked as though it might burn under the most benign of suns. It was no surprise then that she began to apply a liberal amount of sun cream, its whiteness only emphasising her doughy complexion.

Cat looked over to Amy, engrossed in her novel.

'I think I'll read for a bit. Could you pass the bag over please?'

Without tearing her eyes away from the latest page-turner, Amy reached down and grabbed the striped canvas bag that contained all of their sunbathing paraphernalia.

Two pages in and Cat lost interest. She pressed the book closed. For a moment she considered simply letting the warm morning sun suck the energy from her, but she knew that, as soon as she tried, the stillness would gnaw away at her like the tedium of a long motorway journey.

She reached for the laminated snack menu on the small table next to her sunbed and cast a bored eye over it.

'Do you still fancy going into town for dinner tonight?'

'Huh?'

'Tonight—do you want to go into town to eat?'

'If you want,' Amy mumbled.

Cat threw the snack menu back on the table.

'I think I might just nip over to reception and see if they've got any recommendations. Do you want me to get anything while I'm there?' she said, pulling her t-shirt over her head as she pushed her feet into her flip-flops.

'Nah, I'm fine,' Amy said, and carried on reading.

Cat entered reception though a set of glass double doors, the cool air hitting her like a welcome breeze. As she approached the desk, raised voices cut through the quiet, sounding as out of place as a lovers' spat on Valentine's Day.

'You can't do that! Nobody asked me,' Michael Vostanis shouted.

'But sir, your mother, she cancelled it this morning.'

'She had no right to.'

'I'm sorry sir, but the booking was in her name.' The receptionist gave him an anxious smile.

'You'll just have to make a new booking in my name then,' Michael said.

'Of course, sir. As the trip leaves tomorrow, I'm afraid I will need to take payment in full,' she said calmly.

'Oh, forget it. Stick your trip! I'll find another way of going.'

'Michael!' Jaclyn shouted from the other side of the lobby. 'I'm sorry if he's been any trouble,' she said to the receptionist while shooting her son a look of pure fury.

'Why did you cancel it? You know how much I wanted to go,' Michael said.

Another young woman in a smart suit crossed the floor and slipped behind the desk. She flashed Cat a smile.

'Miss McKenzie, how can I help?'

'I was thinking about eating in the Old Town tonight and wondered if you had any recommendations?'

'Of course, there are many places to eat. There is information here.' She pointed casually to a selection of advertising cards and flyers on a small console to the side of the reception.

The argument playing out to Cat's side grew louder.

'Your father has just died and you want to gallivant off on some stupid trip. For Christ-sakes show some respect.'

'I don't believe it! Even now he's stopping me from doing what I want,' he shouted in a final fit of pique before storming off.

Jaclyn watched him go with red-rimmed eyes. Now there was someone who looked like she hadn't slept a wink.

The receptionist attending to Cat reached down under the counter and brought out a flyer. She slid it across the desk. 'But if I was to recommend just one, I would say Georgis. It is the best.' She lowered her voice, 'It is my uncle's. Tell him I send you and he will do you a very good price.'

Cat took the leaflet, noting the promise of free wine with every order of meze. She thanked the young woman and went over to the table and began to flick through the rest of the information.

'I'm very sorry about that,' she heard Jaclyn say. 'If he gives you any more trouble, just call me.'

Out of the corner of her eye, Cat could see Jaclyn start to walk away.

'Excuse me. Mrs Vostanis,' the receptionist called. 'Please, you are wanted by the manager.'

Jaclyn turned back.

'I'm sorry?'

'The manager. He asked me to call you.'

'But... I thought...' Jaclyn looked in the direction her son had walked off in.

'If you don't mind waiting, one minute, I will get him for you.'

The receptionist walked briskly to the manager's office. When she returned, she was accompanied by an olive-skinned man wearing a light khaki-coloured linen suit. Cat recognised him as the hotel's owner who had been there on her arrival, dishing out smiles along with the complimentary chilled drinks.

'Ahh, Mrs Vostanis. I apologise. I was speaking on the telephone,' he said, approaching the desk. 'The gentlemen over there are with the police.' He signalled to two men who were sitting stiffly on a pair of sofas nearby. 'I believe they wish to speak with you about your husband.'

On seeing him gesture, the man facing them jumped up and started to walk over. Young and keen-looking, he was lean and wiry, with a hooked nose and hooded eyes that gave him a hawkish appearance. But it wasn't him Cat was interested in. Her attention was focussed on his companion, a not so young, solid bull of a man. A man who, when he turned around, seemed as surprised to see Cat as she was to see him. He called over to his colleague. For the briefest of moments, the two men conversed in hushed tones. Cat waited. The younger man gave Cat a cursory look over before ushering Jaclyn into the manager's office.

The second the office door was closed Cat broke out a smile.

'Glafcos!'

'Cat!'

The two engaged in a friendly embrace. The Cypriot detective took a step back and threw his hands wide.

'I can't believe it. How are you? And your...' He flicked a finger in the direction of her midriff, causing Cat to once again reach for her now healed wound.

'I'm fine now thanks. They fixed me up pretty good.'

'Sofia and I couldn't believe it when Alex called to tell us what happened.'

Cat remembered the glut of warm words that had flooded in, wishing her well after her run-in with the wrong end of a boning knife of a since-convicted killer.

'So, you are on holiday here?'

'Yes. I got here yesterday.'

'You should have let me know. You know you are always welcome to stay with us.'

Cat thought back to the hospitality that Glafcos and his wife had extended to her and Alex when they had visited Cyprus only six months earlier.

'I didn't think. My friend organised it.'

'Sofia won't believe it when I tell her.' Glafcos looked over to the closed office door. 'Unfortunately, I have business to attend. Perhaps if you are around later?'

'Sure. Will you be taking statements?'

He gave her a puzzled look.

'Statements?'

'The dead man... Me and my friend were the ones who found him.'

Glafcos's eyes opened wide.

'I heard it was two English ladies on holiday. So that was you?' He paused and looked again at the closed door. 'I don't expect this will take long. If you like, I can come and look for you outside?'

'I don't mind waiting here.'

'Are you sure?'

'Yes, it's no problem.'

'Okay. I will see you shortly.'

Glafcos disappeared into the office. Less than five minutes later, Cat cast a longing look through the glass doors, at the sun-washed walls and azure sky, already regretting her offer to wait indoors. She wandered around the reception, picking up and subsequently discarding flyers advertising local attractions. She had ambled towards the dining room, stopping to read the day's menu, when out of the quiet came a man's laugh, deep and resonant. She turned full circle but the lobby was deserted. The laugh rang out again, followed by a familiar voice, youthful with a laid-back Californian lilt. It was coming from the direction of the kitchen.

'Staff only' a black on silver sign advised.

A hand was clasped around the door's opening edge, holding it ajar. Cat walked slowly past. Just then Andreas and Michael emerged. The barman gave the young American a gentle shove in the direction of the doors to the terrace. Michael turned, and grinning, gave Andreas a friendly shunt with his shoulder, and the two of them walked away, jostling each other and sniggering at some shared joke.

She glanced back at the closed office door through which a tired-looking Jaclyn had been shown, wearing the previous night's tragedy on her pale and lined face. Reasoning the meeting was unlikely to be quick, she followed the two men into the heat, to the terrace bar.

Michael was already sitting at the counter when Cat got there. She perched on the stool next to him. The place was otherwise empty.

Andreas acknowledged her arrival with a polite nod.

'Two beers?'

'Just a Coke please,' she replied.

Andreas walked over to the large chiller at the back of the bar area and returned with two cans of Coke. Cat was about to correct his mistake when he placed one of the cans in front of Michael.

'Ice?' he said, looking at her as he reached under the counter for a chilled glass.

'Please,' Cat said.

He filled the glass one third full of ice then cracked open the can and began to pour.

He turned to Michael.

'So, you are not going now?'

Michael reached for his drink.

'No. She's made her mind up. It doesn't matter what I want.' He snapped open the tab and drank straight from the can. 'Never does.'

Andreas shook his head ruefully but then his expression lifted.

'But now you spend time here, and in the kitchen. It will be fun, no?'

'Sure,' Michael said with a hint of a smile, but just as quickly it was gone, blanked out by a frown. 'I'll tell you something though. If she thinks I'm going to run the old man's business for her now, she can forget it. But you know the stupidest thing?' he said, a flush of colour appearing on his cheeks. 'I bet she won't even ask me because she doesn't think I'm up to the job. Dad was always saying how I didn't understand, how I didn't get it, and she always took his side. But he was the one who didn't get it. He couldn't see what was right under his nose. I knew he'd go ballistic. Wish I hadn't told him now.'

All of a sudden Michael stopped talking and fixed Cat with a look. She realised she'd been staring.

'I gotta go,' he said, slipping off his stool and setting off across the terrace, back towards the hotel.

Cat looked down, embarrassed at having been caught eavesdropping.

'Can I get you anything else?' Andreas asked, his expression giving nothing away.

'No, thanks.'

Andreas presented his notepad on the counter in front of her and handed her a pen.

32

'It's terrible, what happened. His father's death, I mean,' she said, signing for the Coke.

The barman said nothing.

'I had no idea that alcohol could be so dangerous for someone with diabetes.'

He gave her a puzzled look.

'Mr Vostanis do not drink too much even though he act crazy.'

'Oh, I just assumed...'

Andreas picked up a damp cloth and moved to the back of the bar where he began wiping down the worktop.

Nice one Cat.

Back in reception the office door was still closed. She hoped that meant Glafcos's discussion with Jaclyn was longer than her absence. She looked at her watch—it had been a little under ten minutes.

At the desk a young woman with large almond-shaped eyes and hair the colour of polished mahogany smiled up at her.

'Miss McKenzie, hello, what can I do for you?'

'Do you know whether the two detectives are still in the office with the American lady?'

'Yes, they are. Would you like me to tell them you are here?'

'No, thank you. I'll wait.'

Cat made herself comfortable on a minimalist sofa in pale green nubuck. The ten minutes that followed felt more like thirty but eventually the door to the corner office opened and voices emerged. Jaclyn appeared, looking even more drawn than she had. She crossed the smooth marble floor to the terrace without as much as a backward glance.

Cat continued to wait. A further five minutes later the door opened a second time and the two detectives appeared. After a short exchange of goodbyes, they started across the room, conversing with lisping and lilting consonants that sounded

Spanish to Cat's unskilled ear. As they drew level, she looked up, smiling. The chat stopped.

'Cat. Good of you to wait.' Glafcos turned and said a few words to his colleague, who then walked off in the direction of the hotel's front entrance.

Glafcos sat down opposite her. A big man, he sank low into his seat, his knees coming uncomfortably close to his chin. Two hirsute shins peered out from under his trouser legs, above a pair of startling white socks. He shunted himself forward and perched on the sofa's edge, recovering his decorum.

'How are you?' Cat asked.

'Busy. So busy.'

'In this sleepy idyll?'

Cat remembered Glafcos's account of policing on the low crime island and his seemingly perfect lifestyle when they'd first met.

'You'd feel quite at home here at the moment,' he said. 'We've got a drug epidemic in the tourist resorts, an arsonist who's come back for their fourth season and now a sudden death. How does that compare to life in your English CID?'

'Add a few car thefts, a handful of robberies with violence and half a dozen stabbings and you'll be half way there.' She gave him a playful wink. 'Anyway, it's good to see you.'

'If only it was under better circumstances.'

The fact that Glafcos had travelled out to meet with the newly grieving widow struck Cat. She leaned forward.

'Not natural causes then?' she asked, keeping her voice low.

'On the face of it, it certainly looks like he died from hypoglycaemia but more tests are needed.'

'Hypoglycaemia? What causes that... the wrong dose of insulin?'

'Amongst other things, yes. We have sent his empty syringes for testing. His wife seems to have put his death down to the fact that he liked his food and drink too much, on top of which he'd worn himself out playing the fool on the dance floor. The doctor says it's possible those things could have brought on the attack, but...'

He shook his head, clearly troubled.

Cat cocked her head and fixed him with her green eyes.

'Do you think his wife killed him?'

'No. What makes you...? Ahh, the meeting, just now. No, that was just a formality.'

'But you do suspect something.'

Glafcos inched forward on his seat and leaned in closer.

'Mr Vostanis was being looked at as part of an international operation. It is possible somebody got to him before we did and dealt him their own kind of justice.'

Cat's mouth fell open.

'What? What had he been doing?'

'He has an import business. We think it is—'

Glafcos looked up, over Cat's head, and nodded. She turned just in time to see his colleague leave through the front door.

'I'm sorry but I must go,' Glafcos said as he eased out of his seat, tugging the sides of his trousers down.

Cat stood up.

'Of course. We can catch up later. I assume you'll be around as part of the investigation?'

He gave a doleful shrug.

'You know how it is. As much as it pains me to say it, no evidence, no investigation.'

Six

Cat was crossing the terrace, on her way back to the pool, wondering what Amy thought of her extended absence—she suspected it had gone unnoticed—when she spotted a white-haired man peering at her over the top of his broadsheet. She saw him say something to the grey-haired woman sitting next to him, who in response set down her own paper, revealing a half-completed crossword. The woman glanced over at Cat and then turned to her companion. She gave him a vexed look and stern shake of the head before returning to her crossword.

The man's expression suddenly brightened.

'Hey,' he said loudly. 'There's Brian.'

Cat followed his gaze and saw the tall, gangly, bearded man who Amy had taken to calling Mr Beardy-dull. Dressed in a shabby safari suit, sandals and white socks pulled up to his calves, he was carrying enough camera equipment to give a BBC documentary crew a run for their money, ticking all of the boxes of a stereotypical twitcher.

'Hey Brian! Brian!' the man called, waving enthusiastically. 'I bet he won't have heard about what's happened,' Cat heard him say just before she walked out of earshot.

Amy was lying in exactly the same position as when she had left her.

'Hey,' Cat said, settling on the side of her lounger.

Amy lowered her book.

'Hi. What've you been up to?'

'I told you, I went to ask about places to eat out, for tonight,' she said, omitting to mention the Coke in the bar and the chance encounter with Glafcos.

'You've been ages.'

'Sorry.'

'It's alright. It's just that I've ordered us some drinks. I got you a beer.'

'Ugh, I don't know if I can stomach alcohol this early,' Cat said, aware that she was in danger of sounding ungrateful.

'It's not that early. Besides I ordered something to eat as well. And before you say anything, I ordered two different things. You can have whichever you prefer.' Amy turned her attention back to her book, leaving Cat feeling even more selfish. It hadn't occurred to her to get her friend anything.

While waiting for their food to arrive, Cat thought about everything that had happened since her arrival. Recollecting the scene in reception between Jaclyn and Michael, she wondered whether Amy had been busy organising something other than just a bite to eat.

'Have you done anything about going to Cairo yet?'

Amy turned on her side and regarded her friend.

'No. Why? Changed your mind?'

'No. It's just I heard the dead man's wife has stopped their son from going. You might find Ethan will cancel as well.'

Amy hitched herself up on to her elbow.

'Of course. I didn't think of that. How did you hear about the kid not going?'

'I overheard them when I was in reception.'

'Do you think they've been told not to leave by the police?' '

'No. Jaclyn said something about it being disrespectful.'

'Jaclyn?'

'The wife.'

'She might be saying that to save face,' Amy said.

'I don't think so. I spoke to one of the detectives. They're putting Tony's death down to his diabetes.' She caught the shocked expression that appeared on Amy's face and hurriedly added, 'I wanted to know if they needed a statement.'

'I take it they don't?'

'He said not at the moment. Though they're still waiting for some test results.'

'Unlikely then. Good. I didn't much fancy interrupting my holiday to traipse to some dreary police station just to give a statement,' Amy said, before lying back down and returning to her book.

Cat frowned.

'I don't follow. You don't think they'll find anything?'

'No.'

'Why?'

Amy sighed and lowered the paperback.

'They've got a diabetic who died as a result of suspected hypoglycaemia. He'd had a big meal with alcohol on top of his insulin and then spent the evening jumping around. It's not that surprising. They're not going to spend time and money trying to find which of those things brought it on.'

Glafcos's need for evidence suddenly made sense.

Amy lifted her book back up.

'You really should learn to relax more. You're not at work now.'

Cat had to agree. Though she wasn't going to say as much. Instead, she let her gaze roam, taking in the poolside, full of people relaxing and soaking up the sun. Suddenly envious of everyone else's ability to take it easy, she reached for her book and opened its stiff pages but after only a few paragraphs she closed it and set it beside her.

'You know, I don't remember seeing him drink very much,' she said.

Amy answered without bothering to lower her book.

'Cat, the guy was reeling drunk. He could barely stand up.'

'But was he? Isn't it possible whatever killed him made him act like that? It's not exactly the same, but nitrogen narcosis can cause scuba divers to behave like they're drunk.'

'Nitrogen what?'

'Narcosis. It makes you think and act irrationally, as if you're drunk. They call it the raptures of the deep. Pretty dangerous when you're thirty meters under water.'

'Never heard of it,' Amy said, rolling onto her side, turning her back to Cat.

Ten minutes later a waiter arrived with their lunch—two plates of sandwiches and two bottles of beer. Amy even put her book down unprompted.

Cat reached for a sandwich.

'Fancy going for a walk later?'

'Maybe tomorrow,' Amy said mid-mouthful.

'How about a drive then? We could check out the local shops or visit one of the places in the guide book. I think the Baths of Aphrodite are quite close to here. They might be worth a visit?'

'I thought you wanted a week lying in the sun. Recharge your batteries. That's what you said.'

'Well, I've done some of that, now I fancy doing something different. Anyway, I thought you'd be up for a bit of culture. I know it's not exactly Cairo but how about it?'

Amy involuntarily, or maybe voluntarily, let out a sigh.

She held her paperback up to judge how far through she was.

'I was hoping to get this finished today. And besides, I've just got to an interesting bit.'

'And then can we do something else?'

'I suppose.' She didn't exactly sound keen.

Once lunch was over, Cat flopped back onto the lounger, where she lay quietly, despite feeling fidgety. Remembering her book, she gave it another go and managed to stick with it for a couple of pages. Eventually, regretting her impulse to experiment with her choice of holiday reading, she put the book down and sat up.

Most of the sunbeds were now occupied by only a towel, set out to deter all but the most resolute squatters. The only other guests toughing it out under the midday sun were the two American girls. Their slender honey-hued bodies lay like sacrificial offerings to the sun god.

Cat's attention drifted back to her own body, down to her still white legs, which felt strangely restless, unaccustomed to lying idle. She thought of her trainers languishing at the bottom of her wardrobe. It had been two days since they were last pulled on, and for a while she contemplated the weight gain she could reasonably expect with the good food, free-flowing drink and none of the compensating plus points that a five-mile run had to offer.

She stood up.

'I'm going for a swim.'

Not waiting for a reply, she walked over to the pool's edge and, without pause, dropped into the water. She submerged completely until only the tresses of her hair remained, swirling in the eddy that followed. And then she shot back up, emerging from the water like a fishing float, her eyes and mouth wide open in shock—the meaning of *unheated* having hit home. She took a couple of breaths and then slipped back under the water, porpoising into a graceful front crawl, before ending the lap with a tumble-turn that barely created a ripple. Already she had found her pace and for thirty minutes she swam lap after effortless lap.

She slowed and swam over to the side near to where Amy was lying, book in hand.

'Hey, Amy, come on in. The water's lovely.'

'You know I can't swim.'

40

'I know you can swim, you just choose not to.'

'Same difference.'

'No, it isn't. The former would be forgivable as a product of a deprived childhood. The latter is just you being a lazy moo.'

Amy rolled onto her side, turning away from Cat, and carried on reading. Cat realised then, no amount of cajoling was going to entice her friend into doing anything different. She climbed out of the pool and padded back to her sunbed. Sitting on its edge, she pulled a comb through her hair, gently working through the knots. Over on the other side of the pool, Jaclyn and David Foulds started down the steps from the terrace. They stopped at the bottom, deep in conversation. In stark contrast to his relaxed demeanour at breakfast, David Foulds seemed agitated. Doing most of the talking, he was leaning in close to Jaclyn, her pinched expression doing little to discourage him.

'I'm just going to stretch my legs while I dry off,' Cat said.

She jumped up and pulled her t-shirt and shorts on over her damp bikini and started around the pool's edge, but by the time she reached the steps, Jaclyn was getting comfortable on a sunbed and David Foulds had disappeared. Not wanting her interest in them to look too obvious, Cat continued past, climbing the few steps up to where a handful of diners were enjoying a late lunch. Phil and Bethany were among them, sitting on one of the wicker sofas, bent over a large drawing pad. He looked up and smiled. Fine lines fanned from his eyes and mouth. Did he laugh a lot, she wondered?

He'd switched his shirt and linen trousers for a t-shirt and board shorts and without his glasses looked less bookish, more rugged and masculine. Cat returned the smile, then glanced down at the colourful crayoned picture the young girl was busy creating.

'That's very good. Aren't you clever?' she said.

A podgy finger pointed to the three lollipop-headed figures holding hands across the page like a nuclear family paper-chain.

'Daddy and me and Maria.'

'Would you like to join us?' Phil said. 'I'm sure Bethany would love to draw a picture of you, wouldn't you?'

'Yeah!' the little girl shouted, beaming excitedly.

'That would be nice.' Cat looked at Bethany, 'Where shall I sit?'

'Here.' She patted a flat hand on the sofa. 'Next to Daddy.'

Phil shifted over to make room before waving a hand in the direction of the bar.

'Hey Andreas! Could we have some drinks over here please?'

Andreas, who was busy re-stocking the shelves in the outdoor bar, stopped what he was doing and headed over to their table.

Phil handed him an empty glass, its sides streaked chalky white.

'Another milkshake please and I'll have a pint of lager, and... what is the going rate for life-models these days?' he said, addressing the question to Cat, who shook her head.

'I'm fine thanks,' she said. 'I just had a beer.'

Bethany turned over a new page in her colouring book. She looked up at Cat and began to draw.

'I heard you had a bit of a shock last night,' Phil said. Cat gave him a puzzled look. 'The dead guy...? It was you and your friend who found him, wasn't it?'

'Oh that. Yes.'

'Awful thing to happen. His family must be devastated.'

Cat's thoughts flicked back to Michael, larking around with Andreas in the kitchen.

'I imagine so,' she said.

'Did he say anything, you know before he...?'

Twice in one day.

'No. He was already gone by the time we got to him.'

'At least he can't have suffered much, I suppose.'

Silence began to bloom.

'Have you been here before?' Cat asked, cursing her lack of originality.

'To Cyprus or this hotel? Actually, I don't know why I said that, the answer's the same. This is the first time.'

Phil looked down at the picture that was starting to form from Bethany's painstaking labours. Cat was lost for words. The stick figure in the picture had a head twice the size of its body and was looking more like Mrs Potato Head with every stroke of the orange crayon. Cat gave an uneasy smile. Inspired, Bethany swung the wax stick across the page, giving the potato head a gaping maw of a mouth.

'How about you?' Phil said.

For a second Cat was thrown by his question, having been on the verge of commenting on the disparity between her emerging likeness and the mysterious Maria's: Munch's Scream and Mona Lisa's smile coming to mind.

'First time too,' she said.

'How are you finding it? Are you enjoying it? Apart from last night, obviously.'

'Hmm.' She looked back across to the pool, to Amy, still lying on her sunbed. 'To be honest, I'd forgotten just how much I hate sitting around in the sun doing nothing. I had my fill of that for a couple of years after I finished Uni.'

'How did you manage that? I left Uni and went to work in an office. All I did was make coffee and run errands. I swear I was known as Phil the photocopy boy.'

Cat smiled.

'I was lucky enough to do some post-grad research in the Maldives. Apart from work, there wasn't much else to do other than sunbathe.'

'I bet you were gutted when that ended?'

43

Cat thought back to the fateful phone call that prompted her hasty departure from that tropical paradise and changed her life forever.

'I was sad to leave but it was the right thing to do. It was time to go home.' Aware the conversation had taken more of a reflective turn than expected, she quickly added, 'What about you?' What do you do now? I assume you're not still photocopying for a living.'

'Daddy makes people safe,' Bethany answered, without looking up from the picture.

Cat gave him a quizzical look.

'Armed forces?'

He gave a quick shake of his head.

'Security,' he said, before jumping up to help the approaching barman. 'Here, let me give you a hand.' He lifted a glass of flavoured milk and set it down on the table. 'A strawberry milkshake for missy here and this one's for me,' he said, taking hold of the pint. 'Are you sure you don't want anything?'

Cat shook her head.

'No. I'm fine thanks.'

'Okay, well, cheers.' He took a swig of beer. 'God, that's good.'

Just then Bethany started to tug urgently at the leg of Cat's shorts.

'Finished. Look...' she said, pointing to her drawing. 'You, me and Daddy.'

Phil and Cat leaned over at the exact same time.

'Very good,' she enthused, fighting to suppress a laugh.

Cat returned to her sunbed only find two towels and no Amy. She was even more surprised when she was still on her own some twenty minutes later.

She climbed the steps to the terrace and scanned the occupants of the wrought iron dining chairs and wickers sofas. Phil was still there, sitting next to Bethany, who was crayoning in the outline of a pony with the concentration of a neurosurgeon. No sign of Amy.

She caught Phil's eye. He smiled.

'Lost my friend,' she said.

Phil pointed towards a row of shrubs that edged the terrace.

'You might want to look over there. I'm sure I heard a woman's voice. I think it sounded English.'

'In the bushes?'

Phil laughed.

'The ground floor junior suites are on the other side of the hedge.'

Cat approached the bushy border and looked over into the suites' private patios. Amy was leaning on the balustrade of the second room along, chatting animatedly to Ethan, who was relaxing in one of two patio chairs. He glanced up, and on seeing Cat, gave a friendly wave. Amy followed his gaze. She held up a hand, all five fingers extended. Cat nodded before walking back over to Phil.

'Mind if I join you?' she asked. 'If I've understood correctly, Amy should be here in about five minutes.'

Some ten minutes later Amy made an appearance.

'Howdy,' she said, flopping onto the empty two-seater opposite Cat. She looked pointedly at Bethany. 'Where's...?'

'Little boy's room.'

'Oh, okay.' Amy picked up a large folded cocktail menu from the table, the type made of laminated card with faded photographs. 'Hey, they do margaritas. We could have one before dinner.'

'Maybe,' Cat said. 'So, how's Ethan?'

Amy gave her a big grin.

'Gorgeous as ever. And you were right, he's not going to Cairo. So that solves that problem. You know, he didn't know anything about the detectives talking to Jaclyn.'

'Oh Amy, I told you that in confidence.'

'You didn't say it was a secret. He was—'

Phil's return caused both of them to look up. He walked around the two-seater that now housed Amy and sat on the arm of an empty wicker chair.

'Hi,' he said, smiling. He turned to Cat, 'Thanks for watching her.'

'You're welcome.'

Phil gestured towards the printed sheet in Amy's hand.

'I can recommend the mojito, if you're after something refreshing.'

'Thanks, but I was thinking more for later. Something to get the party started, if you know what I mean.'

She returned the cocktail menu to the table.

'Feel free to join us. For a drink before dinner, I mean. That's if you're around,' Cat said.

'I'm not sure we'll have time. You wouldn't believe how long it takes to get a four-year-old ready. Maybe after dinner?'

'It's a date,' Amy said.

'Great,' Phil said, sounding a little uneasy. 'Talking of getting ready, I think we'd better make a move.' He started to pull their things together. 'Come on Bethany, time to go. Pick up your colouring books.'

With an unquestioning obedience only a child of so few years could demonstrate, Bethany gathered her books in her arms, took her father's hand and began to pull him in the direction of the lobby.

Amy laughed.

'Do you think I frightened him off?'

Cat shook her head and rolled her eyes.

46

'You're incorrigible,' she said, trying to make light of it, though wishing Amy would sometimes be a little less Amy-like.

Unlike the previous evening, Cat and Amy made their way down to dinner earlier than most and had their pick of where to sit. After settling for a large wicker sofa out on the terrace, they ordered a couple of classic margaritas and waited for the evening crowd to gather.

'Maybe we could eat out tomorrow?' Cat said. 'It'd be good to explore.'

'Yeah, whatever. You know me, I'm easy.'

It was beginning to dawn on Cat that she didn't know her friend anywhere near as well as she'd thought.

'Anyway, you might think differently by tomorrow, depending on what happens tonight,' Amy added.

'What do you mean?'

'Phil, the luscious Londoner.'

Cat let out a laugh that sounded more like a cough.

'Don't be stupid.'

'He's our age, he's single, and he's not bad looking. You should go for it.'

'Why don't you go for it,' Cat said, the words out of her mouth before she could stop them.

Amy hitched an eyebrow.

'Maybe I will.'

'Really?'

Amy scooped her legs up onto the seat and tucked them under her.

'Nah. He is nice. In fact, he's quite fit but he's not my type. Anyway, he's got baggage.'

'What do you mean baggage? You don't mean his daughter? Loads of single men have got children.'

'The ones I go out with haven't. It's bound to cause complications.'

'Of course, and there was me thinking you were only after a holiday fling. How silly of me.'

'I am. Why do you think I'm after the guy with a room to himself?'

The one cocktail turned into a few, for Amy at least. Cat made do with just the one margarita. By the time they were ready to make a move, the terrace had filled and since emptied, and was once again deserted save for the two of them. Amy stood up and walked unsteadily toward the hotel lobby. She pushed on the glass door just as Ethan was coming through and stumbled into him.

'Oh, I'm sorry,' he said, putting out a steadying hand.

'S'alright. Come and have a drink.'

Cat shot Amy a look. They needed food, not more drink, but Ethan saved her from having to say anything.

'Thanks, but I can't stay. I'm looking for Jaclyn. I don't suppose you've seen her?'

'No, sorry,' Cat said.

'Forget about that old sourpuss. Come with us,' Amy said, hanging on to his arm.

'Maybe later,' he said, easing her off him. He gave them both a tight smile and strode away.

Cat slipped her arm through her friend's.

'Come on. Let's go eat.'

Throughout dinner, Cat found herself fixated with the Americans. Michael and David Foulds kept each other amused, growing more boisterous as the evening wore on. By the end of the dinner service they were surrounded by a collection of empty wine bottles, both visibly worse for wear and proving to be quite disruptive. As a result, the tables nearest to theirs had all emptied unusually early.

The other Americans all looked understandably downbeat. Jaclyn, who had arrived after Cat and Amy had been seated, seemed especially withdrawn. Cat hadn't seen her talk to anyone other than the waiting staff. For the most part, she had sat quietly, with her head down, staring at a small patch of table in front of her.

The arrival of dessert and coffee brought Cat's attention back to her own table. Amy had eased off the alcohol and had hungrily devoured her dinner and was now tucking into a large helping of baklava with ice cream. Cat toyed with her tiramisu, too full to really appreciate it. Just then Bethany went running past, her sandals slapping noisily on the tiled floor. Phil followed a short distance behind. As Cat looked up, he smiled and stopped by her table.

Bethany turned and put her hands on her hips.

'Come on, Daddy.' She walked up to him and seized hold of his hand, pulling him in the direction of the door. 'Stop being a slow-coach.'

Phil resisted, holding his ground.

'We're just going through to the bar now. You're welcome to join us when you've finished. It should be a lot more civilised than here,' he said, with a pointed look in the direction of the American men.

'Don't bet on it,' Amy said. 'I can be something of a rabble-rouser after a few drinks.' She started to laugh.

Phil gave her an uncertain look before turning to Cat.

'Well, you know where we are if you want to join us.'

'Ahh, how sweet,' Amy said after he'd gone.

'I thought it was nice of him.'

'I was only having a laugh. I think someone's a little smitten.'

Cat shook her head but said nothing.

After dinner, she and Amy moved into the bar. Phil was sitting at a table in the corner, engrossed in a conversation with the man she recognised as one half of the newspaper-reading couple on the terrace that morning. Not wanting to intrude she followed Amy to the counter. Andreas had just taken their order when Cat sensed someone enter the sliver of space between her and Amy. She bristled a little, given the bar wasn't busy.

'Hallo,' came a voice from behind her.

She turned to see a white-haired, ruddy-faced man beaming at her. It was the same man who had been talking to Phil; the one who had watched her as she'd crossed the terrace earlier in the day. His pink head was tufted with white candyfloss hair and his belly, tight as a watermelon, strained at the waistband of his canvas slacks. He looked like a smooth shaved Father Christmas.

He thrust a hand between them, its stubby fingers extended outwards like an inflated rubber glove.

'Tom Collins. You know, like the cocktail,' he said. 'Thought I'd come over and introduce myself.'

'Hi. I'm Amy and this is Cat,' Amy said, transferring her wine glass to her left and shaking his hand.

'Phil said to come over and let you know where we were.' He turned and pointed towards the corner.

Phil spotted them looking, smiled and raised a hand.

'We wouldn't want to intrude.' Amy said.

Cat looked at her friend and frowned. She'd never known Amy to turn an invitation down.

'Don't be silly,' Tom said. 'There's plenty of room. We'll easily squeeze in another couple of chairs.'

Just then a voice, female and refined, called out.

'Tom, are you being a nuisance?'

Tom broke into a broad grin as the owner of the voice arrived, a remarkably tall woman, whose height only served to emphasise his roundness.

'This is my wife, Rose.' He puffed his chest out proudly. 'These are the two ladies who arrived yesterday. Amy and—'

'Cat,' she supplied readily, not waiting to find out whether he'd forgotten her name already.

'Hello. Nice to meet you. Come on Tom. Leave these two ladies to enjoy their evening.'

'They're coming over to join us, aren't you? No fun sitting on your own all night.'

Cat reached for her drink and started after him.

'Grab a couple of chairs and we'll make some space,' Tom said, putting his considerable weight to the side of a large chair.

'It's all right. We don't want to...' Amy started to reply, but Cat had already put her drink down, freeing her hands so she could drag over the nearest seat.

Phil looked up at from a comfy looking armchair.

'Sorry, I'd offer to help but...'

For the first time Cat noticed the little girl fast asleep on his lap. Phil was gently stroking her hair and forehead.

Once they were all settled, Tom wasted no time. He leaned forward in his seat and his face lit up.

'So, come on then, you two were the ones who found old Tony, tell all.'

'It wasn't that exciting,' Cat said. She noticed Rose's eyes widen and reminded herself that most people wouldn't find discovering a dead body quite as commonplace. 'I mean it was more sad than exciting. We had no idea there was anything wrong. It just looked like he'd fallen asleep in his chair. We were going to leave him but one of the Americans had mentioned he was diabetic so we thought we'd better just check he was okay.'

'Was he already gone or...?' Tom asked.

'Oh no, he was dead. Unfortunately. Otherwise we could have at least tried to do something.'

Tom turned to his wife, looking disappointed.

'We only just missed it then.'

'Tom don't be so ghoulish. The poor man simply dropped dead where he sat. There was nothing to see,' Rose said. 'It was probably all that arguing that did it. Used to tire me out just listening to him.'

'Was he always argumentative?' Cat asked.

'Oh yes,' Rose said. 'Never a day would go by without him having a go at someone for something. Nobody could ever do anything right. He'd snap at that young lad of his for not being interested in the business; and at the girl about being glued to her phone; and at the wife about her spending. I said before, he was courting a heart attack. He always seemed as tightly wound as a spring.'

'It wasn't a heart attack, it was hypoglycaemia,' Amy said, drawing a look of surprise from around the table. Cat glowered at her and she shrugged. 'At least that's what I heard,' she said, reaching for her drink.

'Well I must say, that is a surprise,' Rose said.

Tom was nodding.

'That poor boy. He was obviously beating himself up for nothing. I did think he seemed a lot less stressed tonight.'

'What's that?' Cat asked.

'Michael, Tony's son,' Rose said. 'Last night, after we'd gone to bed, there was a bit of a commotion. Our room's next door to his. When David, you know, the blonde gentleman, came and broke the news, Michael made such a fuss it was impossible not to hear.'

'I thought I'd better go and see if I could help,' Tom said.

'More like, you went and poked your nose in, thinking you were missing out on something,' Rose said.

Tom smirked like an embarrassed school boy.

'What sort of thing was he saying?' Cat asked.

'He was going on about how it wasn't his fault. Insisting his father was alright when he left him. I just assumed Tony had a heart attack and the boy thought he'd caused it.'

Rose opened her mouth, about to say something, but paused, distracted by the appearance of the shorter of the two American girls who stormed through the room with a puffed-up swagger. David Foulds, her father, rushed after her, red-faced and tight-lipped.

'Larissa! I haven't finished talking to you. Come back here now,' he hissed through clenched teeth.

She turned abruptly.

'Well I'm done listening. And anyway, who are you to lecture me on morals?' she snapped back. She grabbed the arm of her friend who had just entered the room. 'Come on Issy. I need to pee.' She strode off in the direction of the bathrooms, towing her friend behind her.

David Foulds stood fixed to the spot. If it had been a cartoon, steam would have been coming out of his ears. Gillian, his wife, had followed him in. She walked over and laid a hand gently on his arm. He looked down and brushed her off him as though she were a piece of lint on his sleeve. Cat saw the hurt appear on her face.

'Did you hear what she said to me?' he said. He looked at his wife accusingly. 'What did she mean? What have you been saying?'

Surprise registered on Gillian's face.

'I haven't said anything. I don't know what she meant.'

'I don't believe you. You women can't keep anything to yourselves.'

David Foulds clenched his fists and Cat saw his chest heave as he took a deep breath. Without another word he turned around and strode off. Gillian stood there, staring at the spot vacated by her husband. Shortly she roused herself, as though waking from a trance. Most people had the decency to at least pretend not to have noticed the altercation. For those that hadn't, she looked around at them and gave a sad smile before ambling off.

'Poor woman,' Rose said.

'They never fail to entertain, do they?' Tom said.

'I must admit, I can't say I blame him for being angry. He's probably got wind of what she's been up to,' Rose said. Everyone around the table, apart from Tom, looked at her, wide-eyed with anticipation. 'It's only what one of the cleaners told me. Apparently,' she dropped her voice, 'she's had one less bed to make recently. It seems Larissa has been keeping her toes warm under someone else's duvet.'

'It's hardly a surprise. The girl is man-mad,' Tom said. 'She's gone after anything and everything in trousers since the day they arrived.'

'Whose bed?' Amy asked sharply.

'The cleaner said she didn't know.'

'I'm still waiting for it to be my turn,' Tom said, chuckling. Rose shot him a look. 'Just my little joke, my darling,' he said, patting her on the knee, while directing a wink towards Phil. 'Hey, do you remember how she was making eyes at Andreas when she first arrived?' Tom turned to Cat and Amy. 'Shortly after they got here, it can only have been their second or third day, I was sitting here and Rose was... she was... actually I forget where she was, but that girl, Larissa, well she was on the other side of the bar. I don't think she realised I was here. She was flirting with Andreas, giving him the come on. Well, I'm no prude but I was amazed at how brazen she was.'

'And he wasn't interested?' Amy said, sounding surprised.

'He spelled it out to her as clearly as he could without being rude, but he left her in no doubt she wasn't his cup of tea.' Tom started to chuckle again. 'Well, she left with a face like thunder.

And the language! If I hadn't heard it myself I wouldn't have believed it from a young girl like that.'

'That probably explains what happened in the dining room when we were waiting to be shown to our table last night,' Cat said, turning to Amy, 'Remember?'

'No.'

'Andreas was talking to us, asking what wine we wanted, when the two girls walked past. That one, Larissa, mouthed something to her friend. At the time Tony was just ahead of them. I thought she was referring to him.'

'What did she say?' Rose asked.

'She said prick. Given what you've just said I imagine it was for Andreas's benefit, not Tony's.'

'I suppose she's not used to rejection. Pretty girl like that,' Tom said.

'The arrogance of youth,' Rose said. 'I bet she thought she'd be the one to change the man.'

'She'd have had a job,' Tom said.

'I don't understand. What am I missing?' Cat asked.

'He's gay,' Rose explained.

Suddenly the image of Andreas and Michael slipping out from the kitchen surfaced in Cat's mind. Michael was the last person to speak to Tony—not a happy exchange, either. She couldn't help wonder what the cause of their altercation was. She was busy thinking of a way to get more information without appearing a complete scandalmonger when a loud tapping interrupted the conversation. Twisting in her seat, Cat was surprised to see Ethan, banging an empty glass repeatedly on the bar. She turned back to look at Amy and pulled a long face. Perhaps Ethan wasn't Mr Cool, Calm and Collected after all.

'Well, I have to say ladies, the place has certainly livened up since you arrived. It's usually much quieter than this,' Tom said. 'Though the pool can get a bit busy, especially when there are no excursions on. It can be all mad dogs and Englishmen around here after everyone's spent the day lying in the sun, eating too much and quenching their thirst with the local beer. On the whole, though it's a lovely little hotel. You'll—'

'Can I get some service over here? Service!' Ethan yelled, over at the bar.

Cat glanced over. Ethan caught her looking, gestured to his empty glass and rolled his eyes. She gave him a polite smile and turned back to the table.

'I'll go get us some refills,' Amy said, jumping up out of her seat.

Cat looked down at the half-full glass on the table in front of her friend's empty seat and stifled a sigh. Larissa wasn't the only one who was man-mad.

'How long are you here for?' Rose asked.

'Just a week,' Cat said. 'How about you?'

'We go back Monday too.'

'Back to the drizzle,' Tom added. He turned to his wife, 'Actually I think I'm ready to go home now. I can't wait to get started in the garden. Goodness knows what it's going to be like after such a mild winter.'

'You said that last year and it was fine.'

'How long have you been here?' Cat asked.

'Since New Year.'

Cat's eyebrows shot up.

'You've been here four months?'

'Yes,' Rose said. 'We've had a wonderful time. We've done all of the excursions—'

'We've been to more markets than you can shake a stick at,' Tom added.

Rose continued, 'We were supposed to be visiting Limassol today, only for a bit of shopping and a spot of lunch, but thanks to the late night, someone would not get out of bed when the alarm went off and so we missed the bus.'

Tom gave her a cheerful smile.

'We can always go tomorrow.'

'Only if we get an early night tonight,' Rose said.

Cat noticed her companions' empty glasses.

'Suits me,' Phil said. 'I really should get this little one to bed.' Bethany was still sleeping soundly on his lap.

As they gathered up their things Cat looked back over to the bar. Andreas placed a glass down in front of Ethan who immediately picked it up and gave it a gentle shake. Even from where she was sitting, Cat could hear the ice clinking against the sides. Ethan took a hefty glug and returned the glass to the bar. All while Amy continued to talk.

Cat stood and waved at Amy, hoping to stop her ordering any more drinks but with Ethan taking all of her attention, Amy was as blind as a blinkered horse. But just then Andreas said something and pointed over to Cat.

'They're all going,' she mouthed.

But Amy's gaze slipped past her to the door, to the two American teenagers, Isabella and Larissa. They had just walked in, passing Phil on his way out, carrying a sleepy looking Bethany in his arms. Larissa Foulds went straight to Ethan and started tugging teasingly on his arm, pulling him to his feet. At first it looked as though he wouldn't be swayed, but after a little more coaxing, he glanced down at his glass and downed the caramel-coloured liquid in one go. Cat saw him say something to Amy before letting himself be dragged away.

The bar was suddenly empty apart from Amy, who looked decidedly down in the mouth. And for some bizarre reason Cat was left feeling like it was all her fault.

Seven

Amy placed the napkin on her crumb-filled plate.

'You're not going already are you?' Cat said, trying not to sound snappy. Amy's desire to speed through everything so she could bury her head in a bloody book was beginning to irritate.

'I thought I'd go and bag a couple of sunbeds before they're all taken.'

'I was hoping we could do something different today.'

'Maybe later?'

'Let me guess, you've just seen Ethan head over there?'

Amy let out a derisory snort of a laugh, picked up her bag and room key and left Cat to finish breakfast alone.

Fifteen minutes later, Cat trotted down the steps towards the pool. Amy was lying on her front, hanging over the end of her lounger, reading a book propped open on the floor. There was no sign of Ethan. Cat perched on the adjacent sunbed and stared into the flat blue waters of the pool. It was so quiet. Most people were still breakfasting.

'What do you think then?' she said. 'Are you up for doing something different today?'

'Like what?' From Amy's mumbled response Cat guessed she already had her answer.

'Well we could go into Paphos and do some shopping. Or we could hire a motorboat. There's a place in the next town that does rentals. We could just go out for half a day. Or there's the Roman ruins. Not quite the pyramids I know but... I don't mind nipping back to the room to get the guide book if you're interested?'

Amy made a pathetic moan, making it clear exactly what she thought.

'I'd like to do all of those things before we leave but...'

'But what?'

'Well, I'm enjoying doing nothing. I don't often get the time to read. It's as big a part of the holiday as sightseeing or any of the things you want to do.'

'Unless it involves an eligible male.'

Amy shot her a sharp look.

'Cairo?' Cat said pointedly.

'That's different. That was more of an extension to the holiday, not a stuffy old day trip.'

'And a fit bloke was going.' Cat was determined not to lose the point.

Amy exhaled noisily and turned the page of her novel.

'I'm not saying no more reading,' Cat said, her voice ratcheting up an octave. She took a calming breath. 'I just thought it might be more interesting to do something else today. What about if we just go out for a few hours, have lunch somewhere and then come back and spend the afternoon by the pool?'

But her friend's silence was answer enough.

This time it was Cat's turn to exhale loudly. Enough was enough.

The air grew cooler as she drew close to the beach, fresh smelling with the promise of a new day. She crossed the path and stepped onto the golden sand.

Her feet slipped on the fine, dry grains, so she kicked off her sandals and carried them, dangling from her hand, as she marched along the water's edge, her frustration making itself felt in spite of the serenity of the setting. But soon the sunshine, warm breeze and the sound of the sea dispersed her anger and she slowed to a stroll. At one point she looked up, attracted by the shrill trilling call of a flock of bee-eaters. The sky, a flawless canvas of periwinkle blue, made a perfect backdrop to their distinctive tails, rendering identification easy. Cat watched contentedly until they disappeared from view. And after the bee-eaters it was the swallows that caught her attention, mesmerising her with their aerial acrobatics. She was sitting on a little patch of grass, staring skyward, when they found her.

'Hi,' Phil called.

Cat started.

'Sorry. Didn't mean to make you jump,' he said.

'My fault. I was miles away.'

Phil craned his neck and looked up.

'Enjoying the view?'

She followed his gaze to the empty sky.

'I was. There were a load of swallows reeling around when I sat down.' She gave Bethany a friendly smile. 'What have you been up to?'

'We've been up to the rock pools, looking for mermaids, haven't we?' Phil said.

'Did you find any?' Cat asked.

Bethany shook her head and for a moment Cat feared the little girl might cry.

'But it looks like you've found plenty of other things,' she added, pointing to the pink plastic bucket Bethany was carrying.

The little girl nodded enthusiastically and thrust the pink pail forwards.

'Shells.'

And just to prove it she reached in and handed over one of her finds, which looked suspiciously like a pebble.

Cat smiled and rose to her feet.

'Are you heading back to the hotel?'

'Yes. You're welcome to join us, if you don't mind how fast you walk. We need all the help we can get to collect the prettiest shells. Don't we, Pickle?'

Bethany looked up and nodded earnestly.

'Sounds like fun,' Cat said, dropping the pebble back into the bucket.

They slowly started to make their way back to the hotel, their progress sloth-like given Bethany's enthusiasm for every piece of flotsam found nestled in the sand.

'So, have you been on your own long?' Phil asked, his candour taking Cat by surprise.

'Is it that obvious?'

'Still too raw to talk about, eh?'

'Not really.' She gave a tight smile. 'Well, maybe.' She'd come on holiday hoping to leave behind memories of her and Mike. 'How about you?'

'The same. Though not that recent. I still find it difficult, sometimes.'

'Do you see much of...?' Cat asked, giving a sideways glance in Bethany's direction.

'Penny. Yeah. She's pretty good. We have a flexible arrangement. I work odd hours, so it can be difficult to keep to any routine.'

Cat frowned.

'Penny?'

'My ex-wife.'

'Oh, I thought...'

'What?'

'It's just that I saw the picture that Bethany did yesterday, with you and... well, Maria. I just assumed...'

'Oh, I see. No. Maria's one of the staff here. She sometimes keeps an eye on Bethany for me.'

Cat nodded, unsure how to follow that.

'So, what do you do back at home?' she asked.

'Security.'

'Oh yes, you did say. Are you, like, an actual security guard, or...?'

'More an operations manager. How about you?'

She tucked a wayward curl of hair behind her ear, buying herself a few seconds of thinking time. She cursed herself for not having created a plausible career choice to use for occasions like this, but then Phil came to her rescue, adding, 'Still doing your research?'

'Yeah, well at least something along the same lines. I basically spend my days tracking down various animals.'

As she said it, it occurred to her how true it was. The detection methods used to locate criminals might be different, but both needed a good balance of patience and intelligence.

'Does your friend do the same thing?'

'Amy? No. She works in forensics.'

'That sounds interesting.'

'I suppose.'

'You don't think?'

She shrugged.

'I'm not sure I'd like to be stuck in a lab all day.'

'Maybe that's why you're out here having a walk while she's by the pool.'

'Oh don't,' Cat said, rolling her eyes. 'I know lying by the pool reading is all part of the holiday, but all day, every day? What really annoys me, though, is she was champing on the bit to go to Cairo when she thought Ethan, that American guy, was going. Yet she won't put her bloody book down to go out for just a couple of hours with me. Now, I bet if Ethan suggested hiring a motor boat...'

Phil laughed lightly.

'She'll come around eventually, when she doesn't get anywhere with Ethan.'

'What makes her think she won't get anywhere?'

'I might be wrong, but from what I've seen, he tends to keep himself to himself. It's all about the business with him.'

They lapsed into silence, focussing on scouring the sand for shells to add to Bethany's collection, trying to steer her clear of the dull charmless pieces. Cat smiled at Phil's efforts to persuade the little girl to part with a rough chunk of concrete. Eventually managing it, he flicked his wrist and sent it sailing into the sea.

'Bit of an odd bunch, aren't they? The Americans,' Cat said as they resumed their walk.

Phil shrugged.

'Hadn't really thought about it.'

'When we first arrived Amy and I thought Ethan and Jaclyn were an item.'

'Really?'

'From a distance Jaclyn looks a lot younger than she is. And Tony, well... just shows you shouldn't judge a book by its cover.'

'Yes, but Ethan? Jaclyn's always with that lawyer, David. Why not him?'

'I didn't know that then. He's a funny one, isn't he? Look how he behaved with his wife last night.'

'Probably just had too much to drink.'

Cat thought back to the mounting collection of bottles around Michael and David at the dinner table.

'Maybe.'

For a little while they walked in silence until Cat spotted a figure further down the beach, throwing handfuls of something out for a raucous squabble of gulls.

'Is that the birdwatcher's wife?' she asked.

Phil, who had been helping Bethany refill her bucket after it accidently tipped over, shaded his eyes with a hand and followed Cat's gaze.

'Sura? Yes. I think she comes walking most mornings when Brian goes to bed.'

'Bed? In the middle of the morning?'

'He goes out at the crack of dawn to birdwatch. He comes, has a late breakfast, then goes to catch up on his sleep.'

Cat suddenly remembered the altercation on the dance floor between Tony, the birdwatcher and his wife.

'Did Sura or her husband have much to do with Tony?'

Phil shot her a look of surprise.

'Not that I'm aware of. Why?'

'I just wondered. I don't know if you were there when it happened but Tony had a bit of a go at them on the dance floor the night he died.'

'I'd forgotten about that. Perhaps he had a thing against birdwatching hippies?'

Cat gave him a quizzical look, wondering if he was serious. He didn't appear to notice and glanced down at his watch.

'Twelve o'clock. Probably should think about heading back for some lunch, before the tables all get taken. Fancy joining us?'

Cat looked down to her white feet and untanned legs; even her arms were barely pink from the sun's rays. Suddenly she had an image of her leaving the sun-kissed isle as anaemic-looking as when she had arrived. And then she thought of her friend, frying in the sun, absorbed in her book. The prospect of sitting in silence by the pool cemented her decision.

'Sure, why not. Provided we can sit somewhere where I can be in the sun.'

'I'm sure that can be arranged.'

At a junction of paths, Cat started down the one that led straight on, back towards the pool, the way she had come.

'This way's quicker,' Phil said, gesturing to a pot-holed track that ran away from the beach. He led the way, stopping when they reached a large rectangular building. 'This is actually the back of the hotel.' He approached a green painted door in the white stucco wall. 'The door's always locked but your key card should work.'

He swiped his own card down the magnetic reader and the door clicked open.

Stepping inside, concrete steps rose above them to their right. Phil lifted Bethany up into his arms. He managed to catch the bucket just in time as it fell from the little girl's grasp.

'Reception's this way,' he said, pushing through a fire door into a long corridor. 'These are the ground floor suites. Some of the Americans have got rooms along here.'

Cat recalled Amy chatting to Ethan on the patio to his room the day before. Just then Michael Vostanis emerged from a room on their left. He pulled the door closed behind him and hurried away, barging roughly into Cat's shoulder as he passed.

'Hey!' Cat shouted, but to no effect. The door at the end of the corridor slowly closed.

'You okay?' Phil asked.

'Yeah, I'm fine. Miserable little sod.

Though as she said it, Cat couldn't help but think back to the previous day, to Michael's laughing, laid-back demeanour with Andreas.

They made their way through the lobby and out onto the terrace, back into the heat.

'There's your friend,' Phil said.

Cat followed his gaze and was surprised to see Amy sitting at the terrace bar, a bottle of beer and plate of sandwiches at her elbow. She was chatting animatedly to Ethan. If Cat had been harbouring any guilt at deserting Amy in preference for a drink with Phil, she didn't any longer. She spotted a vacant table at the far end of the terrace and pointed towards it.

'Shall we—'

Only, at that moment, Amy must have spotted them, as she started to wave, beckoning them over. Cat turned to Phil.

'I don't suppose you'd like to join us?'

Before he could reply, Bethany up-ended her bucket, tipping her collection over the floor. Phil sighed.

'Maybe later. I suspect this is going to take a while.'

'Hi,' Ethan said as Cat approached.

'Where've you been?' Amy asked, glancing over at Phil, who was kneeling next to Bethany helping to sort shells.

'I went for a walk on the beach. I thought you'd still be down by the pool, reading.'

'I felt like some lunch.'

Cat pulled a spare stool over and joined them. Andreas looked over and nodded on seeing her there, waiting. He turned back to Jaclyn and Isabella, who were sitting a little further along the bar, behind Amy.

'I was just talking to Ethan about the investigation into Tony's death,' Amy said. 'It looks like we might have to go and give statements after all.'

'What?' Cat said.

'It'll depend on what the latest tests come back with. I was just saying how difficult it is, in cases like these, to prove anything.' Amy continued, directing her comments to Ethan. 'It's always the same when you have a condition like diabetes which causes chemical imbalances of substances found naturally in the body. Sometimes, what appears to be one thing can often turn out to be something completely different. Just as an example, there's a condition called nitrogen narcosis—the raptures of the deep. People affected tend to—'

'I'm not sure it helps to speculate at this stage,' Cat interrupted. 'And anyway, what tests?'

'I was only giving Ethan the benefit of my professional experience. They must think there's something suspicious about his death to bother doing tests in the first place. Sudden deaths of diabetics are relatively common and aren't always easily pinned down on any one thing. I can see how it pays to be thorough but it'll be like looking for a needle in a haystack. It can be—'

Cat gave a subtle nod and accompanied hard stare over Amy's shoulder, willing her to take the hint and look behind her, only her efforts went unnoticed and Amy continued to talk, seemingly unaware of the closeness of the grieving widow.

Cat darted a glance at Ethan. He didn't look too happy.

'Why don't we talk about something else?' she said.

But it was too late as just then Jaclyn stood and hurried off, with Isabella following behind her.

'Excuse me, I've just remembered something,' Ethan said, before hastening after the two women.

Amy rolled her eyes and grabbed her beer.

'He does seem to make a habit of running off, doesn't he?'

'Didn't you see who was sitting behind you?'

'No.'

'It was the dead man's wife and daughter.'

'Oh.' Amy shrugged.

'Don't you think it might have been a little insensitive to suggest there was something suspicious about Tony's death within earshot of his wife and daughter?'

'I didn't say there was something suspicious about it, only how unusual it is for the police to run tests in cases like this.'

'You keep saying that. How do you know?'

Amy shrank back in her seat.

'Have they been in touch with the family?' Cat pressed.

Amy shook her head.

'No. At least, not as far as I know.'

'So? How do you know they're running tests?'

Amy reached down and picked her bag up from the floor.

'I'm only going on what the detective who phoned you said.'

'What...?' Cat snapped. She patted her pockets and realised, for the first time, she didn't have her phone on her. 'What detective? What did he say?'

Amy pulled a mobile phone from the bag and Cat snatched it from her.

'What did you want me to do? It rang and I thought it would be better to answer it. It was some detective. Kafcos or something like that.'

'Glafcos. What did he say?'

'Only that they'd had some of the test results in. The way he talked it sounded like you'd know what he was talking about.' Amy fixed Cat with an accusatory stare.

'Don't look at me like that. You can't turn this around and make me look bad. I'm surprised he said anything to you at all. Who did you say you were when you answered?'

She noticed Amy look away sharply.

'Amy?'

'I didn't say anything. Just hello. He must have just assumed it was you.'

'And you didn't disabuse him of that idea?' Cat could feel her anger swell. 'What exactly did he say?'

'Just they'd had the results in for the syringes, which were as expected. The other tests would be a while. That was all.'

'Shit Amy. I can't believe you sometimes. You knew he thought he was talking to me, yet you still didn't say anything.' Cat shook her head. 'And if that's not bad enough you went and immediately told Ethan and Jaclyn and Isabella.'

'No. That's not fair. As far as I was concerned, I only told Ethan. You don't know, his wife might not have been listening.'

Cat stared at her and eventually she had the good grace to look a little sheepish. 'Look, I'm sorry. I just wanted to impress Ethan. I thought it might look good if he thought I was in the confidence of the local police. You know, like they valued my opinion. How impressed do you think he'd have been if I'd said, of course, I'll pass the message on to Cat?'

One positive to come out of Amy's transgression was that Cat found it surprisingly easy to persuade her of a change of scene that evening and by the time the taxi pulled to a stop and the two friends climbed out, Cat's anger had eased. She stood for a moment, taking it all in. The square was full of people, hustling, bustling, dawdling and milling all over the place. It was buzzing. Compared to the quiet of the hotel, the town was a riot of noise and colour. An ornate fountain dominated the centre of the square. Submerged lights picked out rich hues of gold, turquoise and cerulean blue of the pool's mosaic tiles, bringing a slug of colour to the rapidly diminishing twilight. Tourists and locals were sitting around the fountain's edge, tucking into paper-wrapped snacks from the street-food vans parked nearby. Mouth-watering aromas filled the air, stirring up Cat's appetite. She scanned the square, which was lined with an array of restaurants and bars, but it was the dark passageways leading away that tempted her with glimpses of candlelit tables and colourful shop fronts.

'Why don't we have a wander down some of these side-streets?' she said. 'We're more likely to find the places the locals eat if we go off the beaten track a bit.'

Amy looked at her like she'd just proposed they raid the nearest bin for scraps.

'You don't fancy that idea then?' Cat said.

'What's wrong with these places here?'

'They're just a bit touristy.'

'Perfect. We're tourists.'

Cat looked around. It was growing busier by the second. Reluctantly she conceded and they started a slow lap of the square, stopping occasionally to look at the menus posted by the entrances.

'How about this one?' Amy said.

They were standing outside a small restaurant, the candlelit tables glowing invitingly. It was perfectly positioned to watch all of the comings and goings in the square.

'It's full,' Cat said. All of the outside tables were occupied.

'Wait, over there...' Amy pointed to an elderly man and his companion who were slowly rising out of their seats. 'They look like they're just about to leave. 'Come on, quick, before someone else gets in.' And before Cat could even register what she was saying, Amy was at the table.

Ten minutes later they were enjoying a bowl of complimentary olives and a surprisingly good house white.

'See, this is perfect,' Amy said.

Cat stabbed at an olive with a wooden pick. It was in a good spot—right in the middle of things.

'So, are you pleased we came out?' she said.

'I suppose,' Amy mumbled, busy scrutinising the menu.

'Don't you feel the need to explore at all?'

Amy shrugged. 'Not really. I'm happy just chilling by the pool, reading.'

'But you can sit and read at home anytime. You live on your own.'

'It's different here. It's more relaxing in the sun. I'm surprised you don't want to just take it easy. I know I've said it before but it's true, your problem is, you just don't know how to switch off.'

Cat was about to defend herself when Amy suddenly sat up and started to wave.

70

'Looks like someone else has opted for a night out,' she said, a wide grin on her face.

Cat turned to see Ethan dig out some coins from his pocket and pay the driver of an idling taxi.

She looked at Amy, disbelieving.

'You told him we'd be here?'

'Of course, I didn't. Oh...' Amy slumped back in her seat. 'He's gone the other way.'

Ethan had started a slow stroll away from the square. Soon he disappeared around the corner.

Amy was still casting an occasional glance in the direction of the taxi rank when Ethan appeared from her left, having walked full circle around the back streets. He looked over and, on noticing them, smiled and gave a little wave, while continuing to walk.

'Ethan!' Amy called.

He stopped and looked back over at them. Amy beckoned to him.

'Are you on your own tonight?' she asked once he reached their table.

'Yes. Thought it would do me good to get out.'

'Same here.'

He cast a quick look around.

'Good choice of restaurant. This place has got an excellent reputation. In the high season you need to book weeks ahead.'

'You're welcome to join us if you like. We can always get them to lay another setting.'

'I couldn't impose on you like that.'

'We wouldn't mind, would we Cat?'

Cat looked up and gave an unconvincing smile.

'No, of course not.'

'Sorry about rushing off earlier... at the bar,' he said, pulling over a spare chair from a nearby table. 'I'd just remembered that

71

Tony had got an appointment for tomorrow. I thought I'd better check it'd been cancelled. It was lucky I did, Jaclyn didn't know anything about it. I went back to the bar afterwards but you'd already gone.'

Amy gave a happy grin.

'Well you found us eventually.'

The waiting staff set up the extra place without complaint and soon Ethan was sipping an aged Scotch and consulting the menu.

'It's a good thing you didn't go to Cairo. It seems you're needed here,' Amy said, causing Ethan to frown. 'The appointment—it sounds like you're the only one with your eye on the ball.'

'Well Michael's new to the business and Jaclyn's never really taken much interest.'

'Presumably she's going to have to now,' Cat said.

'Jaclyn? No way. It's not her sort of thing.'

'Will it just be you and Michael then?' Amy asked.

'No. He's not really interested either. He didn't want to go into the business in the first place. But Tony always got what Tony wanted. I always thought he would have been better recruiting Isabella. I think she was secretly hoping she'd be brought into the business once she graduated.'

'Really?' Cat said. From what she'd seen of the teenager, she thought it seemed unlikely.

'Sure. She was pretty upset at the old guy when he first announced his decision.' Ethan continued, 'Don't get me wrong, I get on fine with Michael and we'd have made it work, but the kid's heart isn't in it. He's always wanted to be a chef. He was horrified when Tony told him the plan.'

'Will she sell up then, do you think?'

'Cat!' Amy said.

'That's alright. I don't mind talking about it,' Ethan said. 'I don't know what she's going to do. Maybe she'll take David up on his offer.'

Cat casually speared another olive.

'He's offered to buy it?'

'No. I doubt he could afford to. No, he's offered to take over as MD.'

'Does he know the food business well?'

Ethan shook his head and took a drink.

'No. Well, not well enough to act as managing director, in my opinion at least. He's really only ever focussed on the legal side of the import business. I suppose he must think that's enough.'

'It must be complicated having to know the legal requirements for different countries,' Cat said.

'He sure makes out it is. Always going on about regulations and import controls. I understand it's probably a ton of work to get a new product approved back at home—there's a mountain of certification processes that have to be followed—but once you've done it once...?'

'And he does it all himself, does he? I mean, he's not part of a bigger firm?'

'No. Just him.'

'So, he'd be your new boss?' Amy said.

'Well, I don't know about that. He might not want me working for him.'

'But I thought you more or less ran the business,' Amy said.

'Well, parts of it.'

'All the transport arrangements and making sure the stock levels are right. That's a big part. Surely he'd need you for that side of things, wouldn't he? There can't be much you don't know.'

'I wouldn't say that. No. I imagine he'd be keen to find someone else. David and I don't exactly see eye to eye on everything. Not like Tony. Tony gave me my first break when I needed to pay my way through college and when I graduated, he didn't hesitate to give me a full-time position. I loved working with him.' Ethan let his gaze drop to his hands, which were busy playing with the napkin on the table. He shook it out and laid it over his lap. 'He was like a father and a best friend to me.'

Amy reached over and lightly placed a hand on his arm.

'He must have thought a lot of you to have given you so much responsibility.'

Ethan gave a listless smile and nodded before beckoning to a passing waiter. He skimmed through the extensive wine list before flicking back to the first page.

'How about this one... a full-bodied red, bursting with dark fruit flavours and a hint of pepper?'

Cat preferred white or rosé. Her veggie main would be overwhelmed by a robust red.

'I—'

'That sounds perfect,' Amy said. 'I love a man who knows his wine.'

Ethan rattled off some long-winded name, complete with year of bottling. The waiter gave him a respectful nod.

Amy toyed with an olive.

'Have you thought about buying Jaclyn out?' she asked.

Ethan let out a snort.

'I've got nowhere near enough collateral.'

Cat looked at him. The question had clearly touched a nerve.

'I'm sorry,' Amy said. 'I shouldn't be offering solutions when I clearly don't know the details.'

'It's not your fault. You know what it's like. You have an image in your head as to what the future holds, and how things are going to go, and then something happens and blows those plans apart. What the hell Tony wanted to retire for anyway I don't know.' He stared despondently at his empty whisky glass.

'Was he looking forward to retiring?' Cat asked.

Ethan raised his eyebrows.

'He seemed to be. God knows what he thought he was going to do with all that free time. It's not like he had any interests outside of work and Jaclyn's an independent lady. She certainly wasn't looking forward to having him under her feet. She made that clear.'

Cat and Amy both said nothing. The waiter's appearance with the wine, followed by the arrival of their food, brought a welcome relief.

On finishing his first mouthful Ethan took a drink and looked over the rim of his glass at both of them.

'Tell me more about you two. Are you enjoying your R and R here?'

Amy rested her knife and fork on the side of the plate and took a drink before replying.

'Well, funny you should say that but rest and recuperation sum it up nicely.' She turned to Cat, 'You'd had a really rough couple of months, hadn't you? And I was due some leave. It seemed a good idea to book something together.'

Ethan's brows knit gently together. He looked at Cat.

'A rough time?'

'She exaggerates.'

'No, I don't. You were really stressed when we booked the holiday. And there's nothing wrong with admitting it. I mean a close shave like that would have freaked most people out. I mean I freaked when you told me how you nearly wound up—'

'...married to my cheating boyfriend,' Cat jumped in, concerned that Amy was on the verge of accidentally mentioning her run in with a six-inch boning knife in the process of arresting a multiple murderer. 'I'd just gone through a messy break-up after I found out that my ex had been playing around. With anyone and everyone, it seems. After I kicked him out, I thought a holiday with a friend was just what I needed.'

'Have you been friends long?'

'Since we were eighteen,' Amy said. 'We met during our first week at Uni. We sat next to each other in our first lecture and that was it. We just gelled. We even shared a flat for a couple of years. We did have some laughs.'

Cat smiled as memories of their student days came flooding back.

'What did you study?'

'Biology,' the two friends said in unison, causing them both to let out a giggle.

'Ah, that figures. Now you're a police scientist, like CSI.'

'Forensic biologist,' Amy corrected.

'That must be really interesting.'

'It is. Sometimes on the surface it looks like there's nothing there, but you learn not to make assumptions. You have to be patient and keep digging.' She paused and ran a finger around the rim of her wine glass. 'I sometimes forget that I'm not at work. That's why, you know, earlier today, I'm sorry if I spoke out of turn. I didn't mean to be insensitive or anything.'

'Don't worry about it. I wasn't offended. In fact, I was very impressed. I can tell you really enjoy your job.'

'I love it. Trying to make sense of what's happened at a crime scene is so rewarding.'

'Doesn't it get a bit gruesome?'

'You get used to it.'

'I'm not sure I would.' He gave Amy a smile and then switched his attention to Cat. 'How about you Cat? Are you a forensic biologist too?'

She shook her head.

'No.' She picked up her water glass and took a drink.

'So, what do you do? Wait, let me guess...' he gave her a look so intense that goosebumps started to pick their way up her arms until the hairs on the back of her neck stood on edge like iron filings on a magnet.

'I'm not a psychic, if you're trying to tell me telepathically,' she said, looking away.

'Not too far off what I was actually going to say.' Ethan laughed as Cat frowned. 'Don't look so worried. I was going to say psychotherapist.'

'What makes you think that?'

'I don't know. It was the first thing that came into my head.'

A smile played on his lips, which suddenly looked very knowing, and Cat was forced to suppress a shiver as the pimples reappeared on her warm flesh.

'You're way off the mark,' she said.

'I give up. What do you do?'

She'd anticipated the question, known it was coming, but was nonetheless unprepared. The only thing she was sure of was that she didn't want him to know the truth. The words Serious Crime Squad tended to frighten the life out of people. Cat looked at Amy, whose normally smiling features looked flat, and saw the first signs of her friend's growing displeasure.

'Nothing quite as exciting as Amy, unfortunately,' she said. 'I left university and went into research.'

'Well you did,' Amy said, 'but now—'

'Now nothing,' Cat replied quickly. 'I'm between projects at the moment.'

'What sort of thing did you research?' Ethan asked.

'My last big assignment was tracking whale sharks in the Maldives as part of a community conservation programme.'

'Whale sharks? Are they what, whales or sharks?'

'They're the largest fish in the ocean... in the world, in fact.'

'And you had to track them. Wasn't it dangerous?'

'No. Whale sharks are like massive hoovers. They suck in plankton and small fish, like sardines and anchovies.'

'What did you do with them?'

'We just followed them, took dimensions and fitted them with a tag so we could trace their movements. It was an amazing experience.' She had a faraway look on her face and eyes that twinkled with the memory.

'It sounds awesome. I mean I surf off the Big Sur back home, but man, the biggest thing I come close to are elephant seals.'

'You surf!' Amy said. 'How cool is that!'

'Not really. In California everyone surfs. Now being a CSI, that's what I call cool. You must have some great stories.'

'Might have,' Amy said.

She put her hand to her wine glass and tipped her head to the side. A coquettish look that Cat had seen her use before, usually to great effect.

'Why don't you tell him about the guy with the stocking fetish?' Cat said. 'I'm sure I remember someone telling me it was your analysis that broke the case.'

Ethan didn't need to know it was Amy herself who had told Cat the story.

Amy broke into a grin.

'I can't believe you remembered that.' She leaned forward, until she was inches from Ethan's face. 'This story is funny. Sick, but funny...'

Eight

Cat glanced at her mobile phone. 6:00 a.m. She lay back down and blew out a sigh. Darkness still hung heavy in the recesses of the room but it was receding fast, losing the battle against the early morning light that bled through the gaps in the curtains.

She sat up and threw off the covers.

The morning air was cool, the cloudless sky having done little to stop the heat of the previous day leaching out. She thought back to the bone-chilling frigid water of the pool the day before. In the Maldives the sea temperature had been warm all year round. She'd been spoilt.

There was no one at the pool when she got there. She placed her towel onto a sunbed and tucked her phone and key card underneath. For a second it occurred to her she might be wrong—perhaps David Foulds didn't swim *every* morning? Then she thought of his toned physique and the fact he'd turned up to breakfast wet-haired and carrying a damp towel, and reassured herself she was probably right to assume he'd make an appearance. She stripped out of her t-shirt and shorts to reveal a one-piece swimming costume, slipped her goggles on to her head and made her way to the pool.

The water was breathtakingly cold but she soon fell into a rhythm that was almost meditative. Her breathing and heart-rate steadied with the slow release of endorphins. She turned her head to take a breath and drew in a mouthful of water as it lapped out of synch with her strokes. She slowed and looking back, saw a dark shape moving powerfully through the water, heading straight for her. She reached the shallow end and made a pretence of doing a few stretches. Sure enough, it was David Foulds. He turned and pushed away for a second lap without registering her presence. Cat dived back under and followed in his wake.

She stayed in for a further thirty minutes before slipping out and wrapping herself in her towel, relishing the warmth. She was patting her hair dry when David climbed out. She saw him glance over in her direction as he reached for his towel.

'Feel better for that?' he called over as he began to rub himself dry.

'I do now that I'm warm.'

He flashed her a smile.

'I like it. Refreshing. The cold tends to put a lot of people off.'

'I normally run but I didn't bring my trainers. This seemed like the next best thing.'

'You could have enjoyed some extra time in the sack. You are on holiday. Or does work bring you here?'

'Oh no. Just a holiday.'

Cat watched as David Foulds pulled a t-shirt over his towel-dried hair, wondering how best to engage him in conversation. She noticed him glance at his Omega dive watch.

'Nearly seven. They won't have started serving breakfast yet but I'm sure I can get someone to fix us coffee, if you'd like to join me?' he said.

She couldn't believe her luck.

'Coffee sounds great.' She ran her fingers loosely through her tangled hair, pulled on her jogging bottoms and t-shirt and rolled up her towel.

It didn't take him long to smooth-talk one of the kitchen staff into making the two of them a drink and soon they were sitting on the terrace nursing a couple of large café lattes.

'Do you swim every day?' Cat asked.

'Sure do. I like to keep trim. You run, you say?'

'Yes. Same reason. Plus, I like the way it sets me up for the day.' She looked around at the scenery; the rising sun practising its alchemy, turning the landscape into gold. She sensed the air warming as the shadows shortened. 'This is definitely my favourite time of day. I love watching the sun come up.'

'You're right. It is beautiful. I don't think I've actually stopped to look at it before.'

'I expect you've been too busy with business.' David Foulds cast her a curious glance. 'Ethan mentioned you worked for Tony. Said this was more of a business trip than a holiday... apart from the women—he said they were only here for the shopping.' Cat gave him a wide smile, hoping a lighter tack might keep him chatting.

'Yes, well that's all changed now.' His gaze fell to the floor.

'Had you worked together long?'

'Over thirty years.'

'Wow. You must know an awful lot about the import business. I imagine it's a minefield, with all the different regulations.'

'It's like most things, once you know what you're doing, it's not that difficult.'

'I bet the family are glad to have your expertise to rely on.'

'I don't think they'll be needing it. It looks like none of them are prepared to take over the reins.'

'Oh. I imagine they're looking for someone else to take it on then?'

He hooked an eyebrow up.

'Ethan said something, has he?' Cat said nothing. David Foulds continued, 'I thought as much. I don't think now is the right time, though. Jaclyn has got more than enough on her plate, especially with the police calling the manner of Tony's death into question.' Still Cat said nothing. 'At least, that's what your friend was telling Ethan yesterday. It sounds like she's quite an authority on the topic. What else does she know?'

'Nothing,' Cat said, more sharply than she intended. 'All she knows is they're doing some tests. I don't know why they even told her that. It's not like she's—'

Just then a waitress approached, carrying a large flask.

'More coffee?'

'Not for me, thank you,' David Foulds said, handing the waitress his half-empty cup. 'I'd better be going.' He picked up his towel and nodded to Cat, who absentmindedly passed the waitress her cup as she watched him walk away.

As with the previous day, Amy rushed through breakfast and settled in for another morning by the pool. With no alternative on the cards, Cat joined her. She laid her towel on the sunbed and began to search through her bag.

'I must have left my suntan lotion in the room. Can I have some of yours?'

'Course,' Amy said, squeezing out a generous amount of the white cream into the palm of her hand.

'I bumped into Tony's lawyer when I was down here having a swim this morning,' Cat said.

'I still can't believe you did that. Anyone else couldn't sleep with the heat would just open a window,' she said, handing the tube over.

'He mentioned the call from the police yesterday.'

'I told you, I'm sorry about that.'

'It's okay, but tell me again, exactly what did you tell Ethan they'd said?'

'All I said was the tests on the syringes came back as expected, the other tests might take some time and they'd be in touch if they wanted statements. Hardly anything to get excited about.'

'It might be if you're the person who killed him.'

Amy gave her a disbelieving look.

'If there was anything to suggest someone had killed him, the police would have been here double-quick and we'd be in the middle of a murder investigation. I don't know if you've noticed, but they're not.' Amy lay down on her lounger. She raised a hand to her brow and looked over at Cat, who was still applying sunscreen. 'You need some counselling. It's not healthy to be so fixated on murder.'

'You're one to talk. Isn't that all you've talked about in your efforts to impress? Perhaps we should both give it a rest?'

'Fine by me,' Amy said, picking up her book.

Cat looked at the bag by her feet and sighed, realising it wasn't only her suntan lotion she'd forgotten to bring with her.

'I'm going to have to go back to the room. Do you need anything?' she asked, pushing her feet into her flip-flops.

She took Amy's grunt as a no.

She jabbed a finger at the button and stared at the light above the lift's closed door. The sound of raised voices in the direction of the hotel's entrance caused her to look over. Jaclyn was having a stand-up row with a tired-looking, middle-aged Cypriot man.

'I explained all of this when I booked the bloody taxi,' she snapped. 'The American Embassy, Nicosia. You do *know* where the American Embassy is, don't you?'

The taxi driver narrowed his eyes and gave her a hard look, but he evidently decided to take the fare as after a few seconds he turned on his heel and headed for the door, muttering to himself.

'And don't even think about over-charging me. I'm not paying a dime more than what I was quoted,' Jaclyn called as she followed him out.

Cat turned back to face the lift and punched the button again. The light hadn't moved. Fed up with waiting she pushed through the door into the corridor that led to the stairwell. Two doors away, a cleaner emerged, a white laundry bag in one hand and a bundle of towels under her arm. It was the same room that Michael Vostanis had rushed out of the previous day. The cleaner gave Cat a warm smile and deposited the towels into a large sack attached to the side of the linen trolley and placed the laundry bag on top.

'Morning,' Cat said, as the cleaner wheeled the trolley past. She glanced at the name on the laundry: *J Vostanis.*

A pile of dirty plates remained stacked up by the doorway and Cat was immediately reminded of the American woman's absence at breakfast. She continued past and slipped up the two flights of stairs, back to her room. Five minutes later, she was trotting back down the stairs, clutching a bottle of suntan lotion and her book. At the bottom she re-entered the corridor, this time at its opposite end. The cleaner and her trolley were both gone, unlike the dirty plates, which still lay on the floor outside of Jaclyn's room, the door to which was now ajar.

Cat looked up and down the length of the corridor. All of the other doors were closed. With Jaclyn's comments to the taxi driver fresh in her mind, she was about to report the open door at reception, when she heard a loud metallic click come from within the room.

She stepped towards the door and knocked.

'Hello...?' she called through the gap.

Another click, followed by another, different sound.

'Hello...?' she called again.

No reply.

She reached for the handle, took one more look about her and then pushed the door open.

'Hello, Mrs Vostanis...?'

84

Nine

Cat stepped tentatively over the threshold.

'Is there anyone there? The door was open.'

At the far end of the room, the privacy-giving voile curtains hanging over the French doors billowed out on the back of a gentle breeze. Behind her, the door to the corridor caught on the through-draft and banged shut, snuffing the life out of the curtains. The voile dropped back into position, once again shrouding the open door. Cat walked over, intending to close it. She pushed the curtain to one side and reached for the handle, taking the opportunity to peer through the uncovered glass. On seeing no one on the patio outside and no movement beyond the confines of the room's small terrace, she fastened the lock on the French door and was about to make her exit when she heard a noise in the corridor beyond. Frozen on the spot, she cocked her head towards the door but the only thing she could hear was the thumping of her heart, banging inside her chest like a hammer drill.

Maybe it was the cleaner, returned for the breakfast tray?

She leaned toward the door—muffled voices—there were people talking right outside. And then she heard the unmistakable sound of a key card being inserted into the lock.

She looked behind her—the way out to the terrace was now locked—and then back at the solid wood door and mouthed a silent expletive. With no obvious alternative, keeping a firm hold on her book and bottle of suntan lotion, she threw herself under one of the room's two queen-sized beds and scooted across until she judged herself to be roughly in the middle. She only just made it in time. The door opened and suddenly the room was filled with voices and the sound of footsteps on the hard-tiled floor on which she was now lying.

She reached up and gathered her hair together, praying there were no stray wisps poking out, and tempered her breathing, concentrating on keeping it silent and even.

'I remember leaving it on the door, that's all I'm saying,' Jaclyn Vostanis said.

'It was probably the cleaner,' came David Foulds's voice. 'It would have fallen off as soon as she opened the door. Give it to me. I'll hang it on there now.'

'What's the point?' Jaclyn snapped.

'To stop her interrupting when she comes back for the dirty plates.'

'I told you, I've got a cab waiting outside. I only came back to get Tony's passport.'

Cat held her breath as a pair of slender, perfectly manicured feet, strapped in pale purple heels, started towards her. They continued past, stopping at the desk by the window. With her back to her guest, and to the bed under which Cat was hiding, Jaclyn reached for something on the desk. Cat heard a familiar click: the same metallic snap that had enticed her into the room in the first place. With intrigue winning over caution she stretched to the far side of the bed and craned her neck to get a better look. Jaclyn was leaning into a large briefcase. Cat recognised the source of the sound she had heard—the bag's metal fastening—confirming her suspicion that someone had been in the room. A growing pressure in her chest gave her a pressing reminder to breathe. Despite an overwhelming urge to take a hungry gulp of air, slowly, very slowly, she let her breath out, amazed the noise of her heart beating and the whoosh of her blood pumping couldn't be heard as far as reception.

'Where the hell is it? It should be in here somewhere.'

Cat could hear Jaclyn tut and sigh as she rummaged through the bag.

'Let me see.' David approached, walking into Cat's line of sight as Jaclyn stepped back. He started to pick through the bag's contents. 'Could Ethan have it?' he said after a short time.

'Why on earth would he have it?'

'I don't know. It was just an idea.'

'Well it was a dumb-assed one,' Jaclyn retorted as she muscled past him and reached into the bag for a second time.

A loud knock at the door made all three of them jump.

'Who's that?' David asked, sounding more suspicious than the situation warranted.

'I don't know. Why don't you answer it?' Jaclyn moved from the bag to the desk drawers, which she tugged open and slammed closed as she searched for the missing passport.

Cat watched the trainer-clad feet stride to the door. It opened to reveal a second set of white Nike running shoes, socks pulled tightly up to mid-calf.

'David.'

'Ethan.'

The two men greeted each other stiffly.

'What's going on?' Ethan asked.

'Jaclyn's trying to find Tony's passport. She's got to go to the American consulate to make the arrangements to fly his body back home.'

'Did you get it back from the police?'

'What?' Jaclyn snapped.

'The police. They took Tony's passport the other night,' Ethan said. 'That detective came back here with you to get it. Don't you remember?'

Jaclyn came to an abrupt stop.

'Oh Christ.' She exhaled noisily. 'I need a drink. David, get me a shot of something strong from the mini bar.'

Cat watched the purple sandals approach the bed under which she hid and felt the push of air as Jaclyn sat down, her heels only inches from her face. Thankfully the American's tiny size-zero frame weighed next to nothing and the mattress barely dipped as she rested on its edge.

David Foulds bent down and opened a built-in cupboard next to the wardrobe to reveal an undercounter fridge. He peered at its contents before calling over his shoulder to Jaclyn.

'Whisky okay?'

'It'll do. Oh, and help yourself.'

'I'll pass thanks.'

Cat heard him twist open the lid on the miniature as he straightened up.

At the same time Ethan's trainer-clad feet reappeared from a room Cat took to be the bathroom.

'Here... I've given it a quick rinse.'

Cat saw David take the clean glass. She then heard him tut as a small metal cap landed on the floor by the bed and spun towards her. Cat shrank back as a hand came into view. It scooped up the lid and disappeared from view. But rather than feel relief, she was frozen rigid, a chill having wormed its way up her spine. While moving away from David Foulds's advancing hand she had rolled over onto her phone—her phone that wasn't set to silent. The same phone that Glafcos had called her on, only yesterday.

What if he called with more news? How long had she been gone from the pool? What if Amy called, wondering where the hell she'd got to?

She felt her breath constrict in her chest.

'David, go and tell the cab driver there's been a change of plan,' Jaclyn said. 'I need to go to the police station on the way to the Embassy. Tell him I'll be out in a minute.'

Just go! Cat implored silently.

He put the glass of whisky on the dresser and crossed the floor in half a dozen easy strides. After he left, Cat felt the pressure ease on the bed above her as Jaclyn stood up and reached for her drink.

'Did you want something?' she said, her voice sounding hard-edged. 'I've got to go.'

'I came to see if you'd made a decision,' Ethan said.

'Decision? How can you expect me to be able to think of business at a time like this?'

'Cut the bullshit. My offer—are you going to accept it or not?'

'Well, seeing as you asked so nicely,' Jaclyn replied. She knocked the spirit back and brought the glass down with a bang.

Cat grimaced at the thought of drinking whisky so early in the day.

Once again, the mattress above her dipped as Ethan eased his weight on the bed. This time the springs dropped a couple of inches.

'Why do you always have to do that?' he said.

'I don't know what you mean,' Jaclyn replied, though it was clear to Cat she knew exactly what Ethan was referring to.

'I need to know. I've already got suppliers lined up. If you do nothing, Tony's orders will stand. You do realise you'll have to pay them, don't you?'

The room was quiet.

'I thought you'd jump at the chance,' Ethan continued. 'You made it clear you don't want to carry on with the business. It'll take time to find another buyer and anyone with half a brain will see it for the fire-sale it is. You'll be lucky to get a fraction of the price back. Or you can do a deal with me. I'm offering it to you on a plate.'

'On an empty plate! You seem to be forgetting, I'm a rich woman now. If you're not prepared to make it worth my while why the hell should I sell to you?'

The dent in the bed lifted and Cat watched Ethan's feet pad towards the French doors. He parted the curtains and peered through the window.

'A bit of slack, that's all I've asked for. Some acknowledgement of everything I've done for Tony... For you. I could have made life difficult for you but I didn't, did I?'

He let the curtains drop and turned back towards Jaclyn.

'Are you done here?' Jaclyn asked in an acid voice.

Ethan moved away from the window towards the door.

'Maybe you need more time to think it over. You know where to find me.' He left, pulling the door closed behind him.

'Arrogant shit,' Jaclyn said.

After Ethan had gone, Jaclyn didn't hang around. Cat grabbed her phone and set it to silent then stayed under the bed until she was sure enough time had elapsed for Jaclyn to have reached the taxi and departed. Conscious of the risk, not only of Jaclyn returning, but also of the cleaner coming back, she slid out from under the bed, and was debating which door to exit through, when the briefcase caught her eye. She was pretty sure it was the bag's clasp she'd heard from outside the door.

She checked the time on her phone. Since they'd left, she'd already been in the room for two minutes... two-ten... two-fifteen... two-twenty...

She made straight for the worn, tan leather Gladstone bag. She looked about her, spotting a box of tissues on one of the bedside cabinets she pulled a handful out, intending to use them to mask her fingerprints. She laid a tissue over the clasp and snapped it open. The bag was brimming with jars and sandwich bags filled with vibrant green herbs, shrivelled brown lumps and slices and slivers of vegetables bound in oil or natural juices of all different shapes and sizes. It looked like the spoils of a smash and grab from the local deli.

Working as quickly as she could, her dexterity severely impeded by the tissues, she quickly removed each item and set it down on the surface before photographing it with her phone. One by one she captured a whole host of different specimens, some she recognised: kalamata, the big juicy black olives that she loved, and morels, easily recognisable even without a label thanks to their wrinkly honeycomb cap. Then there were others she'd never even heard of: tsakistes, a variety of green olive; and giant fennel mushroom, a creamy, fleshy-looking fungus that resembled a large oyster mushroom to Cat's untrained eye. Eventually the only thing left in the bag was a large leather-bound Filofax.

The A5 organiser read like a Yellow Pages of Cypriot restaurateurs and food distributers. Appointments spanned the whole of the previous three weeks up to the day Tony had died and a few beyond. With no idea whether she'd found anything—in fact, no idea of what she was looking for—Cat caught on camera page after page of names and addresses and scribbled notes she assumed represented the dead American's order book. For good measure she also took copies of the half dozen paper orders she found in the organiser, which appeared on first glance to match the entries in the book.

With everything captured on her phone she returned the Filofax to the bottom of the bag and started to put the samples back, trying, as best she could, to replace them in the same order that they came out in. She was almost through when she stopped and reached back into the bag for one of the samples labelled mixed mushrooms. She held up the zip-lock bag and examined the shrivelled, coarsely chopped contents through the see-through plastic. A deep woody brown, they certainly looked like mushrooms. With difficulty she opened the packet, stuck her nose in and had a sniff. The earthy notes were instantly recognisable. It certainly wasn't dope.

A shame. A drug smuggling link could have provided a lot of answers.

She tossed the mushroom sample back into the leather bag and checked her watch. Fourteen-minutes elapsed time.

Time to get out.

She threw the last few items back into the briefcase and snapped the case closed.

Then she noticed the desk drawer.

The drawer opened easily. She quickly glanced over its contents, an array of odds and ends: chargers and plug adaptors, headphones and i-pods, sitting alongside the standard hotel-provided bible and finally, three syringes and an equal number of small vials of colourless liquid, which according to the label had been Tony Vostanis's insulin prescription. She quickly snapped the information on the labels before closing the drawer.

Aware she'd violated enough laws to be career-limiting, if not freedom-restricting if anyone ever found out, her jangling nerves were at breaking point. She took a final look around the room. Her gaze came to rest on the wardrobe.

She took a deep breath. What was it everyone always says of her? She's nothing if not thorough. Normally it was a compliment, today it felt like a curse. But the large built-in closet held no secrets, though she had to accede defeat to the small safe that was secreted behind its sliding doors. Lastly, a quick look in the bathroom revealed a cornucopia of feminine beauty products but very little else. There was nowhere else left to look. Finally, she could make her escape.

She moved to the window and peered out from behind the voile panel. Scanning the small terrace and the pathway beyond, a wave of relief passed over her—there was no one in sight. With her hands visibly shaking, she reached for the latch and cracked open one of the doors, just wide enough to be able to squeeze through. Her legs felt weak and trembly. She pulled herself tall and stepped out, closing the door behind her. With a confident stride, she quickly crossed the small distance to the stone pathway, heading in the direction of the terrace bar, wondering if it really was too early for a stiff drink.

Ten

'You took your time,' Amy said as Cat approached.

'I got you a drink,' Cat said, putting down two glasses of chilled orange juice on the small plastic table.

'What've you been up to?'

'Just went to fetch these.' She pulled her book out from under her arm and slipped the bottle of suntan lotion out of a pocket in her shorts.

'All this time?'

'I got caught chatting on the way back,' she said, thinking Amy wasn't really interested. But she was wrong.

'Anyone we know?'

She'd started the lie, now she had to finish it.

'Just Phil and Bethany. I was barely with them a few minutes though.'

'You seem to have spent a lot of time chatting to Bethany and her dad since we've been here.'

'Don't go reading anything into that. Unlike you, I prefer to spend my time in the company of people, rather than with my nose buried in a book.'

'I wasn't saying anything.'

'Good.'

And, for once, Cat was actually pleased when Amy reached for her latest choice of literary entertainment. With her adrenalin level having returned to normal, all she wanted was to be left in peace, with time to think about what she'd seen and heard. She was sure that news of someone breaking into Jaclyn's room would be of interest to Glafcos but where was the evidence? And what exactly had she seen? An open window, that was all. Okay, there was the sound of the briefcase being opened—and closed—but what if she'd really heard something else? With the window being open, wasn't it even possible the noise had come from outside?

She looked across at Amy, who was already engrossed in her book, and reasoned it safe to look at her phone. She pulled it out of her pocket and a few seconds later was scrolling through the images taken of the dead man's things. They told her nothing.

What did it matter anyway? It's not like she even knew the guy. She reached for her bag, trading her phone for her book, but with the stifling heat and everything playing on her mind it was impossible to concentrate. Minutes later she returned the book to the bag, stripped down to her bikini and sought refuge in the cool—make that *cold*—waters of the pool, sharing it only with the swallows that dipped and dived over the large blue drinking trough. A few laps were all it took to acclimatise to the breathtakingly icy water and she soon found her rhythm.

A quick dip turned into a marathon swim, until eventually her energy levels began to ebb. She climbed out at the shallow end and started to walk back around the pool to her towel, which lay neatly folded on the end of her sunbed. Only her towel wasn't the only thing resting on her lounger. Ethan was sitting on its edge, chatting to Amy, who, just at that moment, threw back her head and gave an exuberant laugh. Realising she wasn't going to be able to hide in the pool all day, Cat reluctantly continued her approach.

'Sorry,' Ethan said, jumping up. 'Here, this must be yours.'

He handed her the towel.

'Thanks.' She wrapped the blue cotton around her shoulders and began to pat at her hair. 'You can sit back down. I don't mind standing.'

'No, please,' he said. 'I only stopped by for a quick chat.'

'Honestly, it's no problem. I need to dry off first anyway.' Cat pulled the towel tight around her.

Ethan eased himself back down.

'God, is it just me? It feels a lot hotter today than yesterday,' Cat said, fanning herself with a flat hand.

'Stop complaining,' Amy said. 'It's why we came. I love it hot.'

'I wasn't complaining. I was just saying. And anyway, you might love it hot, but you won't love it burnt. You're already going red.'

She pointed to her friend's shoulders, which were the colour of rare lamb.

Amy dipped her chin and slipped a thumb under her bikini strap to examine the damage. There was a stark contrast between the white strip of skin that had been covered by the strap of her bikini and the ruddy flush that covered the rest of her shoulder.

'Shit!'

'Did you remember to put more sunscreen on after your swim?' Ethan asked.

'Amy, swim?' Cat said in a jokey tone.

Amy stuck out her bottom lip into an exaggerated pout.

'It's impossible to do your own back properly.' She slid along on her lounger and turned to Ethan with a seductive smile. 'You wouldn't be able to rub some sun cream in for me, would you, please?' She patted the newly created space on the bed next to her.

'Sure,' he said, moving across.

Amy passed him the tube and leaned forward, presenting her back to him. She slipped her fingers under the straps of her bikini and pushed them off her shoulders.

'This smells nice,' Ethan said, as he rubbed the cold cream in.

'Mmm,' Amy murmured. 'Cat, you should put some more on given you've been for a swim.'

'Do you want...?' Ethan asked, offering her the tube.

'Oh, no thanks, mine's in my bag. I prefer a higher factor,' she replied.

'That's why you're still as white as the day we came,' Amy said, over her shoulder, as Ethan continued to work the cream down her back.

With Amy contentedly covered and Cat efficiently applying her own lotion, Ethan wiped his hands together, rubbing in the residue.

Cat returned the bottle to her bag and on turning back, caught Ethan looking at her.

'Here, you've missed a bit.'

He leaned across and gently skimmed her shoulder with his hand, letting it continue upwards to trace the line of her neck. Cat felt a small shudder run up her spine.

'Oh, thanks.'

'You're welcome. I think you were right about the heat. I sure am feeling it a lot more today. Tell you what, why don't I get us all some drinks?'

'Oh, I'd do anything for a beer,' Amy said. She turned her head and made eye contact with him.

'Cat?'

'Just a bottle of water for me thanks.'

'Really?' Amy sounded genuinely shocked.

'I'm thirsty. I might have a beer later.'

But Amy's interest had already waned. She'd switched her attention back to Ethan and was watching him as he climbed the few steps up to the terrace bar. In turn, Cat watched Amy, aware of a mild but growing apprehension about her friend's increasing attraction to the good-looking American.

She sighed and let her gaze roam lazily around.

Across the pool Isabella and her friend, Larissa, were reclined on their sunbeds, their heads turned to one another as they lay chatting. Gillian Foulds was sitting on the edge of a sunbed nearby, reading under the shade of a large umbrella. Beyond the pool, up on the terrace, Tom and Rose were also sensibly steering clear of the midday sun, sitting at a table dappled with the shade cast by a large fig tree. They laughed at something as a waiter brought over a bottle of wine and a cooler. Everyone appeared to be happy in their own little world.

Suddenly Cat felt very alone.

She leaned over and reached under the lounger and grabbed her bag and dug out her phone. She flipped it open and started to scroll through old messages, which were all either from Mike, her recent ex, or Alex her current boss. That was it. No one else. Not surprising really. One explained the other. Work came first, last and accounted for most of the middle. She never made time for anything or anyone else. As though to prove it, she navigated to her address book. Her heart sank at the handful of entries. Feeling hollow inside she locked the phone and threw it back into the bag.

She slumped back onto the sunbed and sighed again. She didn't like having so much time to ponder and she wasn't used to being so inactive. Now, with more time than she had plans for, she sadly wondered how she had come to find herself alone with her thoughts and a bag of books she had no intention of reading.

She let her head loll to the side and looked across at Amy who was snatching five minutes with her latest paperback while waiting for Ethan's return. Cat cast her mind back to when they had booked the holiday. Then they had talked about sightseeing, and hiking, and even cycling. Everything except what they had been doing. She had been so excited. The holiday had seemed just what she'd needed but sitting for hours on end by the pool watching someone else read, or flirt, wasn't what she'd had in mind. She was beginning to wish she was back at work. At least there she was constantly challenged. Never a day would go by without some sort of problem to solve or puzzle to figure out.

Life in the Serious Crime Squad was anything but dull, apart from the paperwork, and even that wasn't *that* bad. Although she hadn't expected it, her research experience had proven a useful training ground. The need to dig lay somewhere deep inside her. It's what made her happy.

'Sorry I've been so long,' Ethan said as he approached. He put a tray with two pints of beer in plastic glasses and a visibly chilled bottle of water down on the small table and drew over a white plastic chair. 'The bar was packed,' he said, setting a beer down in front of Amy, who immediately downed a quarter of it.

'Someone's thirsty,' Cat said.

'Call it a liquid lunch,' Amy said, whilst smiling at Ethan.

'That's a thought,' Cat said. 'Any idea what time it is?'

'Nearly one,' Ethan said.

'God, is it really?' Cat said. 'Maybe we should go and grab something to eat?'

'Didn't you say it was busy up there?' Amy said, looking at Ethan. 'We could leave it for a while. Get something later, from the snack bar.'

'Fine. I'll go on my own,' Cat said, barely concealing her irritation.

She stood up and hastily threw on her t-shirt and shorts. She gave a little salute in Ethan's direction with the unopened bottle of water, managing to squeeze the word 'cheers' out through clenched teeth, and walked away.

As she approached the terrace, faced with the option of eating alone or foisting herself onto other guests, Cat's appetite abandoned her.

With the exception of the reception staff, the lobby was deserted and Cat was grateful for the quiet. She headed over to a pair of settees sitting either side of a low coffee table in the furthest corner, where she was less likely to be interrupted, and plugged in her tablet. The air in the marble-tiled room was cool, bordering on cold, and the area where she was sitting devoid of windows, giving it all of the appeal of a stationery cupboard, but she was comfortable enough.

Availing herself of the hotel's free wi-fi, she quickly found the network and within ten minutes had enough recommendations to be able to eat out every night that remained of her holiday. She drummed her fingers restlessly on the clip-on keyboard, waiting for inspiration to hit. After a few seconds she began to tap away at a pace that suggested a familiar routine. Her email account opened up and she spent a further five minutes trawling through spam missed by the filters before logging out, mildly disappointed but not at all surprised to have found nothing of interest in her inbox.

She thought for a minute and then began to type:

Hypoglycaemia

She pressed enter and selected a link.

Low blood sugar occurs when glucose absorbed into the bloodstream after a meal drops below normal levels. It can be caused by meals or snacks that are too small, delayed, or skipped, increased physical activity, or alcoholic beverages.

She continued to scan the text.

Hypoglycaemia can happen suddenly. It is usually mild and can be treated quickly and easily by eating or drinking a small amount of glucose-rich food. If left untreated, hypoglycaemia can get worse and cause confusion, irritability, clumsiness, or fainting. Severe hypoglycaemia can lead to seizures, coma, and even death.

'Well done Cat. Tell me something I didn't know,' she said quietly to herself.

She let her fingers reach for the keyboard once again and typed:

Hypoglycaemia effects of alcohol.

She selected one of the more promising search results:

Hypoglycaemia can mimic the effects of alcohol.
Some of the early warning signs of low blood glucose levels, such as dizziness, disorientation and sleepiness, can mimic drunken behaviour. This could cause others to mistake hypoglycaemic symptoms for the effects of alcohol, and they may not realize they need to seek help. Make sure friends and relatives know that low blood glucose and drunken behaviour share common features...

'Hmm. So, the diabetes itself could have been what made Tony appear drunk.'

She frowned.

Surely his family would have known that? She then remembered Ethan's initial concern at Tony's behaviour on the dance floor, but even he had been reassured after conferring with Jaclyn. Everything pointed to the fact that Tony had been on top of his condition and had taken his prescribed doses of insulin at the right times that day. In that case, what the hell had caused the hypoglycaemia? She tapped her fingers lightly yet impatiently on the keyboard.

She stopped drumming and typed:

Mimic the effects of insulin

She skim-read the first screen of search results and immediately knew she was out of her depth. Even if she could be bothered to

101

wade through the numerous academic postulations, with the amount of chemistry referenced in them they may as well have been written in Sanskrit. But then two of the results caught her eye. The first related to the effects of mercury poisoning, which amongst other things could impact on insulin production. The second was a more obscure entry for epinephrine, which initially seemed promising until Cat got to the bit where it was revealed that rather than promote excessive insulin, which would have had the same impact as copious amounts of alcohol, adrenalin actually inhibited insulin production. It was a non-starter.

'What *am* I doing?' she muttered. 'Why can't I relax like a normal bloody person?'

She folded the tablet, snapping the keyboard closed and stood up. There was nothing else for it, other than to bite the bullet and return to the pool. The contrast—a hike of twelve degrees into the thirty-degree heat—was marked. She walked languidly down the stone steps to the pool. Ethan and Amy were where she had left them, heads bent, deep in conversation.

'Hey,' she said.

They both looked up at her but there was something in their expressions that roused Cat's suspicions.

'Did you get lunch?' Amy asked.

'No. I didn't feel like it in the end.'

'What've you been up to then?' Amy asked, staring at the tablet in Cat's hand.

'I've been looking at restaurants in the area,' she said. 'I've produced a list of the top ten with the best reviews. I thought we could book one for tonight. What do you think?'

Ethan shot a glance towards Amy, leaving Cat in no doubt that something was going on.

'What is it?' she said.

Amy looked sheepishly away from Cat and down at her feet. 'Well, it's just that... Ethan has asked me... Well...'

Ethan came to her rescue.

'I've been given two tickets for the opening of a local restaurant and it seemed a shame to waste them. Amy has kindly agreed to accompany me to dinner tonight.'

Cat let out a deflated 'Oh.' The expletive that should have followed, remaining trapped in her throat.

'I didn't think you'd mind,' Amy said, but she could barely bring herself to look Cat in the eye.

Cat knew her friend hadn't given her a second thought when she'd agreed to go and was now feeling guilty.

'I think I should go and let you two talk,' Ethan stood and set off towards the terrace before either of them could respond.

Quiet filled the space.

After a minute Amy cleared her throat. 'I thought you'd gone to talk to Phil.'

Cat remained silent.

'You could use this as an opportunity to get to know him better.'

Cat bit her tongue. If she started speaking now, God knows what she'd say.

'Aren't you in the slightest bit interested?' Amy asked, making it sound as though she was some sort of freak if she said no.

Cat had no choice. She either answered or bit the tip of her tongue clean off. She took the least painful option.

'Interested? Interested in what... some seedy holiday romance? You might be happy throwing yourself at the first bloke to come along but don't judge everybody by your own standards.'

Amy looked at Cat. Her features slowly clouded over.

'You fancy Ethan, don't you?'

'What?' Cat said, shaking her head.

'Are you saying I'm wrong? Apart from the fact that Mike was blonde and Ethan's dark, the pair of them could be twins.'

'I don't believe you sometimes.'

Cat snatched her things up and marched off. As soon as she was out of view of the pool, she slowed to a stroll as she mulled over Amy's words. Grudgingly, she had to admit, Amy did in fact have a point. Ordinarily she would have fallen for Ethan's charm and would have pegged him as someone she'd definitely want to get to know better. A lot better. His looks, his build, the way he dressed, even the way he carried himself. No, *especially* the way he carried himself. He oozed confidence. He was someone who looked good and knew it. Mike had been the same and Cat had bought the image, and the lies. And what had made it even worse was that she never guessed about his roving eye, not to mention his other wandering body parts, which she'd come to hear about over the last few months since their break up. Suddenly she felt the disappointment, anger and, stupidly, shame, wash over her all over again. How come she had been the only one never to have noticed? She was supposed to be a detective for Christ-sakes.

It was a relief to finally reach the room. All she wanted to do was to secrete herself away and give in to the tears that were beginning to prick at her eyes. She felt about in her shorts' pockets for her key card but it wasn't there. She reached into her bag and began to fish around until her patience finally snapped.

'Stupid fucking thing,' she cursed under her breath, setting the bag down onto the floor and pulling it open.

'Looking for this?' Amy asked, holding the card aloft, a rueful expression on her face.

Cat stood up and took the offered key card and, with no energy for words, she opened the door and entered the room.

Amy followed her in.

'Cat, I'm sorry. I really didn't mean to upset you. I was just so pleased he asked me. I'll tell him I can't go. That I've changed my mind.'

Cat sat down on the bed, shoulders slumped. She knew her friend was in the wrong but they were only friends and it wasn't like they were particularly close. Cat knew she didn't have any right to expect much. But then how much was too much?

'I don't know what to say Amy. Tell me if you think I'm over-reacting but I've been looking forward to this holiday for weeks and to be honest it hasn't been that much fun so far. And now, the thought of having dinner on my own...' As she said the words, their meaning clutched at her chest.

'You're not over-reacting.'

Amy laughed, a spontaneous infectious sound, and embraced Cat in a hug.

'Come on, let's go get a drink and talk about what we're going to do the rest of the week to make this holiday a lot more fun,' she said, pulling Cat gently by the arm, back through the open door.

Eleven

With the promise of better things to come, Cat tried to look positively on the evening ahead. Starting with a long soak in the bath with Amy's abandoned page-turner, she added half a bottle of champagne on room service for a bit of Dutch courage. Squeaky clean and slightly tipsy, she took her time getting ready and still managed to be at the bar, a margarita at her lips, by seven. The combination of salt and lime made her taste buds zing. And she was feeling pretty zingy herself, the pre-prandial pampering having done the trick.

A stray tress escaped from the loosely tied top knot that attempted to tame her auburn curls. She tucked it behind her ear. As she moved, she noticed how the fabric of her dress gave gently, exposing the curves of her cleavage. She reached down and picked and fussed at it, until she was once again comfortably covered. She eased back in her seat; her fingers toyed with her mobile that rested on the countertop, a physical crutch to compensate for her crippling reserve.

'A dry white wine, please,' a quiet voice at her shoulder said.

Cat turned as Gillian Foulds clambered onto the stool next to her. Not for the first time she noticed how different she was to the rest of the American women. Short and softly padded, she wore her dun-coloured hair flat over her full round face, its complexion looking sore and blotchy where she had inconsistently applied sun-protection to her super-sensitive skin.

Cat waited for her to settled before turning and introducing herself.

'Hi, I'm Cat.'

A look of surprise registered on the other woman's face.

'Oh. I'm Gillian Foulds. I mean, just, Gillian.'

'Beautiful night, isn't it?' Cat said.

The dowdy American gave a smile, unexpectedly lighting up her whole face.

'Isn't it?'

After a brief pause, Cat said, 'It's very quiet tonight. For a while I thought I was going to be the only one down for dinner.'

Gillian looked around, only then appearing to notice they were the only people there.

'I suppose a lot of people must be on the Cairo trip.'

'Oh, I'd forgotten about that. That's today is it?'

'Yes.'

'You didn't fancy it then?'

'It's too hot for me here. God knows what it would be like there. The sun plays havoc with my skin.'

'Oh.' Cat couldn't think of anything else to say so reached for her glass and took a slow sip.

She was beginning to regret her decision to come down early, until it occurred to her, she might be able to learn more about the dead American.

'I'm sorry about your friend, Tony,' she said. 'It must have been a real shock. It happening suddenly like that.'

Gillian nodded keenly.

'I know. It doesn't seem real. To be honest I don't think it's quite sunk in. They always say diabetes can be dangerous but Tony was always so careful with his meds.'

'I saw his wife earlier. In the lobby. She seems to be taking it pretty badly.'

'She'll be fine. Jaclyn's just too used to being in control of everything, that's her problem.' Gillian must have caught Cat's shocked expression as she went on, 'I'm sorry, that must sound bitchy but I've known her a long time.'

107

'Had you known Tony very long too?'

'Oh forever. He and David were just starting out when I first met them. I was barely twenty. The two of them were business partners back then. All full of hope and big ideas.'

'You must have a lot of fond memories.'

'Yes. Tony could be so charming. I guess a lot of entrepreneurs are. He was a very handsome man in those days too.' She paused and stared into the distance. A smile re-emerged, only this one was small and sad. 'That was all a very long time ago.'

'And you've been friends all these years,' Cat said.

Gillian simply nodded and turned her attention to Andreas, who placed a large glass of white wine in front of her.

After the barman had left, Gillian turned to Cat.

'Are you looking forward to the opening tonight?'

'The opening?' Cat frowned, though quickly it lifted. 'Oh, no, that's my friend, Amy.'

'Oh, I'm sorry, I thought it was you.'

'That's alright.'

'She should enjoy it. I was hoping to go, but my husband said he's too tired.'

'Is it a new place that's opening?'

The other woman shook her head.

'No. It's been refurbished following the arson attack last year.'

'Arson?'

'I know, I was surprised. A little out of the way place like this. They think it's some animal rights extremist. The first week we were here, one of the wholesalers Tony did business with, had his warehouse burnt to the ground. Tony wasn't too impressed when they were forced to cancel his order.'

'What are they protesting about?' Cat asked.

'I'm not entirely sure. Some sort of local speciality. Pickled birds. It has a fancy name I can never remember.'

Any hope of turning the conversation back to Tony and the circumstances surrounding his death swiftly died as just then David Foulds arrived. He eased himself onto a bar stool, barely acknowledging his wife.

'A glass of the usual,' he called over to Andreas.

'I take it you couldn't find it?' Gillian asked.

'What?'

'The map. That's what you went looking for, wasn't it?'

'Oh that. Yes, it was in the car.'

'It took you long enough to find.'

'It had slipped down the side of the seat. I couldn't see it at first,' David's expression suddenly lifted. 'Hello there,' he called to Jaclyn, who had just rounded the corner. 'We're having a pre-dinner drink. What would you like?'

'Something strong,' she said, joining them at the bar. 'I'll have a dirty martini.' David slipped off his stool and immediately repositioned himself to stand between both women.

'What's happened now?' Gillian asked.

'You won't believe the day I've had. The hoops they made me jump through just to get Tony back home. It's been an absolute nightmare.' She reached for her drink as soon as the barman set it in front of her. 'Can we go and sit inside? I feel a chill coming on.'

'Would you like to borrow this?' Gillian offered, holding out a generously sized cornflower blue bolero jacket.

The other woman shot her a look of contempt.

'Of course we can go inside,' David Foulds said, saving Jaclyn from coming up with some ungrateful response to go with her acid expression.

Jaclyn immediately started walking and David Foulds fell into step beside her. Gillian picked up her glass and followed behind them, shoulders sagging.

Cat was still staring after them, wondering whether it was just her lot in life to be alone, when she heard footsteps approach.

'Hi,' Phil said, as he joined her at the bar.

Cat patted the stool next to her.

'Come and join me.'

Phil pointed a finger towards a set of rattan chairs. Wide-eyed, Bethany returned their gaze.

'Of course, sorry,' Cat said.

'Actually, I came to see if you'd like to join us,' Phil said.

'I'd love to.'

She grabbed her bag and her phone and slid off the stool. Phil paused and looked back towards the hotel lobby.

'No Amy?' he asked.

Cat gave a tight smile.

'Not tonight.'

'Surely not the Germans again?'

'Worse. The Americans.' In response to the puzzled expression on Phil's face she was able to elaborate in a single word. 'Ethan.'

'Oh. I see,' he said. 'Well, go and say hello to Bethany and I'll get us some drinks. Same again?' He gestured to the empty cocktail glass.

Cat looked down, surprised to see she'd already finished her margarita.

'Nuh-uh, one's enough. I'll have a beer, thanks.'

Soon the invitation to join them extended to dinner and before long the company and the effects of the alcohol had made her all but forget that Amy had left her high and dry.

'Doesn't look like Brian's planning an early start tomorrow,' Cat said. She'd spotted him with Sura looking excitedly on as the waiter cracked open a bottle of champagne.

'It's their tenth wedding anniversary. I heard them talking about it earlier. Sura read Brian the riot act if he so much as thought about going birdwatching tomorrow morning.'

'I don't blame her, poor woman. Hey, talking of birds, have you heard of a local delicacy, something to do with pickled birds?'

'Birds?'

'Gillian Foulds—you know, the American lawyer's wife—she was just telling me how some arsonist has been targeting places that sell them. Pretty extreme don't you think?'

'The pickled birds or the arson attacks?'

Cat frowned.

'I was thinking of the arson attacks. Why would the birds be extreme?'

'They use quite barbaric ways to trap them.'

'Barbaric?'

'So I heard. How come you were talking about that, anyway?'

'I can't remember how it started. Just passing the time really.'

Phil gave her a sympathetic look.

'I take it the holiday isn't quite panning out the way you hoped?'

'That's one way of putting it. To be honest, if I'd have known it was going to be like this I wouldn't have come.'

'It's a bit soon to write it off, isn't it?'

'Actually, Amy has promised to do something different tomorrow. I'm sure it'll be an act of contrition for gallivanting off, rather than because she wants to, but I shan't be complaining. As long as I don't have to spend another day around that bloody pool.'

For the rest of the meal they explored their mutual love of books and films, and found a shared taste in music, both liking an eclectic mix of rock and grunge; though, for the most part, they talked about the areas where their tastes diverged, taking the opportunity for a bit of gentle ribbing. After dinner they retired to the bar. Bethany was playing animatedly with her doll, swooping it up and down the length of the coffee table. Cat gave Phil a quizzical look.

111

'It's the Little Mermaid. She's swimming,' he said.

Bethany looked up at her father and grinned. ''wimmin'.'

'She'd watch the film every minute of every day if she had the chance. She's rationed to once a week.'

'It's amazing they can keep themselves occupied for so long with so little. I don't know what I would have done if you hadn't let me join you tonight.'

'I should be thanking you. It's nice to have some adult conversation.'

Cat smiled.

'Can I get you another drink?' Phil gestured to her empty glass.

Cat was staring into space when he came back from the bar. She started as he put her wine on the table in front of her. He returned to his seat and Bethany snuggled up next to him, mumbling away to the doll cradled in her arms.

He lifted his glass.

'Cheers. Here's to the holiday taking a turn for the better!' He touched his glass to hers. 'So, what do you do to keep busy now that you're single?' he asked. Cat must have looked surprised by the question as he quickly went on to add, 'If you don't do sitting around I mean. I sometimes find it difficult to fill the void, especially the evenings. Less so now, but when Penny and I first split up it was hard.'

Cat didn't need to think about it.

'I work. There's always something to do. But too much work makes Cat a very dull girl. Or at least that's what my boss keeps telling me.'

She recalled Alex's comments as he dropped her off at Gatwick. At the time she thought he was over-exaggerating her tendency to use work to avoid dealing with things. On reflection perhaps he was right.

'I can't imagine that for a minute,' Phil said

'Imagine what?' Cat asked, having forgotten her original comment.

'Cat being a very dull girl.'

She looked at him. They locked eyes for a moment. Sensing her quickening heart, she turned away. Phil looked down at Bethany, who lay close to him, her head resting on his lap and her doll clutched to her chest. Cat took a drink and returned her glass to the table, looking around she noticed that most of the seats were now filled.

'It's suddenly got really busy.'

Phil looked around.

'I guess everyone's finished dinner.' He glanced at his watch. 'I should really think about getting Bethany to bed before she gets too comfortable.'

Cat remained quiet.

Phil looked down at his nearly full pint and turned towards her.

'I don't mean this to sound like a come on, but we've both got drinks to finish. We could take them back to my room and carry on talking? Feel free to say no. I won't be offended if you don't want to.'

'Make yourself at home. I'll just get Bethany ready for bed.'

With his daughter bundled over one shoulder, Phil picked up her nightclothes from underneath a pillow on one of the room's twin beds and disappeared into the bathroom. With the door slightly ajar Cat could hear him coaxing the little girl through her nightly routine.

After taking a cursory look around the room—nosiness second nature—she walked over to the window, pulled the curtain to one side and let herself out onto the balcony. The night was balmy. The moon's waxy light formed a ghostly path across the shimmering inky black water of the bay.

She slipped the cashmere shrug off her shoulders and draped it over the arm of a white plastic patio chair before returning her gaze to the night's sky where she stared into the moon's ashen aura; a perfectly round silver orb. It was so beautiful. So quiet. The only sound to be heard was the shushing of the sea below; the waves coursing in and out like the breath of a sleeping serpent.

Cat sighed as a feeling close to contentment crept over her. She turned and stepped back into the room just as the bathroom door opened, emitting a shaft of light into which Phil emerged, Bethany trailing, tired-eyed and smelling of toothpaste.

'And she'll sleep okay with us sitting here talking?' Cat asked.

'Yes, she can sleep anywhere.' And, as though picking up on the unasked question, added, 'But at least she'll be more comfortable here and I won't have to try to get her undressed when she's fast asleep.'

Cat kicked off her sandals and picked up her drink. She moved slowly, unlike the thoughts which raced through her head. She was aware of Phil watching her intently.

She looked at him.

'What? Is there something there?' she asked, gently running her fingers through her hair.

'No.' Phil laughed quietly.

'What is it?' Cat was beginning to feel uncomfortable under his scrutiny, although there was something about the warmth radiating from his eyes that made her want to trust him. Again, his eyes locked on to hers.

He shook his head and let out a small snort of a laugh.

'I can't believe I'm sitting in my room with such an attractive woman and can think of absolutely nothing to say.'

Cat laughed softly.

'You're joking right?'

'About which bit? The fact you're attractive or that I've got sawdust for brains?' Cat felt herself blush. 'No?' Phil said, a lop-sided smile having settled on his face.

He leaned up against a cushion at the head of his bed.

'Tell me more about the Maldives.'

'There's not a lot to say. I spent a lot of time bobbing around in a boat. You'd think it would be easy looking for something the size of a double-decker bus but believe me it wasn't. Mind you, saying that, they are a bit like buses. You could go hours without seeing one then all of a sudden three would go past.' Suddenly animated, Cat continued, 'It was such a fantastic experience and it really felt like I was making a difference. At least that's what I thought then. Whale sharks are on the red list. Their population is expected to decline by as much as fifty per cent over the next century. But nobody knows the true number of whale sharks in the world, or whether that number is really in decline. We tracked them, tagged them, measured them, photographed them. We even named them.'

'What do you do now? Now you're not in the Maldives.'

'Similar sort of stuff. One-off projects aimed at protecting vulnerable species.'

She saw his eyebrow give a little twitch.

'Is that why you were interested in the pickled birds?' Phil lifted his glass to his lips and took a drink. 'You mentioned them earlier.'

'Oh that. No, I was just intrigued. It sounds gross.' She picked at a loose thread on the hem of her shirt. 'Anyway, enough about me. What sort of things do you like to do when you're not working?'

'I do a bit of cycling, and I run a little.'

'Road cycling or off-road?'

'A bit of both but mainly on-road.' He drained the last of his pint and stood up.

'You're not one of those blokes who spends every Sunday morning hanging around in Lycra with your mates?' Cat asked, trying hard to suppress a giggle. 'What are they called? Man something... Oh I can't remember.'

Phil's smirk gave him away.

'You are!' she said a little too loudly and clamped her fingers to her lips. 'You are, aren't you?' she whispered.

'Not *every* weekend.' He made his way over to the far end of the room, to the wardrobe doors. 'Well, most, maybe. And the name you're looking for is MAMILs. It stands for middle-aged men in Lycra. Although I'd argue I've got some way to go before I'm happy being called middle-aged.'

'Do you compete?'

'Occasionally.'

He bent down and reached into the bottom of the wardrobe and began to rummage around.

'Another drink?' He pulled out a bottle of wine and brandished it with a flourish. Holding it at arm's length, he glanced at the label and affecting a plummy Home Counties accent, read, 'A 2003 Keo Heritage made from a grape native to the Troodos mountains. Rich with flavours of cherry, chocolate and probably some of the local dirt, it perfectly showcases the local terroir.' He dropped the accent. 'I bought it to take home as a present for my wine snob of a brother. It's a thankyou for looking after the cat while I'm away. I can easily get hold of a replacement. Unless you don't want another?'

Cat paused. Her head already felt swimmy with alcohol. Then she thought of her empty room and, letting her actions speak for themselves, held up her glass.

'Go on then, seeing as it's got such a good pedigree.'

With Cat's glass replenished Phil fetched a beaker from the bathroom and poured himself a good glug of the deep berry-coloured liquid.

'Cheers,' Cat said, raising her glass.

'Yamas.'

'So, do you ever win?' she asked as their glasses gently touched.

'Win?' He looked confused.

'Your races... do you ever win?'

'Sometimes. If I'm lucky.'

'Yeah? I bet the more you train the luckier you get, right?'

He laughed and seemed humbled by her comment.

'There speaks the voice of experience.'

'No. Not me. I run to keep fit, not to win medals. No, I was thinking of my brother. He, unlike me, was very competitive. He trained bloody hard and he used to win a lot.'

Phil sat forward on the edge of the bed and looked at her.

'Was?' he asked in a hushed voice.

'One day his luck ran out.'

Cat's eyes misted over and she dropped her gaze to her glass.

She could sense Phil's trepidation, his reluctance to ask the question that had jumped to his lips, but she knew that to sidestep it would reveal their evening's conversations for the sham that she hoped it hadn't been. He didn't disappoint.

'What happened?'

'He was killed in a road accident. Actually, it was a hit and run. They never did catch the bastard,' she said in little more than a whisper. 'Bit of a shock really.'

'Bloody hell, I bet it was. Was that recently?'

'Five years ago. Recent enough.'

'God, I'm sorry. How awful.' He reached over and took her hand.

Cat felt the breath catch in her throat. She leaned towards him. Her gaze flickered between his inviting eyes and just parted lips. Lips that met hers with perfect resistance. The first tentative touch of his tongue drew her in, sending her already racing pulse off the chart. He reached a hand gently behind her neck and softly pulled her closer. A small groan escaped her throat. She could feel her sexuality awaken. Unfortunately, it wasn't the only thing.

'Daddy...' a tiny voice called.

They both jumped, reinstating the distance between them.

'Go back to sleep darling. It's still bedtime.'

He looked wide-eyed at Cat and it wasn't until they both heard the little girl settle back down, they stopped holding their breath.

Cat tucked her hair behind her ears, a small but significant movement; a business-like gesture that signalled an end to their dalliance.

'I should get going,' she said, slipping on her sandals.

'You don't have to. Look, she's fast asleep again.' He looked back across at his daughter, as though doubting his very words.

'It's late. I really...'

'It's okay. You're right. It is late,' Phil said, saving her from any further embarrassment. He looked around the small and sparsely furnished room.

'Did you have a jacket?'

'A little cardigan thing. I must have left it on the balcony.'

Cat stepped out into the cool night air. Phil followed her out. She looked at him, sure she could see disappointment in his eyes. She let her gaze fall to the floor. Frowning, she bent down and picked up a pair of expensive-looking binoculars from underneath the plastic patio table.

'Here,' Phil said, holding out a hand. 'I'll take those in with me. They shouldn't really be left out all night.'

Cat hefted the black aluminium object in her hand before putting them up to her eyes.

'Bloody hell! These are amazing.'

She lowered them and looked at Phil, who reached over and took them from her.

'Night vision binoculars?' she said.

'I'm trialling them for work.'

'What are you... like a spy?'

He reached for the pale beige shrug and passed it to her. His hand touched hers and lingered a moment longer than necessary. Cat shrank away and cast him a murmured goodnight along with an embarrassed glance, before slipping through the door and making her way out of the room.

Her room was still empty when Cat returned. It seemed strange, being there on her own, and she wondered whether Amy would actually be back that night or whether she'd have to wait until morning to hear all about the hot date. She undressed and got ready for bed. Lying there, staring at the ceiling, her thoughts slipped back to that kiss. Her heart danced a little jig at the memory. She let out a loud sigh and banged her head back on the pillow. Such lack of willpower! She'd come on holiday for some time on her own, to get out of the house and away from the memories of another failed relationship. The last thing she needed was some meaningless holiday fling.

A soft scuffling noise in the corridor saved her from any more musing. She raised herself up on an elbow and listened. Muted voices filtered through the door, too muffled to hear what was being said. Then came the sound of the fumbling of a key card being fed through the reader. Slipping the covers up to her shoulder Cat turned over just as the door swung open. For a brief moment, light streamed in, then the door clicked closed.

'Cat,' Amy whispered. 'Cat, are you awake?'

For a moment she considered feigning sleep but then relented.

'Yes,' she said, turning over, blinking as Amy turned on the light. She hitched herself up on one elbow. 'Good night?'

'Oh Cat, it was the most fantastic night ever. It was brilliant. Ethan was amazing. He's such a good listener. I can't remember the last time I talked so much on a date. And you should hear him talk Greek. He's so fluent you'd mistake him for a local.'

Cat lay back down.

'I can't wait to hear all about it at breakfast.'

Undeterred, Amy came over and sat on the side of Cat's bed, trapping her under the covers.

'We went to this bar owned by one of the suppliers they've been doing business with. I'm not joking, they treated us like royalty. We had champagne—on the house—and these little dim sum things. It felt so exclusive. And then we went on to this gorgeous little restaurant. We should go, you'd love it. It was a real local's sort of place but they all seemed to know Ethan. I swear I've had one of the best nights ever. I thought I'd died and gone to heaven.' Amy gave a wide yawn, the excitement of the evening evidently taking its toll.

'You can tell me all about it in the morning,' Cat said, gently pushing her away.

With Amy in the bathroom, Cat lay back down and closed her eyes. Once again, she thought back to her evening with Phil. This time, another part—the romantic in her—inveigled itself into her thoughts, painting pretty pictures of what might have been. Soon she drifted off, a serene smile settled on her lips, wondering whether she would ever get to find out.

Twelve

Standing at the open window he looked out at the brightening sky. Only ten minutes earlier and the landscape had appeared as though etched in charcoal, the white-walled buildings defined by shadows. And then the sun reached a tipping point and light seeped across the rooftops, reaching out and banishing the dark from all but the deepest recesses.

'Come on...' He held the phone to his ear, the monotony of the ring tone stretching his patience.

He heard a click, then a thin slice of silence before a voice at the other end asked sharply, 'You have news?'

'No, nothing.' He stepped back into the folds of the curtain on seeing a figure walk across the path away from the pool towards the hotel. 'I take it nothing's come up at your end?'

'No. It looks like you were right about him not doing anything last night. You will be ready tonight then?'

'Of course.'

The line went dead.

Thirteen

Amy prodded and poked at the contents of her plate whilst staring dreamily into space, while Cat returned to the buffet bar, despite having already devoured a helping of scrambled eggs on toast. Minutes later she was back in her seat tucking into a stack of blueberry pancakes smothered in Greek yoghurt and drizzled with honey.

Amy stared at the full plate of food.

'You did actually go to dinner last night, didn't you?'

'I just fancied something fruity, that's all,' Cat said, though she was really after something to soothe her hungover head and unsettled stomach, the alcohol from the previous night taking its toll. She poured herself a third cup of tea. 'So, last night then... am I going to get to hear the rest of the story?'

'Oh Cat, I felt like I was in some Hollywood blockbuster. Everything was so perfect. We went to this quaint little bar first and had champagne cocktails. Olive Grove or Olive Garden, or something like that anyway. Then we went on to the place he had tickets for. Ethan said it used to be one of the best restaurants in the whole of Cyprus before it closed last year.' She gazed into the distance, a soft curve on her lips.

'And...?' Cat said.

'Sorry. What was I saying?'

'You were telling me about the restaurant last night. Wait, let me guess, it was *fantastic*?' Cat said, her terrible imitation of her friend making them both laugh.

'Honestly though, it was. Really beautiful. Apparently, it had virtually been burnt to the ground only last year.'

'I heard about the fire.'

'You did?'

'I bumped into that American woman, Gillian, in the bar last night. She mentioned it.'

'The blobby one?'

'Oh Amy, that's not nice.'

'Yes, but you knew who I meant, didn't you? What did she have to say for herself? Is she as dull as she looks?'

'She's all right. She told me the fire was actually arson.'

'Yeah, a lot of people were talking about it when we were there. There have been more attacks recently.'

'Did you hear what they think the motive behind it is?'

'No.' Amy took a bite of her toast.

'They suspect it's an animal rights activist protesting against restaurants that sell a certain delicacy.'

'What sort of delicacy?'

'Pickled birds.'

'What... like chickens?'

'No. I looked it up on my phone this morning. It's song birds—robins, blackcaps, thrushes, that sort of thing.'

Amy wrinkled her nose.

'Well, I certainly didn't see anything like that on the menu. I know I'm not into birds like you but even I don't think I could bring myself to eat pickled thrush.'

'They're hardly likely to have it on their specials board. It's illegal.'

'Oh.' Amy's confused expression was quickly replaced by a smirk. 'So, this is the sort of scintillating conversation that the lovely Gillian has to offer. Poor you.'

'Don't worry about me. I enjoyed myself.' Amy fixed her with a dubious look. 'Honestly I did. Anyway, I didn't think we'd be spending quite as long discussing how I spent my evening.' Cat could feel the colour flooding into her face and knew she needed

123

to divert Amy's attention. 'You haven't finished telling me about your date. I'm dying to know; how did it go?'

Like a child bribed out of a tantrum with the promise of a large ice cream, Amy was easily distracted and a smile tugged at the corners of her mouth, lighting her face.

'You didn't?' Cat said theatrically.

The smile turned into a beam.

'We only kissed,' Amy said hurriedly.

'And is there going to be a part two to this romantic tale?'

'I bloody hope so,' Amy said. 'Ethan's had to go to Paphos today, something to do with business, but he said he'd drop by the pool as soon as he gets back.'

'Oh good,' Cat said, trying hard to hide her disappointment. 'Another day by the pool.'

'Morning,' Phil said, as he settled Bethany into her seat at an adjacent table.

'Morning,' Cat said.

'On your own again?' He was looking at the empty seat that Amy had briefly occupied. Then he looked at Cat, his eyes twinkling with mischief. 'Or is she not back yet?'

'No, she's been and gone already. Got to go and get a sunbed. You know what it's like.'

'The Germans?'

Cat laughed and nodded.

'I thought the two of you were going to do something different today. Wasn't that part of the deal?'

'I've come to the conclusion that sunbathing, books and good-looking Americans are always going to trump whatever I'd like to do.'

He gave her a sympathetic look.

'So, what about you? Have you got any plans for the day?'

'Not at the—'

'Sorry, excuse me,' Phil said, interrupting the conversation at the arrival of a waiter, who stood expectantly with his order pad poised. 'A pot of tea please. No orange juice today but can I have a couple of hard-boiled eggs, freshly boiled. Not the ones from the buffet. Thanks.'

'I like your pigtails Bethany, they make you look very pretty,' Cat commented, pointing to the little girl's plaits. Bethany giggled and squirmed from side to side at the compliment.

'She was feeling a bit under the weather this morning. Upset tummy. I'm just hoping it's nothing serious. Food poisoning and four-year-olds do not go together.'

'God, I bet.'

'That's one of the reasons we go full-board. I'm not saying the standard of hygiene in the local cafes and restaurants isn't great but at least the food here is definitely fresh.' Phil paused as the waiter arrived with the tea.

'Daddy, breakfast. I want yogit. Now, Daddy,' Bethany wailed, having grown impatient at their casual chat.

'No darling, no yoghurt today. We're going to have a nice chucky egg and toast. You like that, don't you?'

The little girl nodded vigorously.

Cat stood up and pushed away her chair.

'I should get going and leave you to it. Amy's going to think I've deserted her.'

Like she did to you? She imagined Phil thought but was far too tactful to say.

From the top step, Cat looked across the pool to where her friend was lying, book in hand. She headed over.

Amy turned on hearing her approach.

'Hey, you've been ages. I thought I was going to have to come looking for you.'

Cat's attention picked up.

'Why's that?' She barely dared breathe life on to the glimmer of hope that was borne on those few words.

Amy sat up and, for what seemed like the first time that week, put her book to one side.

'Well, you know how yesterday you said you wanted to do something different today? How about going into Paphos for lunch?'

Her words were like oxygen to a glowing ember of happiness.

'That would be great. I don't mind driving if you wanted to drink. Or maybe—'

'Don't worry. It's all sorted.'

The smile fell from Cat's face.

'It is?'

'Yep. A taxi will be here at eleven.'

She started to smell a rat.

'You were going anyway?'

Amy looked uneasy.

'Ethan called and invited us *both* to have lunch with him. I assumed you'd want to go. You did say you wanted to get out more.'

'But on a date?'

'It's not a date. I told you, Ethan had to go into Paphos anyway. He's got some business to deal with this morning and he thought it would be fun if we joined him afterwards.'

Cat suddenly realised there was no right way for things to end—an afternoon playing gooseberry or one spent on her own.

'I suppose it would be nice to get out for a while,' she said, although she couldn't quite keep the grudging tone from her voice.

Amy looked at her watch.

'Come on then. We'd better go get ready, otherwise we'll be late.' She picked her sunglasses up off the table and propped them on her head, grabbed her book and set off, leaving Cat to follow behind. Again.

The taxi ferried them from door to door. Cat climbed out and looked around as Amy paid the fare—her treat. The restaurant was stunning: lime-washed walls contrasted harmoniously with the red-tiled roof and troughs of geraniums and bougainvillea flooded the patio with colour. A waiter stood by the entrance, eager to greet them, looking as smart and dapper as the white linen-robed tables, which were finished perfectly with centrepieces of green and cream foliage.

At their table Amy immediately took up a watchful vigil.

'You are so besotted,' Cat said.

'I'm not.'

'You are. You can't sit still for looking for him.'

'I was just checking the place out. It's gorgeous here, isn't it?'

And it was. Set in a corner of a small cobblestone square, the restaurant rubbed shoulders with an ornate gothic church. An antique shop and a deli-cum-bakery-cum-grocer completed the picture of a sleepy, well-heeled Mediterranean village. All tucked away in a quiet corner of bustling, boozy Paphos.

But Cat wasn't buying any of it and fixed Amy with a stare. Her friend responded by letting her head drop before giving a shy shrug of the shoulders.

'Okay, maybe a little smitten.' She looked back at Cat. 'But do you blame me?'

'What are you going to do when Monday comes?'

A small pucker appeared on Amy's brow.

'Monday?'

'When we go home. You can't take him with you, you know.'

'Oh don't. Let me enjoy it while it lasts. Maybe I'll do a Shirley Valentine and stay.'

127

'I doubt that will help you for long. Not unless he's planning on staying too.'

'You never know. After all, he's got nothing to go back for now.'

Cat was about to reply but paused, unsure of what to say. She feared her friend wasn't entirely joking. The waiter arrived with their bottle of wine and a cooler, which he set next to the table.

'Mr Garrett says he is nearly finished. He will be with you soon,' he said, pulling a bottle opener from his pocket.

He paused and reached for Amy's handbag, lifting it from the back of her chair. He set it on the seat next to her and pushed it in under the table.

'Madam, your bag, you must not leave it unguarded like that. The thieves... already Mrs Vostanis. Please, not you.'

He opened and poured the wine then offered it to Amy to taste.

She flapped a hand towards the bottle.

'Just pour it.'

'What happened to Mrs Vostanis?' Cat asked.

'Her bag, taken, you know?' the waiter said.

'Mrs Vostanis had her bag stolen?' Cat said.

The waiter nodded, before hurrying away. Cat tucked her own bag down by her feet.

'Did you know about that?' she asked.

'No,' Amy replied, before taking a sip of her white wine. 'It's not exactly the kind of thing you talk about on a first date.'

'I just thought...'

Cat paused mid-sentence on seeing a grin spread across Amy's face. She turned to see Ethan striding across the floor towards them.

'I thought I heard your voice,' Amy said, suddenly animated.

He leaned towards her and gently embraced her shoulders with long slim fingers. He touched his lips lightly to one cheek and then the next.

'Am I that loud?' he joked.

'No, just distinctive,' she said, by which time, he was repeating the gesture on Cat.

Very Mediterranean.

'Have you ordered yet?' he asked.

'No, only wine,' Amy said. 'We were waiting for you.'

'Sorry. Things took a little longer than I expected.'

He pulled out a chair and almost sat on Amy's bag.

'Here...' she said, taking it from him. 'I'll put it down by my feet.'

'The waiter told us to be careful of our bags,' Cat explained. 'He mentioned Jaclyn had hers stolen from here.'

'Oh, of course. I'd forgotten about that.'

He held up a hand and within seconds the waiter was by his side.

Cat waited for him to finish ordering a scotch before asking, 'Was that recently?'

'What?'

'The stolen bag.'

'Oh that. Yes. A couple of days ago. The day you arrived, in fact.' He rubbed his hands together. 'Anyway, let's order. I'm starving.'

While waiting for their food to arrive, Amy and Ethan shared idle chat. Cat listened with half an ear as she thought through the implications of the stolen bag.

'Did Jaclyn carry her husband's insulin in her bag?' she asked as soon as there was a lull in the conversation.

Ethan looked at her blankly.

'I just wondered whether Tony's syringes were in the stolen bag?'

He shrugged.

'I don't know.'

'It doesn't really matter now does it?' Amy interrupted. 'Just keep an eye on your own bag,' she said before turning the conversation back to more frivolous matters.

A complimentary bottle of champagne, courtesy of the restaurant's owner, arrived with their lunch plates.

'Champagne. Wow!' Amy said.

'Are we celebrating something?' Cat asked as the waiter poured her a glass.

'It's just the owner's way of saying goodbye.' Ethan said. 'This will probably be the last time I'll be here, you know, with what's happened and all.'

Amy's happy, smiling face suddenly dropped.

'But I thought you were going to try to go into business for yourself. Isn't that what you said last night?'

He shrugged.

'That was what I was hoping but based on my meeting this morning I don't think I'll be able to get enough equity together.'

'What will you do instead?' Amy asked.

'I guess I'll have to find a job.' He held his champagne glass up. 'Here's to... well, to new beginnings.'

It was late afternoon by the time they got back to the hotel. Amy suggested making the most of the last few hours of sun by the pool and for once even Cat didn't have the energy to object.

Ethan pointed to a couple of unoccupied sunbeds next to Gillian and the girls.

'I'm sure we can squeeze another lounger on the end.' He looked around the poolside.

Just at that moment Larissa looked up and waved.

'But they've got towels on them,' Amy said.

'Someone's probably just left them there. I'll go and find out.' Amy laid a hand on his arm.

'Why don't we go for a walk along the beach instead?' she said. 'It would be good to work off some of that lunch.'

'I think I'm just going to head to the room and grab a bit of me time,' Cat said with a smile that disappeared as soon as she turned her back.

Cat started a slow walk to her room. In no hurry, she passed the lift and pushed through the double doors into the ground floor corridor, making her way to the stairs. Her pace slowed slightly as she approached Jaclyn's room, the memory of the previous day still strong. This time though, there was no sign of the cleaner and the door was firmly closed. So when it opened and David Foulds stepped out into her path he took them both by surprise. He quickly pulled the door closed behind him and scurried off in the same direction as she was headed, a hare to her tortoise. She looked back to the closed door, a frown puckering her brow.

Back on the balcony to her room, her book lying untouched on the small plastic table, Cat stared into the distance, where rolling hills melded into one another: a mixture of browns, cleft from a palate of sand and clay, dotted with green scrubs of grass and long swathes of gold and yellow rape. A small flock of swallows gate-crashed the view, coming close to wheel around the eaves of the hotel. They flashed quickly through the shared space of her balcony, taking her breath away with their speed and audacity, seeming oblivious to her presence. She watched for a few minutes as they swooped and swirled above her, before expanding the circumference of their route to take in the pool below, mapping a perfect trajectory into the still water, drinking on the wing, before rolling up and out into the sky above.

And then they were gone.

She leaned forward, her arms resting against the hot metal of the balcony. The second-floor room gave an excellent view over much of the hotel's grounds and the beach beyond. She looked over to the pool. Most of the American party appeared to have packed up for the day, with the exception of the two girls, and there was no sign of Amy or Ethan. Over on the sun terrace, Phil, as usual, was bent over a low coffee table helping Bethany with her colouring. Cat's gaze strayed past them towards the bar. A chalkboard placard announced half price cocktails between four and six pm. She looked at her watch: just after four. That probably explained Amy and Ethan's whereabouts, though the awning over the bar meant it was impossible to tell.

She looked back at Phil and the little girl, now engaged in a lively conversation. She smiled as Bethany broke into a fit of giggles as her father lifted her up onto the sofa to tickle her into submission. The girl's squeals pealed around the walls of the hotel.

A little further along David Foulds and Michael Vostanis were sharing a table and a couple of beers. Cat watched as David leaned forward in his seat and waved in the direction of the ground floor suites. She looked over and spotted Jaclyn, perfectly attired in a buttercup yellow and white chiffon sun dress, relaxing on the patio of her room. Jaclyn raised a casual hand in reply. Cat looked back at David Foulds, who now appeared to be gesturing and mouthing something. Jaclyn dismissed his attention with a flick of the hand and returned to the pages of a glossy magazine.

It was obvious to Cat that the American woman's room was clearly visible from parts of the terrace as well as to the half a dozen rooms that shared the same south-facing aspect as her own. She felt her stomach lurch and once again found herself praying no one had actually witnessed her escape from the room the previous day. Although there was always a chance whoever had been in there had hung around long enough to see her, she hoped their own subterfuge would prevent them from exposing hers.

Feeling the need for a distraction, she turned to her book. Two pages later it lay discarded on the table. She picked up her phone and scrolled to the photos taken in Jaclyn's room.

Since his arrival on the holiday isle, Tony had appointments with suppliers pencilled in for every day; two or three on some days. She noticed a number of them had been annotated with a note written in a tidy script and a price against it, which she took to relate to either orders placed or quotes obtained. Others simply had a neat hyphen against them. She looked at the entry for Monday, the day that Tony had died. It confirmed his lunch appointment at Kostas, the same restaurant where she and Amy had lunched earlier, at Ethan's expense. Unsurprisingly, there was no reference to the stolen handbag. It wasn't that type of diary.

'Busy boy,' she murmured.

She scrolled back through the photos until she got to the first of the samples from the large Gladstone bag. The same reference system was in evidence on the samples' labels as had been used in the Filofax. She squinted at the image, the contents of the polythene bag unrecognisable due to the haste with which the photo had been taken.

She returned her phone to the small plastic patio table and went back into the room. On the dressing table, a faux-leather folder, embossed with the hotel's name, contained a range of items. After extracting a small pad of paper and a pencil she returned to her chair in the sun.

She took a moment to consider what she'd found and then started to sketch out an outline of the facts as she knew them, as well as a few she could only guess at.

Tony:

Diabetic
Successful businessman
Domineering, traditionalist
Died of hypoglycaemia. Accident or induced?
Linked to his proposed retirement?
Motives: money, hate (Michael?), love (Jaclyn & David?), revenge

Jaclyn:

Independent lady. Marriage of convenience?
Main beneficiary?
Bag stolen day Tony died.
Intruder in room. What were they doing?

Isabella:

Tension with father (normal for a teenager?)
Unhappy at being passed over in the business

Michael:

Angry young man
Resented Tony's insistence at going into business
Possibly gay? How would Tony react?
Confusing response to father's death
Budding chef. Maybe knows what food causes hypoglycaemia?

David:

Has lost client and old friend yet appears to be happier
Deals with imports. Is he involved in illegal activities?
Offered to take on MD role. Possible motive?
What is his relationship with Jaclyn?

Gillian:
No obvious motive

Larissa:
"man mad"—surely not with Tony?

Ethan:
Strained relationship with Jaclyn
Likely to be privy to family secrets. Knows more than letting on?

Other:
Supplier—what benefit if Tony is regular customer?
Arsonist—was Tony involved in bird trade? Could have made him a target.
Birdwatcher—did the incident on the dancefloor mean anything?
Phil—binoculars???

Reviewing the list, Cat thought about the tension that appeared to exist between the different members of the American party. She had heard so many irate and angry exchanges in such a short space of time she'd almost become immune to the tantrums and had rarely paid attention to what was being said. She made a note to be more observant in future.

What else?

She cast her mind back to the conversation in the restaurant over lunch. To Jaclyn's stolen bag. Could one of Tony's party have taken the bag, removing a doctored syringe? Cat gave a tiny shake of her head. Glafcos had said they had tested the syringes and found only what they expected to find. The syringes can't have been in the bag.

She added:

Is the theft of Jaclyn's bag relevant?

She tapped the sentence with the blunt end of her pencil and for the third time opened her phone and scrolled through the photographs, struggling at times to read the American's unfamiliar handwriting. Cat stared at the page and added two new lines:

Who broke into Jaclyn's room and why?
Someone planting something or someone taking something away?

Fourteen

Cat looked at her watch. 4:45pm. It would be two-forty-five back home.

Maybe he was out?

She lowered the phone and was about to hang up when his voice came through, small and tinny sounding.

'Hello?'

Hurriedly she put the phone back to her ear.

'Hi Alex. It's Cat.'

'Cat?' It seemed to take him a minute to place her. 'Why are you phoning? You are still on holiday, aren't you?'

'Yeah. Are you okay to talk?'

'Sure. I'm in the office. Is something wrong?'

'No, I'm fine and before you ask Amy's fine.'

'But the weather's shit?'

'No, the weather's fantastic.'

'So what the fuck are you calling for?'

'I just wanted to ask a favour.'

'What?' A statement of disbelief, rather than an offer of assistance, but Cat ignored his intonation.

'I just wondered if you had Glafcos's mobile number. I thought I'd got it on my phone but I haven't.'

She'd tried to keep her voice light and cheery but couldn't help give a small grimace as she waited for him to respond, hoping he wouldn't want to know too much.

'Glafcos? Sure, I'll have it somewhere. He'll be pleased to hear from you. Are you planning on paying him and Sofia a visit?'

'No. It's... well actually I might, but first I need to talk to him about a case he's working.'

'What? A case? You're working a case?'

'No. I'm not. He is. One of the guests here was found dead on Monday night and something's come up I think he ought to know about.'

'Are you serious?'

She laughed. Nerves, she thought, the conversation wasn't that funny.

'Look, it's not a big deal. Let me start again. This guy died suddenly; an American here on business. The Cyprus CID is dealing with it. I bumped into Glafcos when he came to talk to the dead guy's wife. We had a bit of a chat and he said something about the tests taking some time to come through. Things are the same the world over, eh?' When her boss and mentor remained silent she pushed on. 'Anyway, on the face of it, it looks like a straightforward hypoglycaemic attack. He was a diabetic who drank and ate too much and, well, no one was really too surprised when it happened. So then—'

'You're like that Murder She Wrote character, Jessica someone,' Alex said, interrupting her. 'Wherever she went someone would wind up dead. What was it, poisoned meze or did someone clobber him over the head with that banjo thing they play?'

Cat let him get it out of his system. He was clearly enjoying the joke.

'First of all, it's Jessica Fletcher. And for the record, I'm nothing like her. Secondly, it's a bouzouki, not a banjo. And finally, I didn't say it was a murder. I just happen to have noticed one or two, well, I don't know, odd things I thought Glafcos might be interested in.'

'Cat,' he said, his voice taking on a warning tone. 'You know what I'm going to say, don't you?'

'You're going to tell me to mind my own business. I know it sounds like I'm meddling but I'm not. I just—'

But her attempt at persuading him otherwise fell on deaf ears and he quickly cut in.

'Too damn right I am. Firstly,' he was mimicking her earlier tone, 'you may be a murder squad detective, but you're not a murder squad detective in Cyprus. Secondly, you are a murder squad detective taking a much-needed holiday. And finally,' he said, stressing it to such an extent that Cat knew her boss was close to terminating their call, 'you just said yourself, you haven't even got a murder!'

'I wasn't planning on doing anything other than give him a call and letting him know what I heard today. I think it might be important.'

After a drawn-out silence she finally heard Alex sigh and knew there was a chance. She just needed to give him a gentle nudge.

'Look, all I'll do is call him, tell him what I heard and let him make his own mind up. That way it's up to him. If the tables were turned, you'd want to know, wouldn't you?'

'Oh fine. But you'll have to wait. I haven't got his number on me. I'll call you back with it later.'

Cat gave a subtle fist-pump that would have done any British tennis player proud.

'Thanks Alex. When?'

'Christ Cat, when you get back we'll need to work on your ability to know when to stop. I'll call you as soon as I get chance.'

'But today, yes?'

'Tonight,' he acceded.

Ten minutes later, sitting on her balcony enjoying the last of the day's sun, Cat closed her eyes and listened to the waves rolling onto the beach below. Soon the noises of the outside world grew muted and distant and she drifted as gently as a falling feather into an easy sleep.

The sun was still comfortably warm when Cat stirred. Amy had returned and was talking to her.

'What?' she mumbled.

'I said, I wondered where you'd got to,' Amy repeated, loudly.

'I told you I was coming back here.'

'I didn't think you meant all afternoon. I thought you hated being cooped up.'

Cat closed her eyes again.

She felt, rather than heard, Amy sit on the adjacent chair. After a minute's silence she gave up and opened one eye to see her friend staring into space, a faraway look on her face.

'What's up with you?'

'Beer?' Amy asked, reaching over to the table where there were two full bottles.

Cat took the offering.

'So?'

Amy turned to look at her with a puzzled expression.

'What?'

'The drink, the moony smile... you're leading up to something. What is it?'

Amy simultaneously shrugged and shook her head but Cat saw through the feigned indifference.

'You've agreed to go out with Ethan again, tonight, haven't you?'

Amy stood up and leaned on the balcony and for a few seconds appeared to have forgotten the question, feigning an interest in the swimming pool below, but eventually said, 'He has asked me but I said I'd talk it over with you first.'

She turned around and looked at Cat who was openly wearing her disappointment. Amy looked away and took a swig of her drink.

'Right. Of course,' Cat said. 'Let's discuss it then. What if I say I'd prefer it if you didn't leave me on my own for the second night running?'

They both knew she'd rumbled Amy's pathetic attempt to make it seem anything other than a done deal.

Amy had returned to staring over the balcony. The sun was hovering lazily above the hills in the distance, causing a riot of reds and oranges to tinge the late afternoon sky.

Without turning around, she replied, 'Okay, so I said I'd go. I thought you'd be okay about it. I'm sorry.'

She didn't sound sorry. A bitter edge had crept into her voice.

Amy picked up her drink and walked back into their room. Cat followed her as far as the doorway and watched as Amy shed her clothes and walked naked into the bathroom.

'Aren't you getting ready a bit early?'

'I told Ethan I'd meet him outside by the front doors at half-past.'

'What, five?'

'Yes.'

'And I'm supposed to do *what* tonight?' Cat called. 'Have dinner on my own... again?' Her voice trembled from the hurt and anger that had her chest in its grip.

Amy reappeared in the bathroom doorway, wrapped in a towel.

'Cat, come on,' she said, somehow making it sound as though Cat was the unreasonable one. 'I've told you how much this means to me. I didn't exactly plan for it to happen but I can't let a chance like this slip through my fingers.'

'A chance like what, Amy? You've only just met the guy.'

'Sometimes you just know.'

'What do you know?' she asked. 'You don't know the first thing about him. You've had one lousy date and you're prepared to—'

'What?' Amy snapped. 'I'm prepared to do what?' She fixed Cat with eyes that seethed with anger—no hint of any remorse for leaving Cat high and dry. She took a step back and slammed the door.

'Well forgive me if I don't rush out to buy a hat!' Cat shouted before snatching up her key-card and storming out.

She left the hotel by the side exit and marched the length of the pot-holed road. Once again, she found herself walking the sands. Only this time she remained alone. The fresh air and brisk pace soon sapped her anger and extinguished the fire in her belly. Only without it there was nothing. Just a feeling of hollowness; a manifestation of the loneliness that seemed to be the only constant in her life. Despite that, she didn't venture back to the room until quarter to six. A combination of slow-burning resentment and concern over what impact any further conflict might have on their friendship, prevented her from wanting to see Amy before she left. Even then, she entered cautiously, just in case her friend had had an uncharacteristic prick of guilt and had decided not to go to dinner with Ethan after all. But she knew it was a false hope.

Inside the room, a wet towel lay discarded on the floor; nearby, a puddle of after-sun dribbled from an open bottle. Cat sighed and gathered them up, setting the bottle on the dressing table, in amongst the lotions and potions that made up Amy's vast collection. She returned the towel to the bathroom. The small room was cloyingly warm and the moisture from Amy's shower hung heavy. Fighting a feeling of claustrophobia, Cat made for the balcony and savoured the fresh, dry air. Slivers of voices and snatches of music slipped out of the open windows of the rooms around her.

In stark contrast to earlier, the terrace below was deserted. Or so Cat thought, until she spotted Phil, partly hidden under the canopy that shaded the bar. Her stomach gave a little flip. She could see he was talking. Moments later, she watched as he walked away and once again found herself wondering what might have been. And then he was gone and the terrace was empty. She headed back inside, hitting the play button on her MP3 player en route to the shower, stopping only to make a call to room service. For the second night in a row, confidence came courtesy of cheap champagne.

She took her time dressing. Cursing her pedestrian fashion sense, she rooted through Amy's half of the wardrobe trying to find anything that wouldn't swamp her, given her friend's fuller figure. After much deliberation she settled on a silk shirt the colour of chartreuse, liking the way it brightened the rich copper tones in her hair and accentuated the green of her eyes. She paired it with a long, loose-fitting skirt, in a rich paisley of peacock blues, which, rather than cover up the shape of her legs, clung gently. The pairing made a flattering combination, eye-catching even. It was a world away from her normal plain Ts and jeans, which was exactly why she felt like a fifteen-year-old waiting for her date to the high school prom.

She stood in front of the mirror and repeated a turn and tiptoe move for the umpteenth time, peering at her back and bottom, the clothes' clinging lines making her nervous. It was time to go. In fact, it had been time to go for a full fifteen minutes. Fifteen minutes during which she had been dressed and ready to walk out of the door, if only she could get her head in as good a place as her body was.

'Oh, for God's sake!'

She unzipped the skirt and stepped out of it, dropping it onto the bed on the way to the wardrobe and her jeans. At least the silk shirt softened the effect of the dark denim. This time, in front of the mirror she allowed herself a small smile, happy with the compromise.

On entering the dining room, any feeling of self-consciousness was momentarily forgotten as she searched the room for a friendly face, but there was no one who she would even consider a potential dinner companion. Reluctantly she took a seat at the same table she'd sat at the previous night and tried to remember what time the three of them had come through for dinner then. She looked at her watch—it was seven-thirty. Surely it had been earlier?

Just then she heard a familiar voice and relief washed over her as Tom and Rose approached, taking the table next to hers.

'Good evening Cat,' Tom said, his usual cheerful self. 'How are you today?'

'I'm fine, thanks.' She waited for them to settle in their seats, then asked, 'How are you two? Have you had a good day?'

'We went to the market over in Paphos Old Town. It was good wasn't it, Tom?' Rose said.

'It was alright. Very busy.'

'How about you?' Rose asked, turning to Cat. 'Did you and Amy have a good day?'

'It was okay. We were in Paphos as well. We had lunch there.' The words came out flat. 'Actually, the restaurant was really nice,' she admitted grudgingly.

'Where did you go?' Rose asked.

'Kostas. Do you know it?'

'Yes. The place in a little square, right on the corner, by the church?'

'That's right.'

'We've been there a couple of times. I remember the food being really quite good.'

Cat's thoughts jumped back to lunch.

'You're right. The food was excellent. Actually, it was quite interesting—we were chatting to one of the waiters—he was telling us how Jaclyn had her bag stolen when they were there on Monday.'

'We heard about that, didn't we?' Rose turned to Tom, 'Do you remember? We hadn't long been back from Nicosia and were enjoying a bit of peace and quiet with the crossword when they all came barging onto the terrace as though world war three had broken out. She was all in a tizzy about her bag and he wasn't having any of it, having some bee in his bonnet about being ripped off.'

'Ripped off?' Cat said.

A gleeful look crossed Tom's face.

'Seems like the two boys had cocked an order up or something. Tony was having a rant about it. Said he'd never get to retire if they kept making stupid mistakes without him being around to check.'

'So, what happened?'

'It all kicked off. Michael had a go at that Ethan, who retaliated, saying something about Michael setting hares running. Well that set Tony right off. The old boy was hopping mad and started to have a go at Ethan about not picking up on something sooner. How he didn't die of a heart attack there and then I don't know.'

'Especially when Jaclyn started on about her bag,' Rose said. 'That nearly pushed him over the edge. I still don't know what all the fuss was about. She got her blessed bag back, surely that should have been an end to the matter.'

'She got her bag back?' Cat said.

Rose nodded.

'She had the police out. They turned the place upside down trying to placate her. Apparently, it's some Louis Vuitton limited edition which means it's virtually irreplaceable. One of the waiters found it at the back of the restaurant, down the side of a bin.'

145

'Bloody lucky, if you ask me,' Tom said.

'I know,' Rose said. 'Turns out she only lost a few euros. Now, if they'd taken the bag, I could understand her being upset, given it cost over a thousand dollars.'

'How much?' Cat gasped. 'A thousand dollars for a handbag?'

'I know. It's obscene. Funny lot. Best to steer clear,' Rose said sagely.

The three of them fell quiet and turned their attention to their menus. But Cat had already decided what she was having and used the time to think how best to enquire about Phil without it seeming obvious. She was deep in thought when she heard Tom speak.

'Cat...?'

She looked up and smiled.

'Yes Tom.'

'I said, where is the lovely Amy? She's not ill as well is she?'

'No, she's fine. She's out fraternising with the enemy.' Her companions exchanged puzzled looks. 'Sorry, that was my terrible attempt at a joke. She's out with Ethan, the American guy.'

'And you didn't want to go?' Rose asked.

'I was surplus to requirements.' Cat looked down, aware of a slight colour flushing her cheeks. 'They're on a date.'

'It's like the war all over again. The GI always gets his gal.' Tom laughed.

'Oh, poor you,' Rose said, 'having to sit and have dinner on your own. Why don't you join us?'

'It's okay. It's not really that bad,' she lied. 'We could have a drink together in the bar later?'

'Of course. We'd be more than happy to join you for a nightcap.'

'Thanks.' Cat paused and looked around the now full room. 'I'm surprised Phil and Bethany aren't down for dinner yet.'

'I doubt we'll see them tonight,' Rose said. 'We bumped into them earlier. Bethany's a little under the weather. Phil was arranging to have something sent up to their room.'

'Oh. I hope it's nothing serious,' Cat said, trying to hide her disappointment.

Dinner was spent pleasantly enough. Rose and Tom kept the conversation flowing, doing their best to include Cat in their discussions. Afterwards, the three of them decided to make the most of the warm evening and retired to the terrace bar. Cat was listening to Tom and Rose bicker agreeably about nothing in particular when her mobile rang. Surprised by the interruption, she snatched it up and accidentally knocked over her glass. Wine spilled over the table.

She put the phone to her ear, not bothering to check to see who it was.

'Hello?' she said, rushing over to the counter and grabbing a handful of paper napkins.

'Cat. It's Alex.'

'Hang on a sec...'

She gave Tom and Rose a look of apology as she began to hurriedly mop up the spill. She dashed back across to the bar and threw the wet napkins into the bin before walking off in the direction of the pool where there was less chance of being overheard.

'I'm free now. Go on,' she said.

'You wanted Glafcos's number.'

'You've got it? Can you text it to me?' Silence filled the airwaves. 'Alex?'

'Are you sure you're doing the right thing calling Glafcos?' he said. 'I'm not telling you what to do, and it doesn't really matter to me if you make yourself look like—'

Cat let out an exasperated sigh and perched on the edge of a sunbed a safe distance away.

'Alex, what do you think I am?' she said, louder than she'd intended to. She lowered her voice. 'I'm not doing this to get brownie points off Glafcos. I'm just doing what I think is right. Like I told you before, I think if he knew what I know, it might help with his investigation.'

'What's so important you have to tell him?'

'There's a couple of things. First, I happened to be at the restaurant the dead guy ate lunch at on the day he died. I found out his wife had her handbag stolen when they were there. The bag then turned up. I wouldn't be surprised if his insulin syringes were in that bag.'

'You think someone faked the theft to tamper with his meds?'

'Yes.'

'I'd have thought the first thing the police will do, is test the syringes. It'll be pretty obvious what happened if they find something other than insulin in one of them.'

'Glafcos said they'd already tested the syringes. There was nothing wrong with them. But isn't it possible someone intended on switching his meds but got interrupted and had to abandon their plan?'

Alex sighed loudly.

'They could have got another opportunity later,' she added quickly.

'But then the syringes wouldn't have tested normal, would they?'

Cat fell quiet.

'Did the theft of the bag get reported?' Alex asked.

'Yes, she had the police out but what does that... Oh, I see, Glafcos probably already knows about that. But that's not the only thing...'

She took another look around. Deciding it was too risky to continue with the conversation in such close proximity to the bar, she rose and started a slow stroll around the pool.

Keeping her voice low, she continued, 'Someone broke into the dead guy's room.'

'Before he died?' Alex asked.

'No, afterwards.'

She waited for Alex to comment but then realised he was waiting for her to elaborate.

'Maybe they took something incriminating,' she said.

'What was reported as being taken?'

'I don't think it's actually been reported.'

'Then how do you know it happened?'

'This isn't as bad as it's going to sound but...'

Alert to any other guests enjoying a relaxing postprandial stroll, Cat told Alex of her adrenalin-packed encounter.

'For Christ's sake Cat, what were you thinking? Please tell me you didn't take anything. Trespass is bad enough but burglary?'

'Just a few photos. I know it doesn't sound good but I didn't exactly go in on purpose.'

'They'll only have your word for that. It wouldn't take much for someone to argue that you broke in through the patio window yourself.'

'I was only going to tell him I noticed the open door and thought I heard someone in the room.'

'Well then you're more stupid than I thought. Fucking hell Cat, if anyone finds out what you did you could be facing charges. I'm guessing you didn't have time to wipe the place clean of your prints?'

'Actually, I used a tissue to handle everything.'

'Including the door handle, or window, or whatever it was you touched when you first walked in or when you dived under the bed?'

She stalled.

'I take it that's a no. So, you've got a possible break in but no evidence of what was taken. What we do know is that you've left

149

more than enough evidence to implicate yourself, which even though well-meant could get you into serious trouble.'

Cat started to feel her chest constrict.

'Just let it go,' he said. It was an instruction, not a plea.

'But if Tony was murdered... I don't...' She realised the futility of her words before they were even out of her mouth. 'Shit. What was I thinking? You're right as usual.' Cat felt her confidence abandon her.

'Look, just keep your mouth shut and you should be okay. I've got to go. I'll see you next week... Oh, and Cat, try not to get into any more trouble.'

Fifteen

After the call from Alex, Cat returned to Tom and Rose. Despite her downbeat mood, she summoned up every morsel of small talk she could muster and the evening passed comfortably by. Rose finished her glass of wine, the last of their bottle from dinner, and put a hand to her mouth to stem a yawn.

'Oh dear, I think I'm ready for bed. I'm struggling to keep my eyes open.'

Tom gave her a peculiar look, 'But I haven't...' He looked down at his empty glass. 'I haven't got a drink.'

'Well that's good timing then isn't it? Come on,' Rose said, reaching for her cardigan.

'Well, not really. I wouldn't mind a little night cap.'

'You could always take a drink back to your room,' Cat said.

'I'd rather have it here.'

'Tom,' Rose said, sounding serious. 'I'm tired and really not in the mood.'

He shot a worried look across at Cat, who realised what he was trying to do.

'Don't stay on my account,' she said. 'I'm more than happy to crash out now. Honestly.' She picked up her bottle of wine, which was still half full. 'Maybe I'll get lucky and there'll be a film on one of the satellite channels.' She stood up and gathered her glass and key card off the table. 'Goodnight, and thanks for the company. I've had a really nice night.'

Back in her room Cat kicked off her sandals and poured herself a glass of wine. After swapping the silk shirt for a cotton tee, she cleared the bed of the remnants of her earlier fashion show and settled down in front of the TV. The choice of English-speaking channels was limited and after five minutes of looking, the only vaguely entertaining thing she could find was a Sandra Bullock action movie. Although she was sure she'd seen it before, she stuck with it for the twenty or so minutes until the credits started to roll. She switched the TV off and turned to look for her book. A quick scan told her it wasn't anywhere obvious. Climbing off the bed she tried to think when she'd last had it. The sight of an empty lager bottle jutting out of the bin jogged her memory and she remembered leaving it on the balcony. Her stomach lurched as the altercation with Amy sprang to mind. She felt so stupid and petty having fallen out over something so trivial.

Out on the balcony the air was a comfortable temperature; no longer warm but not cold enough to draw out goosebumps. Her book was on the plastic table where she'd left it. As Cat walked towards it, her foot accidentally caught on something, sending it shooting across the floor. She looked down and found a single diamante-decorated silver leather sandal. She checked under the table and the two plastic chairs that filled the small space, before peering over the balcony rail. The fallen object lay twinkling up at her from the border below, reflecting the moonlight in its glass-encrusted straps.

Cursing her bad luck, Cat returned to the room, tossed her book onto her bed, and grabbed her shoes. It had to be one of Amy's sandals, rather than one of her own, didn't it? If she didn't retrieve the missing footwear, Amy was bound to think she'd done it deliberately.

Downstairs, she waded into the shrubby border, scouring the area underneath their balcony. Despite the simulated diamonds having glittered like a disco ball from the balcony above, at ground level the shoe somehow managed to evade detection. Five minutes later, with her patience exhausted, Cat turned to leave, prepared to face the music when Amy returned. She stood up and took a step towards the path. And there it was, resting on the top of a sturdy bush, winking at her out of the darkness.

'Fucking thing,' she said, snatching it up and clambering back onto the path.

Out of the corner of her eye, she spotted a movement over towards the pool. She squinted into the gloom and saw a figure silhouetted against the whitewashed walls. They were heading in the direction of the beach. As her eyes became accustomed to the dark, the form began to take a familiar shape.

Her intrigue grew.

So much for nursing a sick daughter.

Images of a late-night tryst—with the luscious Maria, maybe—flashed through her head. Much to her annoyance, she felt her stomach squirm with disappointment. And then the figure turned a corner and disappeared, leaving the landscape empty and still.

For a moment Cat continued to stare into the darkness. She took a deep breath and was about to return to her room when the improbability of what she was imagining hit her. Why would he need to sneak around after hours like a common criminal, when, as she knew only too well, he could avail himself of his own room? Then she remembered the binoculars. If the alcohol and her muddled emotions hadn't made her thoughts all fuzzy, she might have thought to quiz him about the night vision eye-piece. But just because she hadn't, didn't mean she'd forgotten.

She put Amy's sandal on the short wall that bordered the path—it would be safe there until later—and started after him.

It wasn't until she'd left the hotel grounds that she managed to regain him in her sights. Thanks to the shining moon casting a soft glow across the landscape, illuminating her target and lighting her path at the same time, she was able to keep a safe distance. But the light wasn't quite bright enough to prevent her from tripping on a gnarled olive root as she trotted along in

153

pursuit. With her heart racing, she lay on the ground, frozen in place, listening for an approaching footfall.

Nothing.

She climbed to her feet and, quietly cursing, continued her previous course, skirting between the fruit trees as she followed the beach south. She became aware of a noise ahead. A screeching, screaming cacophony of bird call. Picking up the pace she ran ahead, then, all of a sudden, the tree cover ended and she burst out into the clearing.

In the dim half-light, the scene looked so alien it took her brain a moment to properly register what she was seeing.

Nets.

And eyes... Hundreds of eyes.

Out of the shadows emerged a tangle of birds, all fighting for their freedom. Cat felt the bile rise as she made sense of the shocking sight. And in the middle of it all was Brian, the birdwatcher.

Brian?

She looked around. There was no sign of Phil. After all that, she'd been following the wrong man.

Brian turned and noticed her standing there.

'Don't just stand there. Make yourself useful,' he shouted. He held out a small but sharp penknife. 'Use this to cut them free. And be careful!'

Quickly his hands reached for a bird and untangled it with remarkable dexterity. Cat did likewise, timidly to begin with, her confidence growing with each release and between them they gave life back to scores of fragile, frightened song-birds. It wasn't until they were surrounded by empty nets Cat found herself wondering whether there might be a link between Brian's efforts to free the trapped birds and the arson attacks happening in violent protest against the illegal bird trade. She flinched as her unconventional companion slipped a large bowie knife out of a sheath on his belt.

'What are you doing now?' she asked.

With no more birds to release she was acutely aware she may have outlived her usefulness. For the third time in as many days she subconsciously touched the scar at her side but if he did intend to do Cat harm, he had other business to attend to first.

'These nets need destroying otherwise it'll have all been for nothing.'

He started to shred the sheets of fine mesh, pulling the blade through them until all that was left were streamers of shredded nylon hanging like tattered cobwebs on a third-rate horror flick. He stood back and surveyed his handiwork.

'I think that's it. We're done. Thanks for your help.'

He returned the blade to his belt and started to walk away.

'Wait,' Cat said, starting after him. 'What was all that?' she asked, looking over her shoulder, still reeling from what had just happened.

'Mist nets. They use them to trap the birds, which they kill, if they're not already dead by the time they come for them. They pickle them and call it a delicacy.'

Cat looked around at the small clearing in the midst of a thicket of citrus trees.

'How did you know where to find them?'

'They put the nets where there are likely to be a lot of birds. I used to regularly stumble across them when I first came here. It took me a couple of years but now I know where all the trapping sites are. I just have to keep going from site to site until I find where they've actually set the nets.'

'At night?'

'No. I see the poles they attach them to when I'm out during the day. They don't set the nets until late in the day, ready for when the birds go to roost in the evening.'

'Aren't you worried you'll get caught?'

'No one will come back for the birds until after dawn.'

Cat took another look around. The scale of it still a shock.

'How many of these things are there?' she asked.

'Too many.'

'But if it's a local delicacy and the restaurants can only sell it under the counter why so many birds?'

'Who said local? Cyprus is on the main flight path of so many migratory birds. They capture and pickle them here then transport them all over Europe. It's a thriving black market.'

'Does it have a name, this delicacy?'

'Ambelopoulia. But you won't see it advertised. It's illegal.'

'Then I don't understand. Why do you have to come out and do this? Why not just tell the police?'

'Because nothing would happen.'

'But if it's illegal?'

'Has been since 1967.'

'Then surely if you told the police where the nets are, they'd have to do something. Wouldn't they?'

He gave a disparaging snort.

'I'd be wasting my time. They just turn a blind eye. I know for a fact, some of them even order it for themselves. I focus on what gets results. It might not be much but it's better than nothing.'

Suddenly the sound of a branch snapping cut through the quiet like the crack of a gin trap.

'Hide!' Brian hissed as he dived for cover.

Cat jumped behind the same bush and they found themselves shoulder to shoulder. They tilted their heads simultaneously, straining to pick up the slightest of sounds.

Silence.

'Do you think it's them?' she whispered.

Brian shrugged.

They waited and after a couple of minutes Brian straightened up and stretched.

'Probably just a rabbit or a fox. Whatever it was, it's gone now.'

Cat could hear his back crack and crunch. Wary of being caught, she remained huddled amongst the greenery.

'I must go.' And without waiting for a reply he set off, striding through the undergrowth.

'Wait!' Cat called but it was too late, he was already gone. 'Oh great!' She had no idea how to get back to the hotel. 'Well, here goes nothing,' she said, diving into the dark thicket.

Fifteen minutes later, with only blind faith, the moon and the sound of the sea to guide her, Cat was flooded with relief when the rough grass gave way to smooth soft sand. A smile bunched her cheeks as she spotted a row of thatched umbrellas punctuating the beach's length. But as she advanced, the smile slowly dissolved. Hushed voices came to her, carried on the gentlest of sea breezes. Intrigued, she walked quickly to join a small crowd gathered at the sea's edge. Concentration creased her brow as she tried to listen in to their whispered words. She raised herself up on tiptoes hoping to see what the attraction was, but all she could see was the backs of people's heads. Recognising Rose, she pushed her way through.

'Hey Rose, what's going on?' she whispered.

'Cat!' The word leapt from her lips.

Rose stepped forward and turned, blocking Cat's view even further. She laid a gentle hand on her arm and started to steer her away from the water's edge.

'Why don't we go over here and talk?'

Just as gently, Cat pushed Rose's hand away.

'What's going on?' she asked.

Rose darted a look of alarm over to Tom. He took a step towards them but Cat had already started to move through the loose throng of people, weaving her way through until she reached the front of the small crowd.

Whatever she had expected to see, it certainly wasn't Andreas kneeling in the wet sand, oblivious to the foam and froth of the sea washing over his legs. Cat realised he was actually leaning over someone. He had his back to her, unaware of her presence.

'Can I help?' she said. 'I'm trained in first aid. Please, let me take a look.'

Andreas looked up from his ministrations and a look of panic crossed his face. He quickly turned around and began to fuss with the blanket that was positioned over the prostrate figure. Someone coughed, nervously. It was Tom. The clouds cleared from the high moon and she noticed his heavily lined face, radiating worry—his serious expression at odds with the rest of his appearance, standing there in a pair of blue and white striped pyjamas, reminding Cat of the hippo from a TV commercial for something she couldn't remember. Beds maybe?

Instantly the lateness of the hour occurred to her and she felt a prickling of the hairs on the back of her neck. She looked around, taking in the concerned faces. With a growing apprehension she realised that everyone was avoiding her eye. Everyone except Brian, who was standing a small distance away, looking as bewildered as she was.

'Andreas, please,' she said firmly.

The Cypriot turned to look at her and Cat saw the hopelessness in his eyes and in that second, she knew what everyone else standing there was already privy to.

The barman eased up on to his knees. Cat looked down at the blanket-covered form. Two bare legs with pink painted toenails jutted out into the incoming tide. Andreas reached over and lifted the cover, folding it back gently to reveal the face. Cat heard herself gasp. She had already guessed it but seeing it made it real.

Amy. Her features blank, her hair sodden and pasted to her head. The waxy pallor of death magnified in the pale ghostly wash of moonlight.

Was it just Cat's imagination or did time stand still for that moment? Even the waves seemed to stop breaking.

'Cat...' Tom stepped forward and placed a hand softly on her shoulder. 'I'm so sorry.'

'What happened?'

'We don't know. Phil found her. He tried to save her but it was too late.'

Although her senses were dulled and her reactions delayed, the words trickled through to Cat's consciousness and she looked at the Londoner. His khaki shorts had turned a dark moss colour. He was soaked through to the skin.

She bent down and went to lift the blanket to give to him. His need was greater, she reasoned, but as she peeled back the pale blue cover she stopped suddenly.

'Where are her clothes?' She turned back to the crowd. 'Where are her clothes?' she yelled into a crowd of blank faces.

A number of them shrank back, but nobody replied.

Sixteen

The light, more pewter than silver, made Cat's hair look darker and her skin paler than usual. Like a Bronte heroine she seemed fragile, yet somehow wild and dangerous. She scowled at the guests milling around, their numbers having grown since she'd first walked across the beach.

Sordid voyeurs, every one of them.

'Come on everybody,' Phil shouted. 'Start making your way back into the hotel. There's nothing to see here.'

With his arms held out in front of him he began to usher the crowd away from the body.

Cat, standing motionless, stared into the undulating waters. Nearby Rose hovered, offering comfort to the few who remained.

'Andreas, could we get some hot drinks out here?' Phil said, as he made his way back down the beach.

The barman looked down anxiously, seeming uneasy about abandoning his vigil.

'Don't worry,' Phil said. 'I can stay here and make sure nobody touches anything.'

Andreas's absence was short and he soon reappeared with the hotel's matriarch, a large, grey-haired lady of advancing years who looked as though she should be permanently wearing a flour-dredged apron. She brought with her a thin blanket, which she draped around Phil's shoulders. He pulled it close. Andreas, as requested, carried a tray of teas and coffees, which he began to distribute.

Phil took a mug of strong hot coffee and continued to talk to the grey-haired lady. He spoke in hushed tones whilst looking over to where the grass met the sand and tufts of straw-coloured sedge poked out. Cat followed his gaze and noticed Brian, sitting on a small hump of the long grass, his knees tucked under his chin. The sheathed knife hanging from the belt of his trousers rested against his leg. Phil uttered more whispered words to the woman and she turned and began to make her way back to the hotel, stopping en-route to talk to the birdwatcher who slowly stood up and stretched before accompanying her indoors.

Phil looked over to Cat. She could feel his eyes on her, watching her. He started to make his way over. She turned, presenting her back to him and stared blindly out to sea.

'How are you holding up?' he asked. She felt him pull gently on the crook of her arm. 'Cat?' She jerked her elbow free. Her dry eyes roamed aimlessly over the open vista in front of her. 'Why don't you go inside? There's nothing you can do here.'

She shook her head. She felt the rise and fall of her chest, every fibre of her being focussed on keeping control.

She was standing in the same spot when she heard Glafcos. His voice resonated through the night air, rousing her from the quiet place in her head she had retreated to. Back to the nightmare. No. To the day-mare... real and inescapable with no chance of experiencing that wonderful wash of relief on waking up.

She watched the stout-booted Cypriot approach. Two men followed behind. Glafcos bent over and lifted the blanket. He gave a slow mournful shake of his head. Cat looked down at the mug in her hand, its contents untouched. She threw the cold tea on to the sand to her side.

Glafcos straightened up.

'Cat. What can I say? I am very sorry. When I heard that it was your friend, I thought there must be some mistake.'

She looked him in the eye, a hard expression on her face.

'I want you to nail the bastard that did this.'

'You can be assured that we will—'

'Somebody was down here with her, someone who knows what happened. Who may even be responsible for what happened.'

He raised an eyebrow, giving life to the thick black comma of hair.

'You have proof of this?'

'She was naked. What more proof do you need?'

'This is proof, how?'

'Why would she be out here past midnight on her own, naked? And where are her clothes? She couldn't exactly drown and then dispose of them.' Cat was struggling to keep herself from shouting at him.

'Maybe she came down for a swim?' Phil said from over Glafcos's shoulder.

'Naked?' Cat threw him an obvious look of annoyance.

'Her clothes could be somewhere nearby. Nobody's looked.'

Glafcos turned.

'Go and search for the clothes,' he said, seeming to speak to the shadows.

A man in a dark suit stepped forward and started to walk away, heading down the beach.

'Ethan!' Cat cried. In a moment of clarity suddenly she remembered the American's unswerving presence in Amy's life for the last couple of days.

Before Glafcos could even think about reaching out a restraining hand to stop her, Cat was already beyond his grasp. Her feet sank deep into the sand as she ran, slowing her step and frustrating her efforts as though she were running in a dream. At the path, she suddenly speeded up, her exertions benefiting from the added traction. Soon, she burst through the double doors into the hotel. She turned the sharp right into the corridor leading to

Ethan's suite, and, after batting Phil away, who had given chase, began to bang her fists violently on the door to the American's room.

The door opened, just a crack at first. Cat stopped banging and took a step back. Slowly the door inched open wide enough for Ethan to peer around. He looked at Cat with eyes that blinked in protest to the brightly lit corridor.

'Cat? What is it?' He ran his fingers through his dishevelled hair.

But Cat was unable to answer. As she struggled to find the words to describe what had happened, she was struck by images of her friend's immobile body and its lacklustre features. The realisation of what had happened finally hit her and the tears started. Phil placed a hand on her shoulder but she pushed him away just as Glafcos lurched through the door at the end of the corridor, his chest heaving as he gulped large mouthfuls of air to feed his spent lungs.

Ethan's brow knotted.

'What the hell's going on?'

'It's Amy,' Phil said. Glafcos was still catching his breath. 'She's been found down by the beach. It looks like she drowned.'

The look of confusion on the American's face multiplied.

'What? But she's okay though, isn't she?'

'Drowned, as in dead,' Phil said quietly.

Ethan stood blinking for a moment.

'Dead?' He looked at Cat who was struggling to stifle her sobs. His eyes widened. 'Oh my God. Sweet Jesus. But when...? How...? She'd gone back to her room. I was sure she'd gone back to her room.'

'As this gentleman has already explained, she was found on the beach. It looks as though she drowned. This is all we know at this time,' Glafcos said.

'That means she was there all the time. I thought she'd got sick of waiting.' He ran his hand over his face, leaving it cupped over his open mouth.

As they talked, Cat's tears slowed and eventually dried, and she stood listening to the conversation going on around her, seemingly invisible to the three men who talked amongst themselves. She heard how Amy and Ethan had returned from dinner, fuelled by alcohol, buoyed up by their feelings of romance and mutual attraction, excited at the prospect of getting to know one another better. Yes, he'd been hopeful. Amy wasn't backward in coming forward. They had planned to go for a swim in the sea, just the two of them under the stars, backlit by the moon. They'd split up once they got to the hotel, Amy having gone to her room to fetch a couple of towels, whilst Ethan headed to the bar, promising champagne. As he said it, he opened the door and gestured to the unopened bottle on the desk behind him.

'Do you often swim in the sea at night?' Glafcos asked.

Ethan looked up at him, through the hair that fringed his eyes. He gave a small shake of his head.

'Never. It was Amy's suggestion.' He looked down towards the floor. 'She said a midnight skinny dip would be fun.'

Cat thought back to Amy as a student—a real party animal. It seems she never did lose her daring.

'If it was her idea, what made you think she'd changed her mind and returned to her room?' Glafcos asked.

'I was longer than expected.' Ethan said. 'I got caught talking to someone in the bar. I tried to get away but by the time I got to the beach there was no sign of Amy. I walked up and down calling her, but nothing. I figured she was pissed at me and had gone back to her room. I went and knocked but there was no reply.' He looked at Cat. 'I thought you might both be asleep. Amy'd had quite a bit to drink.'

'Who delayed you?' Glafcos asked.

Ethan paused. He looked from Glafcos to Cat and then back to Glafcos.

'Does it really matter?'

'Sir, I don't need to remind you how serious this is,' Glafcos said, fixing him with a look that would have buckled steel.

Ethan paused. For a moment Cat thought he wasn't going to answer, but then he sighed and said, 'Her name's Larissa Foulds. She's one of the group I'm with.'

'When you eventually got to the beach, what did you do then?' Glafcos asked.

'I walked to the end of the path. From there I walked say fifty yards in each direction, like I said, calling out for her.'

'And you didn't see anyone else?'

'No. No one.'

'And then...'

'I went to check her room... their room,' he said, gesturing towards Cat. 'I did knock, quietly. I didn't want to wake everyone up. I even picked up a sandal that was by the steps and took it with me. I thought it was one of Amy's. It was meant to be like a peace offering, you know, prince charming and Cinderella. Cheesy, huh?' He grimaced.

'What happened to the sandal?' Phil asked.

Ethan's eyes flicked to Cat.

'I left it outside their room.'

'Didn't it occur to you that perhaps something had happened to her?' Glafcos asked.

'No,' Ethan said, looking bewildered. 'I turned up late and there was no sign of her. I just thought I'd blown it.' He turned to Cat, 'You didn't answer the door. If you'd have answered the door I would have known something was wrong.'

His words held no hint of accusation yet they hit her as hard as a punch to the gut.

165

'Okay,' Glafcos said. 'As you are the last person known to have seen Miss Reynolds alive, we need to interview you under caution.'

Ethan glanced down at his watch.

'What, now?'

'Yes sir. I'll wait while you dress.'

Ethan glanced down, as though only then noticing he was wearing only a t-shirt and a pair of navy boxer shorts. He sighed, then nodded in acquiescence, before walking back into his room. With legs like lead Cat made her way back to the beach, relieved to see boiler-suited scene of crime officers having joined the party.

With nothing to do but stare into the inky water and the blackness beyond, Cat felt the tears start again. Not the snotty onslaught that had overtaken her earlier, this time a delicate trail of teardrops rolled down her cheeks.

The sound of voices filtering through the open doors caused her to turn. Through the glass she could see Phil and Glafcos deep in conversation in the reception area. A solemn-looking Ethan, dressed in sweat pants and a jumper, sat on a chair nearby, staring at the ground. Phil nodded and Glafcos began to walk away. He pushed through the glass doors and started straight for her. Cat moved a few steps away from the path and looked away. Glafcos continued past, towards the beach. Five minutes later he made his way back. This time he stopped.

'Cat.' Although he said it quietly it still made her jump. She looked at him, her eyes wide and rheumy. 'Cat, why don't you go to bed? There's nothing you can do here now.'

She turned away from him. His hand touched her shoulder lightly.

'Cat, they're going to be coming through here with the stretcher in a minute.'

She went to speak but her voice caught and a strangled sound emerged. She cleared her throat.

'I'm fine. I want to wait.'

'Okay. I'll stay here with you then.'

She shrugged and together they waited, Glafcos with his hands thrust deep in his trouser pockets, Cat with her arms wrapped around her chest, comforting herself in the cool night air. And they remained like that for a hundred and thirty-two breaths. Cat knew, because she counted them, only stopping when Glafcos broke the silence.

'By the way, we found her clothes.'

She looked at him sharply.

'They were on a sunbed, down the other end of the beach. We found them along with two towels, all neatly folded.'

Cat was about to say something but stopped, distracted by the sound of the ambulance crew shuffling their way up the steps from the pool to the terrace. She watched the stretcher advance. As it drew level, she started to walk alongside, accompanying it out through the lobby to the waiting mortuary van. Glafcos walked behind, keeping a respectful distance. The ambulance men rolled the stretcher into position and locked it into place. Glafcos approached one of the two men. They conversed briefly in muttered Greek before Glafcos nodded and stepped away, giving the man access to the cab. As the ambulance drove away, the detective made his way over to Ethan.

Cat watched as he ushered the American into a waiting car, before turning to face her.

'I'll be back in the morning,' he said, climbing behind the wheel.

Finally, Cat was alone. The trees stirred in the breeze that brushed past her cheek, drying her tears into faint silvery tracks.

Alone.

As soon as the word stole into her thoughts she looked around as if to confirm it. And from nowhere a distant memory sprang with burning clarity from the recesses of her mind. That time had ended in tears too, as the reality of her brother's death hit home. She remembered a single moment of lucidity that came with the news of his murder, when she was filled with a driving desire to do something to help other people, people like her, people whose lives and loves had been unjustly torn away from them. That was the moment Cat's life had changed track forever.

Seventeen

The crackle and hiss of the fire drowned everything out, including the shouts from the Cypriot fire crew.

'I can't hear you. You'll have to speak up,' he said loudly, hardly expecting to be heard, but shortly the violent sounds retreated into the background.

'Is that better?'

'Yes. I take it from the commotion there's been another attack?'

'You guess correctly. Any news on your man?'

'I had to abort. You haven't heard?'

'No. What?'

'There's been another death at the hotel.'

'What?'

'The detective's friend. Drowned in the sea late last night. I...'

The wailing of a fire engine horn cut through the call, banshee-like against a back-drop of shouts.

'I've got to go. I'll call you back.'

The shouts and sirens fell silent; the call was over.

Eighteen

Cat groaned and stirred slowly, coming round like a prize-fighter after a knock-out blow. Her eyes, swollen and puffy, opened reluctantly. Gently she sat up, drowsy through lack of sleep and exhausted from the emotional angst. For one cruel second her slow to wake brain put the previous night's events down to a hideous nightmare. But her rising hopes quickly sank.

She took a deep breath.

It juddered into her chest and hung there for a moment before being forcibly expelled. She flopped back onto the bed and stared up at the uneven ceiling. The lumpy surface was covered with a smattering of grey speckles.

Damp probably.

She rolled over. With her ear pressed to the pillow, her breathing sounded deep and resonant, seeming unnaturally loud in a room otherwise deadly quiet. So loud it took her a moment or two to notice a quiet tapping at the door. The tapping grew to a quiet knock. Easing up onto an elbow, Cat looked over. She contemplated lying back down and pulling the covers over her head, but instead blew out a heavy sigh and threw off the bedclothes. She climbed out of bed and padded to the door. She opened it a crack and peered out around its edge.

Phil looked back at her, his face crimped with concern.

'I came to check you're okay.'

'I'm fine, thanks. Well, I'm not, but you know what I mean.'

He nodded.

'What time is it?' she asked.

'Just after nine.'

'Is it really?' She sounded agitated, as though for some reason the lateness of the hour mattered.

'I hope you don't mind but I took the liberty of asking the restaurant to put some breakfast aside for you. Just give reception a call when you're ready and they'll bring it over.'

'Oh God. I don't think I can eat. Just the thought of food...'

She felt the bile swell in her gut as images of the previous night flashed through her mind, opening up her raw emotions and the well of tears that had had all night to fill. It was only because her stomach was empty she didn't retch.

'You don't have to have it. I'm sure they'll be happy to prepare you something else later, if you'd prefer.'

'I'll see how I feel in a bit.' She looked him directly in the face. 'Thanks for last night... For walking me back to the room.'

He smiled, a small sympathetic gesture that barely curved his mouth.

'I couldn't leave you standing out there on your own.'

An uncomfortable silence filled the gap.

Cat leaned through the door and looked up and down the corridor.

'Where's Bethany?'

'Rose is with her. She said if there's anything she can do...'

'That's kind.'

'Same here—if there's anything I can do.'

'Thank you.'

'I mean it. Let me know if you need anything.'

'I'm fine. Honestly. Go back to Bethany.'

After Phil left, Cat gently pushed the door closed and turned to rest her back on the solid wood, glad of its support. She looked around. The soft scent of Amy's perfume still lingered in the air. Her clothes lay strewn around the room. She stared at the dressing table, littered with Amy's things, including a lone sandal. She walked over and picked it up. A strip of light from the gap in the curtains caught on its diamante straps and it twinkled in the dimly lit room. It reminded Cat of Amy, of her effervescence and her love of life.

She remembered how irritated she'd been when the sandal had fallen from the balcony and her relief on spotting it lying in the bushes below, easy enough to retrieve. And if that was all she had done, who knows how things would have turned out. She thought back to Ethan and how he'd come up to the room, believing Amy had simply deserted him for her bed. Cat couldn't help but blame herself— if she had come straight back to the room instead of gallivanting off after a man, and not even the man she thought she was following, they would have realised straight away that something was wrong. She would have suggested they go look for Amy. Maybe it would have been soon enough.

She tightened her grip on the sandal and felt the glass embellishment cut into her fingers. Suddenly she was filled with a rage that erupted out of nowhere. She hurled the sandal across the room. It slapped onto the wall and fell to the floor next to a pile of Amy's clothes spewing out from the open wardrobe.

Her friend may have gone but her stuff was everywhere. Cat felt her chest tighten just looking at it. The sandal, the clothes, the shoes, the make-up, the books, her i-pod... It was all too much.

She reached for an empty suitcase and began to grab armfuls of Amy's things, throwing them into the bag until its heaving seams could take no more. Leaning her full weight onto it she managed to coax the two halves of the zipper together, sealing the physical reminders of Amy inside.

Then it was her turn.

Hot water shot out of the shower and thick steam filled the tiny space, the bathroom's sluggish ventilation unable to clear the vapours of a cathartic twenty-minute cascade. But the rushing waters could only wash skin-deep. Unfortunately for Cat, no soap could reach deep enough to wash away the ache.

But the shower did clear her head. The fog lifted and her anger subsided. Sitting on the bed, a clean towel wrapped around her pink, freshly scrubbed body, she pulled a comb through her tangled curls. She caught sight of a pair of white sandals she'd missed, tucked out of sight down the side of the dressing table. She remembered how Amy had worn them to her first dinner with Ethan. Suddenly the memory of her friend's naked form, lifeless and shoeless sprang forward. Feelings of inadequacy and guilt once again bubbled to the surface, accompanied by a slow rising of acid, sucked up from the pit of her stomach, its bitter, acrid taste bringing life back to Cat's bottled up emotions.

The tears gathered like clouds before a storm but she was determined not to succumb. Not this time. She buried her face in her hands and slowed her breathing, waiting for the urge to cry to pass. More difficult to dismiss were the eruptions in her gut as her stomach demanded food. Grateful for the distraction, she picked up the phone and dialled reception, calling for the breakfast that had been set aside.

Once her physical needs were satiated, Cat let her thoughts return to the death of her friend. The morning was marching on and yet no word from Glafcos. Her thoughts jumped to the inquiry, or lack of, into Tony's death, even though, according to Glafcos, there was something to suggest it might not have been as straightforward as it seemed.

Based on her experience of working with Glafcos before, she had been of the opinion he was a good detective: conscientious, thorough and determined. Now she wasn't quite so sure. She hoped she was wrong.

The reception was quiet. As Cat approached, she noticed the two girls behind the desk exchange glances before looking at her with expressions that were a blend of sympathy and embarrassment.

'Good morning Miss McKenzie. How may I help?' the nearest girl asked.

'I wondered whether Detective Glafcos Theophanus had arrived yet?'

The young girl flashed a glance towards her friend who was doing a good job of appearing to be busy.

'I'm sorry, I don't know. Are we expecting him?'

Cat looked at her sharply.

'Haven't you been asked to set a room aside for the police?'

The girl shook her head but the gesture was lacking confidence.

'Would you check please?'

The receptionist walked over to her colleague and muttered a few words. The two girls spoke in Greek. Cat watched, trying to decipher their body language.

The other girl approached.

'You are looking for Detective Theophanus?'

'That's right.'

'He has already left.'

'Left? What time did he get here?'

'I think about eight o'clock.'

'But it's only eleven now. When did he leave?'

The receptionist looked at her watch.

'I am not sure exactly. I think by half-past nine.'

'Any idea who he talked to when he was here?'

'No, I am sorry.'

'Well, did he ask to speak to anyone?'

The girl shrugged.

'I'm sorry I do not know. Is there anything else I can help you with?' she called, but Cat was already walking away.

Back in her room, she grabbed her handbag from the bottom of her side of the wardrobe. She checked the car keys were in it and was halfway through the door when she remembered her driving licence. Cypriot law required she carry it, along with her passport, if she was going to take the hire car out. She dropped the bag on the bed and looked inside. Her passport was there but no driving licence.

She tried to remember when she'd last seen it. Given Amy's reluctance to do anything other than lie by the pool and read, the hire car had yet to have an outing, which could only mean one thing: her licence was going to be where she'd put it when they'd first unpacked.

She was right. It was sitting amongst her travel documents in her bedside cabinet. She slipped it into her bag and went to leave when she stalled for a second time. Returning to the cabinet, she rooted through its contents. Frowning, she turned and scanned the handful of items that remained on the dressing table after she'd purged it of Amy's things. Finally, she stepped out onto the balcony. A single glance at the empty table and chairs, told her all she needed to know.

She heaved a sigh.

The contents of the case swelled out as soon as she eased it open. Even as she unpacked the items, one by one, she knew she wasn't going to find it. There was no way she would have mistakenly packed her notepad away with Amy's belongings. But if it wasn't there, hastily packed with the bulk of Amy's things, then where the hell was it?

Out on the terrace, Phil didn't disguise his surprise at seeing her. She noticed his expression soften. Before he had chance to issue more words of sympathy, she launched straight into explaining the reason she was there.

'No. Sorry. I don't remember seeing anything like that,' he said. 'But I wasn't there very long and, well, I was only interested in making sure you were okay.' From Cat's reading of his body language he seemed genuine enough. 'Is it important?'

She shrugged.

'Probably not. I just don't like it when things mysteriously disappear.'

Just then Bethany flung up an arm and waved a crayoned page in front of them both.

'Finished. Want to see?' Bethany laid the page on the table.

Cat looked down at the garish mix of azure blue and canary yellow combining to give a not unpleasant green, the colour of well-watered grass.

'Very pretty. What is it?'

'Bird.'

'A parrot?'

Bethany giggled.

'No. That's silly. It's a beeter.'

Cat looked at Phil.

'A bee-eater,' he supplied.

'Wow. I'm impressed,' Cat said, taking a second look at the picture. 'It does actually look like one now you've said it.'

'Bethany loves the bee-eaters. She picked up on their call the first day we were here and she's been fascinated with them ever since.'

The four-year-old resumed her colouring in as Cat took a seat next to her.

'Would you like a bird of your own?' she asked.

'Oscar doesn't like,' Bethany said, without looking up.

Cat looked at Phil.

'Our cat.' He lowered his voice. 'Unfortunately, the problem is, he likes birds a little *too* much. If you know what I mean?'

Cat nodded, before peering at the colouring book.

'What other pictures have you got there? Do you want to show me?'

Bethany didn't need to be asked twice. Together they worked through the jumbo sketch pad. All the while Cat oohed and ahhed, vocalising her admiration for the little girl's pictures. At the end of the narrated tour Cat flicked back to the first drawing in the pad. It was a face, with butterfly halves as ears, two blue scribbles as eyes and a yellow thatch levitating above the ball-shaped head. Shaky letters ran underneath. Cat made a mental note to thank her guardian angel.

'Is this a picture of you?'

The little girl nodded and pulled herself up proudly.

Cat pointed at the scribbled words. 'And you even signed it! Can you read it to me?'

'Show Cat what a clever girl you are,' Phil said.

'Beth...an...ee...' the four-year-old said slowly, breaking the word down into its composite syllables as her finger traced below.

'Bethany,' Cat repeated. 'And how do you say this word?' she asked, pointing to the page.

'Woj....er...z,' Bethany said, sliding her finger along underneath.

'Rogers,' Phil said, enunciating the word carefully for Bethany's benefit.

'Wojerz,' the little girl asserted.

'Well I think it's a good job you signed it as I'm sure this will be worth a lot of money one day, when you're a famous artist,' Cat said.

Bethany left the drawing pad and started sticking self-adhesive glittery shapes in a different book. Cat turned to Phil.

'I don't know much about kids but she seems very bright.'

He looked down at his daughter, pride written all over his face.

'Her playgroup teacher says she's always quick to pick up new things.'

In an attempt to make fast her collection of stickers, Bethany began to bang her fist on top of the loosely positioned papers. The table wobbled and the glasses on its surface trembled precariously. Phil jumped forward and put a steadying hand on the table.

'Careful Bethany. You don't need to bang so hard.' He pushed their glasses into the middle of the table before putting out a warning finger towards his daughter. 'Now be gentle.'

'I should go,' Cat said rising.

'Have you got any plans for today?'

'I'm going to try to find out what the police are up to.'

Phil looked over to her, an arched eyebrow telling of his misgivings before he even said a word.

'Isn't it a bit soon?' he said. 'I wouldn't think there'd be much they could tell you yet. It's been less than twelve hours.'

Cat paused and thought about it. It felt like a lifetime ago.

'You're probably right. Maybe I'll just go back to the room and finish packing Amy's things.' She turned to leave but paused. 'This morning... I forgot to thank you for what you did, last night... you know, trying to save Amy.'

'I only did what anyone would have done.'

'I don't know about that. I'm sure a lot of people would have just raised the alarm. You waded in and tried to rescue her. If there was any chance...' Her voice started to break up. She stopped, taking a moment to regain her composure. '...a chance she wasn't already dead, your being there could have made all the difference. It was a miracle you happened to be walking by and saw her at all. I mean with Bethany and everything.'

Her eyes made contact with his. She waited, letting the unasked question hang between them.

Phil looked away from her and down at his daughter. He brushed a hand gently over her head, smoothing down a few errant hairs.

'She was fast asleep in bed. It was so warm I was sitting on the balcony, having a drink, listening to the sea and thinking about...' For a moment his gaze drifted. He let out a soft sigh. 'Well, anyway I saw someone walking along the beach. A woman. On her own. To be honest I thought it was you. I watched until you, I mean she, disappeared from view. I sat there, watching, waiting for her to walk back. When she didn't appear after a few minutes I decided to nip down and go for a little stroll myself. I kind of hoped I'd bump into you. I was going to ask if you fancied joining me for a night cap. But when I reached the beach there was no one there. I was going to walk as far as the furthest umbrella and then return to the room if I didn't find you. I didn't get that far.' He looked Cat straight in the eye. 'I'm so sorry.'

Nineteen

After leaving Phil and Bethany, Cat crossed the terrace. She looked up at the clock above the bar and slowed her step. She had intended on going straight to the police station, but Phil had a point—maybe it would be better if she waited? She looked again at the clock. It was *nearly* lunch time.

Cat lifted herself onto a bar stool and ordered without needing to look at the menu.

'A four seasons pizza with a house salad and a side order of those stuffed vine leaves.'

'Koupepia,' Andreas added helpfully, as his pencil scratched over the pad. 'And to drink?'

'A beer.'

'A bottle of Budweiser?'

'Yes. Actually no, make that a pint of the local draft beer.'

'A pint of Keo?' He sounded surprised.

Andreas scurried off in the direction of the kitchen to put her order in, leaving Cat at the bar. She was the only person there. She glanced over to the pool area, which appeared to have attracted the entire population of the hotel, thanks to the uninterrupted blue sky and thirty-something temperature. As a result, it was something of a surprise to hear the scrape of a stool beside her. She turned in her seat and was even more taken aback when she saw Isabella sitting there.

The pretty American craned over the counter.

'Is the waiter around here someplace?'

'He's just run over to the kitchen. I imagine he'll be back any second.'

'Right.'

The two of them returned to looking straight ahead, like businessmen in an office block taking the same lift as each other for a decade or two.

'Sorry to hear about your friend,' Isabella said shortly.

'Thanks.' Cat looked at the teenager. Close up and without make-up she was exceptionally pretty, with none of the hard lines of her mother. 'How are you doing?'

'Okay, I guess,' Isabella said.

'Were you close to your father?'

'S'pose.'

'But he didn't always see your side of things, right?' Cat recalled the nineteen-year-old's response when Jaclyn caught her on her mobile phone in the ladies. 'That's fathers for you.' Cat had something of a fractious relationship with her own father so it was easy to empathise.

'He was alright.' Isabella said. 'He was just a little old fashioned.'

Cat thought of her own father. She remembered how proud he'd been when her brother, Pete, graduated from Police College. Cat had hoped her switch from biologist to detective might also win her father's favour one day. She was still waiting.

'Is that why your brother was taking over the reins?

Isabella frowned.

'What?'

'I heard your brother was taking over running the business.'

'He was, but that was nothing to do with Michael being his son. Daddy really wanted the business to stay in the family; he thought Michael's interest in food would be enough.'

'You weren't interested?' Cat asked.

The teenager gave an attractive laugh.

'I can't think of anything worse. Lucky for me Michael never dared to tell Daddy he didn't want to do it. Daddy tended to over react sometimes, especially if it was something he didn't want to hear.' She started to pick at the polish on the edge of one of her nails. 'Like the other night, in the bar.'

Cat was wondering how far she could take things. Could it be a case of simply asking? But before she dared to, Isabella continued, 'Of course, Michael knows Daddy wasn't really mad at him. Though it would have been better if Michael had mentioned the thing with the prices sooner, but he didn't want to because he knew Daddy would go ballistic. Which of course he did. That's what's so terrible.' Isabella dabbed the corner of her eyes. 'Daddy got so wound up about it, he fell out with virtually everybody.'

Cat was so absorbed in what the teenager was saying she didn't hear Andreas approach. It was only when Isabella directed a dewy-eyed smile over Cat's shoulder that she turned. The barman acknowledged Isabella with a nod before slipping back behind the counter, sliding a pint glass under the tap for Cat's lager.

'So, what do you do, back at home?' Cat asked.

'I'm in college, majoring in pharmacology.'

Cat noticed Isabella tilt her chin defiantly, perhaps too used to people's shock reaction that this attractive-looking girl also had a brain? It struck her that a pharmacology student would surely know all about insulin and her father's diabetes. Cat went to speak but paused, distracted by the sight of the brimming pint that appeared in front of her.

Isabella darted a glance at it.

'Just a mineral water for me, please,' she said to Andreas.

A waiter arrived carrying a tray full of food. Andreas gestured towards Cat and the man set down two full plates.

'I didn't realise how big the portions were,' Cat said, suddenly feeling foolish.

'Well you go right on and enjoy,' Isabella said, before taking a sip of the drink Andreas had set on the counter in front of her.

Cat started to cut a sliver of stuffed vine leaf.

'Are you shocked at what happened to your father?' she asked.

'Well yes, I suppose I am. Daddy was always messing around with his mealtimes, you know. He'd go too long between meals, or he'd like have some alcohol, which made him buzzy and hyperactive. It'd screw him up for a while but he was always alright, you know?'

'What if he forgot to take his insulin?'

Isabella gave an emphatic shake of her head.

'He never forgot.'

'Could it have been something he ate?' Cat said, trying to sound casual. 'The food that's exported needs to have a long shelf-life, doesn't it? Maybe the preservatives they use here aren't that safe? Do you know of anything, with your pharmacology knowledge, I mean, that might cause a hypoglycaemic attack?'

Isabella shrugged.

'No. And besides, he only dealt with normal things. You know, porcini, sun dried tomatoes, olives. They just come in jars, in oil. I mean no diabetic has ever died of that sort of stuff, have they?'

But Cat didn't give up that easily.

'What if your father had tried something he wasn't yet importing, something he hadn't got the all clear on? I would imagine some of his suppliers would have tried to get him to expand his range? There is one local delicacy. Ambelopoulia. Ever heard of it?'

Isabella looked vacantly at Cat and shook her head.

'It's song birds, pickled whole.'

As Cat watched, a look of repulsion marred the Californian's pretty features.

'You're kidding, right?'

'No. It's quite popular around here. At least that's what I heard. I've no idea what the pickling liquid is, but I don't suppose it will be regulated.'

'Well I'm sure Daddy would have been very careful. He wasn't stupid.'

Isabella reached for her drink and Cat wondered if she'd pushed too far but after a moment the teenager said, 'Is it because of your friend? Are you wondering whether she and Daddy ate the same thing that killed them, only she happened to be in the water when it happened? I can see why you might think that but we've eaten at Kostas loads of times and never been ill.'

'Kostas?' Cat shook her head. 'No. I don't think it could have been anything from there. For one thing, both Amy and I had the same thing.'

Isabella gave her a peculiar look.

'You went with them? I thought it was, well, a date.'

'Yesterday lunchtime?'

'No. Last night.' Isabella said.

'Amy ate at Kostas last night?'

Isabella took a sip of her drink.

'I'm sure that's what Ethan said. In the bar last night.'

'Kostas is that really smart place in Paphos, in the old town, isn't it? A white-washed old house in a little square.'

'That's right, with flowers growing up the wall around the door and windows. And they have the most gorgeous white linen. And the flowers in the table settings are just adorable. I bet they do the most fabulous weddings there. It's the perfect setting.'

'And Ethan said he took Amy there last night?'

'Yes, but I'm sure that's got nothing to do with it. I mean Ethan's okay, isn't he?'

Isabella, suddenly wide-eyed, shot Cat a look.

'Wait... your friend, she wasn't a diabetic, was she?'

'No.'

'Oh.' Isabella leaned back in her seat. 'I thought maybe they both ate something that only affects diabetics.'

'But I thought you didn't know anything that would have that effect,' Cat said.

'I don't, but that doesn't mean there isn't something. And besides, that won't really help explain how your friend died will it?'

'No, I don't suppose it will,' Cat said, even more confused.

But then nothing seemed to make much sense any more.

Twenty

Cat pushed past beach towels and snorkel and fin sets and stepped into the store's crisp frigid air. Goosebumps pricked their way up her arms. She made for a tall refrigerator and pulled out a cold can of diet Coke, hoping the caffeine would rid her of the lethargy brought on by her mammoth lunch. She headed to the till, past bottles of local olive oil and a plethora of Turkish delight in boxes shaped like the southern half of the island. A stack of writing pads grabbed her attention and she picked one up on her way through.

Back in her room she took a last pull of her drink and threw the can at the waste bin under the dressing table. She missed and it bounced off the rim and went rattling off under Amy's bed. For a second she thought about leaving it there but then kneeled onto the cold tiled floor and reached under the bed. At one point she felt the cool metal touch the tip of her fingers but when she tried to grab it, it evaded her grasp and went rolling out of reach.

She let out a sigh, lifted the bedspread and lowered down onto her front. She easily reached the can and set it on the floor beside her, then went back for a small piece of card that had caught her eye. She sat back on her heels and took a closer look. Across the top of the card, beautifully scripted in an ancient Hellenic-styled font, was the word Kostas, which sat above a delicate sketch of the charming tavern. An address ran along the bottom in small print. The reverse was plain, save for a series of numbers scribbled in black biro. It was a promotional card for the restaurant where she and Amy had lunched with Ethan the day before. The same place that Ethan had apparently taken Amy that night.

Rising to her feet, Cat slipped the card into her pocket, threw the can in the bin, successfully this time, and grabbed her new jotter. For a moment, she contemplated trying again to find her original notes. But what was the point? She'd already given the room a thorough going over.

Walking out onto the sun-drenched balcony she felt her stomach churn as memories of the previous day sneaked up on her. Determined not to get distracted she pushed them away, closing the door to her emotions, and made herself comfortable on one of the two white plastic chairs. Pen poised, she stared at the blank page.

The dilemma was whether to try to recreate what she had previously written—a feat of pure memory—or to start with what she knew now, which, no doubt, would come out different to her original notes. Giving in to the scientist within, she went back to basics.

'Start at the beginning,' she said.

But when was that? That was the million-dollar question. Was it when Tony died or was that supposed to be the end? And how did it link to the arson attacks or the bird trade? Was there a link?

She toyed with the pen, not wanting to commit anything to paper until she had some semblance of order in mind. She wished she had a bigger sheet, that way she could have tried mind-mapping the links, but...

'Okay, let's start with Tony.'

Tony Vostanis
Cause of death: hypoglycaemia
Diabetic, self-medicated with insulin
Residue in syringe suggests correct doses (if Amy was right)
No obvious explanation for hypoglycaemia

187

Questions:
Did Tony have a Cypriot heritage or family?
Did he target a US Cypriot market?
Did he usually do food tastings himself?
Was he (illegally) importing pickled birds?
Who are the beneficiaries of his will?

Cat knew that accidental death amongst diabetics was all too common and it seemed everyone else had resigned themselves to that. But if it was just a sad tragedy then why couldn't anyone explain *how* it had happened, given Tony was a man who, by most accounts, took reasonable care of himself.

And then there was the loose end only she knew about—well, apart from one other person at least. Why had someone taken the trouble to break into his room and what had they achieved while they were there? She thought back to what had happened: the open door, the clicking of the bag's clasp, the bag full of samples. She felt her heart quicken. She couldn't believe what she'd done—it must have been the adrenalin, she reasoned. It seemed so surreal now, looking back, but she had done it and she had the pictures to show for it. But what did they show? With a renewed interest, she returned to the room for her phone. Back in her seat, she turned a new page on her pad and began to slowly scroll through the dozen or so photos of the food samples, jotting down the names written on each of the bags. On cross-checking the samples against the written orders in Tony's bag, Cat found each order correlated to at least one of the sample packets. In fact, the number of samples out-weighed the orders. Presumably something hadn't exactly wowed the discerning American.

'Not a dead bird in sight,' she said, tapping her pencil on the paper.

She added another heading.

Removed a sample—linked to illegal imports? (drugs? pickled birds?)
Removed other item
Left something????

If there had been something in his bag worth taking, it must surely have some bearing on the motive for his murder, mustn't it? Assuming, of course, he'd died at another's hand. But now, with Amy's death, Cat was more certain than ever the dead man had been murdered, though she was no nearer to knowing why. She quickly added a third category to her note.

Motive:

Anger—did the animal rights protester take the arson attacks a stage further?
Blackmail—did Tony have something on someone—a supplier? Perhaps intruder took back evidence?
Revenge—was Tony's death retribution for something?
Protection—did Tony know something that was a threat?
Theft—had Tony taken something that belonged to someone else?
Hate—did Tony's oppressive nature drive one of his family to rebel?
Love—was Tony standing in the way of love?

Cat knew that there was another obvious and much more probable answer:

Money—who gains from his death? By how much?
How widely known are the contents of his will?

But what if the intrusion was to remove an item? Could it have been more to do with how he died rather than why? Cat went back to the list of possible objectives of the intruder:

Removed item that caused hypoglycaemia?

Which spurred her on to compile a new category:

Cause of hypoglycaemia:
Too much insulin—no evidence of overdose or wrong dose
Too much alcohol—not usually enough to kill and no evidence
Too much exercise—ditto
Not enough food—ditto
Other toxins ???

After spending five futile minutes trying to rack her brain for what limited biochemistry knowledge it contained, she gave up and was about to turn the page when a thought occurred to her. She added:

Post-mortem results / toxicology—what do they show?

She picked up the pad and reviewed her handiwork. Her focus gravitated to the entries that documented her foray into the dead man's room. It occurred to her that Jaclyn would ordinarily be prime suspect, assuming she was the main beneficiary, yet she had no need to sneak around, making clandestine trips to her own room.

What if it was a double bluff? What if Jaclyn had wanted someone to spot the partially open door, to then report a potential break-in? It was obvious from the dirty crockery that the cleaner was going to come back though. Cat recalled Jaclyn's

190

apparent irritation at the fact that the 'do not disturb' sign had fallen from the handle.

She thought back to the sequence of events, trying to find any hint the ordinarily confident, cock-sure widow may have been play-acting, but there was nothing to suggest that was the case. And besides, Cat reasoned, it was too complicated. How would Jaclyn have known anyone was going to walk by or the cleaner not take the plates the first time?

She blew out a heavy sigh.

'This is why in real life people don't do murder investigations from their armchairs,' she chastised herself out loud. Though it didn't stop her from starting a new sheet.

Amy
Drowned: accident or murder?
Signs of struggle? Need PM results
Too drunk to swim?
Any sign of other drug/chemical involved?
Cramp after a large meal?

If murder—why?
She saw something?
She knew something?
She said something?

Out of ideas, she set the pad down and pulled the small advertising card for Kostas's restaurant out of her pocket and looked at it again. There was no doubt that someone other than Amy had written the number on its reverse. The angular European style was about as far removed from Amy's curlicued script as it could be.

Cat scored under the figures with her pen as she contemplated the numbers' significance. A date and a time maybe? Perhaps

Amy's date with Ethan had clashed with a rendezvous of a different, more dangerous type. She picked the pad up and added a further entry.

Wrong place, wrong time?

Without warning the memory of her friend's fragile form lying in the sand sprang to mind and Cat felt the swell in her chest. Her throat tightened and then the familiar pin-prick stinging of her eyes started as she began to well up. With her vision distorted, she put her pen down and gave in to the grief she had pushed aside since waking. The tears soon subsided though and after a deep restorative breath she looked again at the scant facts that she'd pulled together. She felt sure there was something there, something nagging away at her. With an overwhelming need to talk to someone she reached for her phone and hit the most frequently called number on her contact list.

'Hi Alex, it's me. Are you okay to talk?' she asked, her voice thick in the aftermath of too many tears.

'Sure. What's up? You're not in trouble, are you?'

Cat gave a groan which Alex automatically took as an admission of guilt. 'Oh shit. Cat, I told you...'

'No. It's not me. It's Amy.' Her voice caught in her throat, strangled by her emotions. Alex waited patiently. She steadied herself with a few deep breaths and continued, taking him through the events of the previous night. The words tumbled out, a confusion of facts and feelings. Occasionally Alex would interrupt and ask a question until eventually he knew as much as she did.

'Oh God Cat, I'm so sorry. Is there anything I can do at this end?'

'No. But thanks. That wasn't why I called. I just needed to talk to someone. I've been going mad trying to make sense of it all.'

'Surely it was just an unfortunate accident, one of those terrible things that happen sometimes?'

'I wish I could believe that. I don't know why but I can't help but think... Oh I don't know. There are just things I can't explain.'

'What sort of things?'

'Well I told you about Tony, the American who died. Ethan, the guy who Amy spent all week chasing, was part of the same group. I heard Amy talking to him about the death as though she knew something and she wasn't exactly discreet.'

'But she couldn't have known anything.'

'I know that but anyone who overheard her wouldn't have. They might have seen her as a credible threat: a forensic scientist who was actually at the scene when the body was found.'

'But Cat there's no evidence to suggest the man was even murdered. And even if he was, anyone with half a brain would have just kept their head down. They certainly wouldn't have put themselves at risk by killing someone on the back of a bit of idle speculation.'

'If they'd already killed once they could be living on their nerves.'

'But what could she have said that was enough of a threat? She didn't know anything.'

Cat remembered the missing notepad.

'She might have pretended she'd spoken with the authorities here. Shared information from them.'

'But how?'

'I made some notes, after talking to Glafcos, just a few bits and pieces. I've looked everywhere for it but my notepad's gone.'

'Shit, Cat, when will you learn? When did you last see it?'

'Yesterday afternoon. I'd been writing in it on the balcony of my room. I noticed it missing this morning.'

'And you think Amy took it?'

'I don't know. All I know is it's not here now.'

'Hmm. Did you see it after Amy had gone out?'

Cat felt a tingle of hope, perhaps he was coming around to her way of thinking? She thought for a minute.

'No. And she did come out on to the balcony. I'd been making notes and then I must have nodded off. When I woke up Amy was there. But if she took it, where is it now?'

'Maybe she had it on her last night? You could ask the police if they found it with her belongings.'

'Uh-hu,' Cat said, annoyed that she hadn't thought of that.

'What else?' Alex asked.

There was more but she knew he wouldn't understand. How could he? All she had was a maelstrom of gut instinct and uneasy feelings arising from a collection of inexplicable and unhappy coincidences.

'I suppose that's it.'

'Are you sure... no more suspicious characters or spurious theories?'

She knew he was trying to lighten things up but she just wasn't in the mood.

'Don't make fun of me Alex. You don't know what it's like. There are some funny goings on around here. There's a whole load of stuff around the illegal trade in pickled birds and then there's an arsonist and—'

'Pickled what?'

'Birds,' she replied, articulating the single syllable clearly. 'There are traps all around the area to catch migrating birds. The local restaurants sell them, even though it's illegal. One of the other guests here at the hotel—a keen birdwatcher—has been going out late at night freeing the bloody things single-handed. I did wonder if perhaps he's the arsonist... though he seems too nice.'

'Arsonist? What arsonist?'

'Someone's going around torching restaurants that sell this delicacy.'

'I'm not sure I follow. How does any of this link to the two deaths?' Alex asked with his typical laser sharp focus.

'I don't know. It might not, but Tony—the dead American— ran a business importing Mediterranean foods into California. He could have been supplying a stateside black market with pickled birds. I would imagine it's a very lucrative business. There must be millions of Americans of European descent living in the US. If he was doing something like that, it could explain why he was murdered. Maybe the arsonist decided to take a more direct course of action.' Cat cringed as she said it. She knew he'd be able to drive a coach and horses through her reasoning. 'Look, I know it sounds a bit loose but there could be a connection.'

Alex cleared his throat.

'I realise arson may be a marker for psychopaths but not all arsonists are murderers.' There was a short pause. 'Now if you suspected the American of being the arsonist that would make more sense. There would be suppliers who'd want him out of the way.'

'I know,' Cat said. 'But why would he be the arsonist if he was importing the bloody birds into the US in the first place?'

'*If,*' Alex said, pointedly, letting the word hang between them for longer than Cat could bear.

'You're not helping,' she snapped.

'I'm sorry but from where I'm sitting you're trying to make the facts fit your assumptions and there isn't even any evidence either of them was murdered. All you've got is a suspicion that someone broke into the American's room after he died. But even that could have just been something blowing off a table if the patio door was accidentally left open.'

'Don't forget the stolen bag,' Cat said.

'Ah, yes. The bag that happened to have been stolen on the same day as he was found dead.' He softened his tone. 'Maybe it was what it appeared to be? Someone took the opportunity to take the bag, strip it of cash and then dump it as fast as possible to avoid being caught with any incriminating evidence.' Cat remained quiet. Alex said gently, 'I'm sorry. I know you want somebody to blame for Amy's death, it's human nature, but I just don't see anything there. It's not surprising you're confused, given all the tales of pickled birds, arson attacks, stolen bags. Not to mention the dead American and now Amy.'

If Alex had been there, he might have been surprised to see the anguish on Cat's face. He was so wrong, she already had someone to blame: herself for not being there when Ethan came looking for Amy.

She took in a deep breath and let it out slowly.

'Well thanks for listening,' she said. 'I should have known you'd put a different perspective on things.'

'I'm glad I could help. Just hang on in there. You'll be back to normality before you know it.'

Not before she'd found out what had really happened, she vowed.

Twenty-one

The bedside alarm glowed blue in the growing darkness. 18:30. Cat walked over to the window and looked out at a sky streaked pink and orange by the setting sun. By the time she pulled into the harbour car park in Paphos the night sky was shrouded in black. She climbed out of the car, spent a couple of minutes studying the rudimentary map hastily scribbled by one of the receptionists, committed it to memory and then set off.

In any other circumstance she would have enjoyed the walk, passing down pleasant streets lined with boutique shops and bars, with couples walking arm in arm, mingling amongst groups of friends, laughing and chatting. But Cat paid them no heed. She walked with a steady stride and a forward gaze. At a junction of roads, she made a final check of the map and turned the corner. And there it was, the restaurant, straight ahead of her. As she approached, her eyes took in the scene. Candlelight cast a soft buttery glow over the tables, the flames' reflections dancing over crystal glasses and polished cutlery. Murmured conversations and gentle laughter spilled out onto the pavement and filled the air as heady as the intoxicating aroma of the night-blooming jasmines that clothed the walls. As beautiful as the taverna had been by day, by night it was doubly so. Cat could see now why Ethan might have chosen to bring Amy back for dinner, despite having already eaten there earlier that day; it was perfect for a romantic dinner for two.

The outside seating area was already full and Cat began to doubt her chances of getting a table. She walked past the alfresco diners and approached the front desk. The maître d' met her with a warm smile.

'Madam?' he said.

'Good evening. Do you have a table for one?'

'Your name?' He transferred his attention to a large reservations book on the lectern in front of him.

A waiter pushed through the door giving Cat a glimpse of the interior of the restaurant. It looked just as busy.

'I'm sorry, I haven't booked.'

Cat looked back at the black and white outfitted man whose smile had evaporated. Sensing an impending eviction, she thought back to a previous time when she had attempted to eat out at short notice in Cyprus, when she and Alex were working their last murder case. Then Alex managed to save the day with some timely flattery. If it worked once…?

'I can see you're busy. It's my own fault. I should have booked, especially as it's my last night here. Unfortunately, I only got to hear about you yesterday from friends of mine who told me what a great place this is.' She would have tried fluttering her eyelashes, only with no mascara on it would probably just look as though she had something in her eye. Instead she made a point of looking around the restaurant. 'I can see they were right. You have a beautiful restaurant. My friends are an American family. Perhaps you know them?'

He closed the reservations book, signalling the end of their brief exchange.

'We will have the pleasure of welcoming you next time.'

Cat was just about to leave when she heard a familiar voice ring out. She turned, surprised to see Ethan emerge from the direction of the kitchen. He spotted her immediately.

'Cat!'

'Hi.'

'Are you alright? You look like you've just seen a ghost.'

She gave an embarrassed smile.

'I wasn't expecting to see you here, that's all.'

Ethan took a quick look around.

'Are you eating here on your own?' he asked.

'Yes, well, actually no. That was the plan but they're fully booked. I was just leaving.'

'Let me see what I can do. Kostas...' He beckoned to the maître d'. 'Kostas, my good friend, this lady tells me you are too full to squeeze in another little table. Is that true?'

The heavy-set Cypriot looked at Cat. His jowls twitched as the corners of his mouth lifted, as though pulled by the practised hand of a puppeteer.

'Mr Ethan is your American friend? Why didn't you say? It is very good to meet you.' He thrust an open palm towards Cat and shook her hand vigorously.

Ethan spoke to the Cypriot in his native tongue. Kostas nodded keenly before enlisting the help of two of the waiters.

'It'll just be a minute,' Ethan said.

They waited together, watching the staff dismantle a table set for three. Soon the tablecloths had been removed and the two small square tables pulled apart and re-laid separately.

Minutes later, Cat was sitting facing Ethan on a table for two. She wondered whether the party of three that would be sitting next to them would comment on their cramped settings.

'Would madam like to order a drink to begin?' the waiter at her elbow asked.

Cat reached for the wine list and then remembered the forty-five-minute drive back to the hotel.

'A bottle of sparkling water please.'

'And sir?'

'A bottle of your best burgundy,' Ethan said.

The waiter whisked away the wine menu and the crystal glass from Cat's place setting and returned moments later with a bottle, peppered with dust and a grimy label that spoke of some age-old vintage. He dusted it off and set it against a linen napkin draped over his arm. Ethan cast an eye over the label before nodding. The waiter expertly eased out the cork, poured a splash into the bottom of an oversized wine glass and offered it to Ethan. Taking the glass gently, with the stem between his fingers, he held it up to the light. Next, he lowered it and with his nose hovering over the rim, inhaled deeply. Slowly he began to roll the deep plum and cherry coloured liquid around the glass, until, after what seemed like an age, he stilled his hand and studied the thick tracks streaked down the sides of the glass as the wine settled. Finally, he took a drink, swilling it around his mouth like a dental rinse, before finally swallowing. He set the glass back on the table and watched as the waiter filled the glass

'An excellent find. Thank you.'

'You're welcome,' the waiter said as he slipped his order pad out of his pocket. He turned to Cat, pen in hand. 'Is madam ready to order?'

Cat took a moment to scan the menu.

'I'm really not sure. It all sounds delicious.' She looked over to Ethan. 'Do you recommend anything in particular?'

Ethan glanced down and studied the menu for a moment.

'The chef's special is probably the most popular appetizer. It's a porcini and black truffle pâté that comes with herb bread. And for entree, well, there are a couple of stand-out dishes.' He looked up at Cat. 'You like seafood?'

'Vegetarian, remember?' she said, trying not to sound apologetic.

'In that case I'd definitely recommend the eggplant. It's chargrilled with a lemon, chilli and herb dressing and a green salad with artichoke hearts. It's light and fresh yet bursting with flavour.'

'That sounds perfect.' Cat turned to the waiter and gave him a warm smile. 'I'll have the mushroom and herb bread appetizer, followed by the aubergine please.'

'Excellent choice madam.' He looked over to Ethan, 'And for sir?'

'The egg lemon soup followed by the grass-fed rib-eye, rare. A side of vegetables. No rice.'

The waiter finished scratching their order on his pad and then left in the direction of the kitchen. He returned moments later to add a soup spoon to Ethan's place setting. When they were on their own, Ethan looked over to Cat with a thoughtful frown.

'Is there something wrong?' she asked.

'I've just realised, I have made a massive imposition, joining you at a sensitive time like this.'

'Not at all. It's a relief not to have to eat on my own.' She smiled yet somehow the action failed to reach her eyes.

His eyes scoured her face.

'Really?'

'Yes, honestly.' Cat looked away and reached for her napkin. She shook it gently and laid it over her lap.

'No, I'm sorry. It was inconsiderate of me to barge in. Would you like me to leave? I promise, I don't mind.'

'No, I meant what I said. Anyway, you'll never get a table now.' Cat looked at him and frowned. 'Were you even planning on eating here?'

'Of course. This is one of the best restaurants in Cyprus. I come here whenever I can.'

'But where...?' She looked around but couldn't see a single unoccupied table.

'One of the privileges of business,' Ethan said. 'There's a small table for the staff to eat at in the kitchen. If I'm on my own and they're busy, they let me dine in there.'

'Ahh.' Cat nodded. She took a drink of water and returned it to the table before looking back over at Ethan. 'You obviously like it here. A lot. I admit, I did find it a bit strange that you brought Amy here last night, given we'd already had lunch here.'

'Yesterday lunchtime was a choice of convenience. I had a meeting here, so it made sense. But last night, well...' Now it was Ethan's turn to switch his attention to the napkin draped on his lap. Picking at a corner, he lowered his voice and spoke slowly, hesitantly. 'Last night I wanted it to be perfect. I reserved one of the best tables outside. Lit by candlelight, surrounded by bougainvillea, with the smell of jasmine and orange blossom hanging in the air. It was... well, it was just magical.'

Cat looked at him. The flame from the candle reflected in his eyes, shimmering on the tears that coated their surface. He closed his eyes and pinched the bridge of his nose.

'You know, I still can't believe what's happened.'

They both reached for their drinks and after a short silence Ethan cleared his throat.

'I feel like I owe you an apology,' he said. Cat's eyes grew wide. Ethan began to roll the stem of his wine glass gently between his fingers. The blood-red liquid swirled slowly around the bowl. 'I meant to come and see you this morning but, oh I don't know... I guess I didn't know what to say.' He took a deep breath and then gave her a tight smile. He looked about him, as though appreciating their circumstances for the first time. 'So anyway, how come you're here, in this restaurant, miles away from the hotel, intending on having dinner on your own?'

'I just couldn't face the hotel. I knew there would be tons of places to eat in Paphos. It seemed a good idea at the time.'

'But here?'

'More accident than design. I parked at the marina and just started walking but nothing seemed to grab my eye. I just kept going until, well... here I am.' The words tripped effortlessly off her tongue. She was becoming something of a proficient liar, she noted.

'Sure you're not just looking for ways to beat yourself up over what's happened?' The dubious look on Ethan's face was a match for the cynicism his voice held. 'If I hadn't been here, you would have been on your own, in the same place that Amy was last night.'

Cat was surprised by his astuteness. Like a masochistic flagellant she couldn't stop whipping herself with what-ifs. She was saved from answering by the timely arrival of their starters. Kostas brought them out himself. *Ethan really was getting the VIP service.*

She took a piece of the herb flatbread and tentatively dipped it into the silky-smooth blend of creamy roast mushroom. Flecks of black truffle peppered the surface of the mocha-coloured pâté. She took a bite and closed her eyes, chewing slowly and indulgently.

'Oh wow. This is amazing.'

Ethan gave a gentle laugh.

'Seriously. Would you like to try some?' She extended her plate towards him.

'No, I'm good thanks.' He looked down at his own bowl. 'Besides, this is a great soup. I can get another spoon brought out, if you'd like to try?'

Cat shook her head.

'Thanks, but I'm happy with this little bit of paradise.'

Throughout the meal, conversation came easily. And for a while Cat was able to relax, content to simply sit and listen to Ethan talk fondly about his life back in California and his friendship with Tony. He told how the two of them had transformed the tiny deli in Tony's small hometown into a thriving business occupying a two-storey turn of the century canning factory with ocean views in one of the city's most visited resorts, where discerning buyers could grab freshly ground coffee and gourmet foodstuffs imported from all over Europe. He even had nice things to say about Jaclyn and the rest of the clan. Though Cat thought that was probably because until Tony had announced his plan to retire, Ethan's contact with them had been limited to the occasional get-together, which, by his own admission, was exactly how he'd liked it.

'Did he do much online business?' Cat asked, wondering how you'd go about selling an under-the-counter item on a mass scale.

'Tony? Online?' Ethan gave a hard laugh. 'He didn't know one end of a computer from the other.'

'I wondered if Michael or you helped him with that side of things?'

'No,' he said, shaking his head, before taking another mouthful of food.

'It's only, I thought he ran a much bigger operation than a single deli-coffee shop.'

'No. Just the shop.'

'Oh.'

Ethan reached for his wine.

'You sound surprised.'

'It's just I got the impression he was something of an entrepreneur.'

'I suppose he was in a way. He was always looking for the next big thing. He could always spot a trend in the making. People would come from all over California to visit the shop. Especially when we'd got new stock in. That's one of the reasons we come out here every spring—to look for new products to add to the range.'

'Have you ever tried the pickled birds? I hear they're a real delicacy,' she asked. Her eyes scanned his face, studying his reaction.

'Wow!' He raised his eyebrows and smiled, shaking his head. 'I wasn't expecting that.' Cat continued to look at him, saying nothing. Ethan shook his head 'A lot of the old-timers here think it's part of their heritage; a tradition that should be allowed to continue. But Tony always said we're a modern American business. He'd rather the suppliers innovate and come up with products that will sell back home rather than hang on to the past.'

'What about you? What do you think?'

'I agree with Tony's take on things. You have to know your customer: most Californians are animal-loving health-nuts. If it isn't free-range or organic, it isn't going to sell, believe me.'

Suddenly enthused, Ethan started to recount some of the businesses' notable successes and failures. He was in the middle of some story about disastrous homemade broccoli bread, when Cat became aware of somebody moving around behind her. She thought of her bag hanging on the back of her chair and reached around for it. A man moved towards her, a large black camera to his face. Just then he crouched down and pointed it straight at her. Cat sensed Ethan lean in towards her. She loosened her grip on her bag and turned back in her seat, giving an uneasy smile for the camera. The photographer chatted animatedly as he bobbed and side-stepped. Occasionally Cat heard him say 'cheese' as he repeatedly pressed on the shutter release. Eventually he stopped shooting and straightened up. He pulled out a handful of small cards from a pocket, scribbled something on the back of two of them and handed them one each. Cat looked down at hers. By the time she looked back up the photographer had already moved on to the next table.

She turned the card over between thumb and forefinger. It was an exact replica of the one that had inspired her to come to the restaurant in the first place. With one exception—the number on the back of the card was different.

'What does this mean?' She pointed to the figure on the reverse.

Ethan took her card and laid it down on the table next to his. The two were identical.

'It's today's date and time. It's so you can find your photo on the website if you want to order one.'

He handed Cat the card back. She took another look then checked her watch.

'That can't be right. It says eight, it's gone nine now.'

'The evening sitting is always put down as eight. Are you always this inquisitive?' he laughed.

'Not always,' she lied with a smile.

They fell quiet and Cat continued to fiddle with the photographer's card, turning it over in her fingers.

'You know earlier, you asked why I was here.'

Ethan looked up at her, mild interest showing on his face.

'Yes.'

'I found one of these on the floor in my room,' she said, reaching into her pocket and pulling out the card she'd found under Amy's bed. She placed it on the table, next to hers. 'It must have fallen on the floor when Amy came back last night, before she went down to the beach. I thought it might be important.'

Ethan looked down at the two cards and then back at Cat with a frown.

He shrugged.

'Important how?'

'I don't know. It sounds stupid now but I wondered if Amy had stumbled across something.'

Ethan's frown intensified.

'I don't understand. What do you mean stumbled across something?' He looked up from the cards and into her face with such intensity Cat felt her skin prickle. 'Do you mean something that could have led to her death?' he asked quietly.

'I don't know.'

Ethan's gaze drifted back down to the cards on the table. He gave a faint shake of the head and reached for his glass.

Cat cleared her throat.

'The first night you took Amy to dinner...'

Ethan returned the glass to the table and looked her in the eye.

'Yes?'

'I heard there was quite a crowd there.'

'It was busy, yes. It was the grand opening.'

'Did you happen to talk to anyone while you were there? Other than Amy, I mean.'

A puzzled expression appeared on his face, but he didn't answer immediately and Cat waited while he thought about it. Shortly he shook his head.

'No.'

'What about at the place you went for cocktails? Perhaps someone joined the two of you for a drink?'

'No.'

'Not even briefly? A supplier you've met with recently or someone else who—'

'No,' Ethan said. 'I would have given anyone trying to talk to me the brush off and told them to call me the next day.' Ethan was looking openly concerned now. 'What's this all about Cat?'

She looked down. *Just clutching at straws.*

'Do you seriously think someone was responsible for Amy's death?' he asked.

She felt her grief resume its grip as her stomach flipped at the mention of her friend's name.

'You okay?' Ethan reached across the table, settling a hand gently over one of hers.

Cat pulled her hand away and hastily wiped the corner of her eyes.

'I'm sorry but it's been a long day.' She reached for the photographer's cards lying on the table, glancing at them fleetingly, before dropping them into her handbag. 'I spent all morning packing Amy's things. It seems strange to think she won't be needing them anymore.' She gave a tight laugh. 'You wouldn't believe how much stuff she brought with her. Actually, that reminds me, I noticed a notepad was missing. I don't suppose she had it on her last night, did she?'

'A notepad? No, I don't think so.'

'It was one of those small pads they provide in the room. In that leather embossed folder along with the pamphlets for local attractions.'

He shook his head.

'No. Sorry. Is it important?'

'Probably not. I just wondered where it had gone.'

'Maybe Amy put it in the trash can and the cleaner emptied it?'

'I doubt it,' she replied, knowing full well that wasn't the case. 'Amy never put anything in the bin. It's like the thing with the towels on the beach.'

Ethan frowned and shrugged a shoulder.

'The police told me they found Amy's clothes and the towels folded neatly on a sunbed. She was the untidiest person I ever met. I don't think I ever saw her fold anything before.'

'Really? You surprise me. From the way she talked, she struck me as a neat, methodical kind of a person.'

'Amy? Neat and methodical?' Cat gave a soft laugh.

'Of course, I'd only known her for a few days, but surely, with her job?'

'Neat didn't come into it. That's why I think it's strange she left her stuff like that.'

'That thing with the towels...' Ethan hesitated. 'That was me.'

'You?'

'I mean, I told Amy to put them on a lounger. I couldn't see the point of getting towels and taking our clothes off if everything was left on the sand to get soaking wet. I guess she must have listened.'

'Now, if I'd made that suggestion...' Cat's words trailed off. After a moment she roused herself. 'How did it go at the station last night? Did you have to give a formal statement?'

'No. They just asked me to go over what we did, where we went,' he suddenly looked all sheepish, '...how much we'd had to drink. I got the impression they were treating it as an accident. That's why I was surprised earlier, when you said you thought there might be more to it.'

Cat opened her mouth but stopped, unsure what to say. She brought her lips together and shrugged her shoulders.

'I don't know what to think. I just want them to do the right thing by Amy, that's all.'

Ethan nodded.

'I know you do. I do too.' His expression ponderous, he reached for his wine and slowly took a drink. 'I hope you don't think it's too presumptuous,' he said, returning the glass to the table, 'but I wondered whether it would be appropriate to send my condolences to Amy's parents?'

'That's a nice thought. I'm sure they'd appreciate it.'

He pulled a pen and slim-line black leather-bound book from his jacket pocket.

'Do you have their address?'

'Oh, I don't, no. I suppose you could send it to Amy's house. I'm sure her parents will be picking up her post. It's—'

'You couldn't just write it down for me? I sometimes find your English pronunciation a little difficult to understand. I wouldn't want to get it wrong.'

Cat jotted down the address from memory and passed the book back.

Ethan opened it to the new entry.

'Rochester.' He pronounced it Row-Chester. 'That sounds kinda quaint.'

'It's okay. I suppose some bits are quaint. The area near to the cathedral is all cobbled streets and old timber houses. Charles Dickens lived there or set his books there. Something like that anyway.'

Ethan opened his jacket and went to return the book to his inside pocket, only he misjudged it and it slipped onto the table and knocked over his glass. Thankfully it was almost empty and only a single drop of red wine dripped in slow motion onto the white table cloth where it blossomed.

Ever efficient, the restaurant staff immediately swooped in and replaced the soiled linen and refilled Ethan's wine glass faster than a Formula One tyre change.

'Shall I get madam a glass?' the waiter asked, indicating the bottle of red wine.

Ethan looked at Cat.

'Please, join me...'

'Thanks, but I won't. I've got to drive back later.'

'You'll be okay with one small glass.'

Cat looked at her bottle of water and then at the wine. As appealing as it sounded, she knew that the consequences of being caught drink-driving didn't bear thinking about.

'It's tempting but I won't. Thanks all the same.'

'You don't talk about yourself very much,' Ethan observed, in the lull that followed.

'Don't I?'

'Not really.'

'You mean compared to Amy. She always was Mrs Sociable— could talk the hind legs off a donkey.'

'Well she was just what I needed. After what happened with Tony. The suddenness of it. She really helped take my mind off

210

it. Well, as much as you can, in the circumstances. You were close, weren't you? The two of you?'

'Used to be.' Cat paused. 'Not so much recently.'

'She spoke very highly of you.'

'Did she?'

'You sound surprised.'

'I suppose I am, a bit.'

'She said you were always sharing stuff, helping each other out.'

Cat thought back to the borrowed halterneck and the green shirt. And then to the harsh words they'd shared the day she'd died.

When she looked back, Ethan was toying with the napkin in his lap. Cat got the impression he was mulling something over. She waited.

After a minute he must have come to a decision and opened up.

'I suppose Amy probably told you some of the things we'd talked about?' He glanced nervously at Cat. 'It's my own fault. I didn't say it was a secret. I know I probably don't need to say it, but I was hoping you wouldn't say anything to anyone else. People might read the wrong thing into it.'

'I'm sorry, I'm not sure what you're talking about,' she said.

'When Jaclyn mistook me for David on the phone?' He interrogated her with his gaze.

Cat thought a little half-truth wouldn't hurt.

'Oh, that. Hmm, yes.' She nodded.

Okay, so she knew it was an out and out lie, but where was the harm?

'You can see why I don't want it becoming common knowledge. I can't see how their affair could have anything to do with Tony's death.'

He reached for his glass only it was empty. He grabbed the bottle. It was also empty. He held it aloft to signal for a replacement, making sure the waiter acknowledged him, before returning it to the table.

'I really shouldn't have been so indiscreet. I don't make a habit of talking about people but Amy had a way about her that made me open up.'

The waiter arrived with a fresh bottle.

'You can just leave the open bottle there,' Ethan said. Once they were on their own again, while pouring himself a refill, he continued, 'I'd suspected something for a while. I don't know whose idea it was to bring David on this trip—he could have just as easily done what he needed to do back home—but once the idea was planted in Tony's head there was no changing his mind. He thought it was the perfect solution. Larissa and Isabella are good friends, and Tony thought Gillian would be company for Jaclyn. But it was a stupid idea, putting temptation in their way like that. I'm only grateful Tony never found out about it, though I think he was starting to have his suspicions.'

'Well you don't need to worry about me. I promise I won't say anything to anyone.'

Ethan gave her a grateful smile and lifted his glass.

Twenty-two

Cat felt tired. More than tired, she felt exhausted. She touched her face with her fingers, running them lightly under her eyes, hoping to smooth away the dark circles she could see in her mind's eye.

'Are you okay?' Ethan asked.

'I'm fine, just feeling the effects of having hardly any sleep last night.'

The restaurant was emptying rapidly. The earlier lively conversations had been replaced by low murmurs interspersed with the occasional clattering and clanging of tables being cleared as diners departed, leaving their compliments and, more often than not, a generous tip.

Cat glanced at her watch.

'Oh my God. It's eleven already. How did that happen? No wonder I'm so tired.'

Ethan caught the eye of one of the waiters and mimed writing into an imaginary pad. The waiter rushed over and placed a small brass dish on the table. In it was a slip of folded paper and a handful of individually wrapped mints. Cat reached for her bag off the back of her chair and started to delve into its depths for her purse.

'Don't worry, I'll get this,' Ethan said, reaching for his wallet.

She looked up at him.

'Please. I insist.' He unfolded the bill, which had topped three figures, and set his credit card on top.

A young waiter approached carrying a credit card machine.

'You are ready to pay now Mr Garrett?'

'Yes. Thank you.'

'I hope Mrs Vostanis is recovered after Monday,' the waiter said while waiting for the card to be accepted.

Ethan looked up at him, a look of disbelief on his face.

'About as recovered as you might expect,' he said.

But the waiter was too busy keying the amount into the credit card machine to pick up on the sarcasm in his voice. He passed the card reader to Ethan and looked on, blankly.

'Good. I would not have liked for it to have ruined her holiday.'

'Not ruined her holiday?' Ethan thrust the machine back to the perplexed-looking waiter. 'Her husband has died and you hope it hasn't ruined her holiday?'

The look of embarrassment multiplied on the young waiter's face.

Kostas, spotting a fracas in the making, came rushing over from the other side of the room.

'Is there a problem?' he asked.

'I am sorry. I just ask if Mrs Vostanis, if she was improved after finding her bag.' The waiter gestured wildly with his hands. 'I did not know about Mr Vostanis. I did not know he die.'

Kostas gave him a contemptuous look and smacked him across the shoulder.

'Get out... Go to the kitchen and help your cousin before I do the same to you as I did to Petros.' The waiter handed over the card reader and scurried away. 'I must apologise for my imbecile nephew. I do not know where he gets his lack of brains from.'

'What happened to Petros?' Ethan asked. 'One of the waiters,' he added, for Cat's benefit.

'I get rid of. I think he is the one who steal Mrs Vostanis's bag.'

'Really?'

'I think, yes. No one else is stupid enough to take the bag down the alley to ransack. It is a dead-end, you know, only the

214

store room is down there. It was Petros job to bring stock in that day. He was in and out of the store room all day.'

'I thought the bag was left by a bin,' Cat said, remembering an earlier conversation.

'Yes. By the storeroom. They are all so stupid.' Kostas walked away, shaking his head.

Cat stood and lifted her jacket off the back of her seat. Ethan jumped to his feet.

'Here, let me.' He held the coat out for her.

'I guess Jaclyn was lucky the guy didn't throw her bag in the bin. If he had, she might never have found it,' Cat said.

Ethan pulled his sweater on over his head.

'I suppose.' He ran his fingers through his hair, smoothing it back into place. 'Let me walk you to your car. Where are you parked?'

'By the marina. But what about you, you're not driving are you?'

There was very little left in the second bottle.

'No. I'll get a taxi.'

'Don't be silly. I can give you a lift back.'

'Thanks, but I promised Kostas I'd stay for a farewell drink after they close.'

'In which case don't worry about walking me to the car. It's not that late. I'm sure I'll be quite safe.'

'I don't know...'

'Honestly, I'll be fine,' Cat insisted. 'Thank you for a lovely night.'

'It was a pleasure. I hope you feel a little, well, better than you did earlier.' He leaned in and kissed her lightly on both cheeks as they said goodnight. 'Make sure you stick to the promenade where there will be more people. Just turn left out of the door, along the cobbled path until you get to the main strip, then turn right. After that just follow the road around. It will lead you straight to the car park. Couldn't be simpler.'

Following Ethan's advice, Cat exited the restaurant, keeping left. Where the building ended, a tarmacked alley ran along the back. She glanced down its short length. Light spilled from a window, illuminating two large paladin bins in the farthest corner. She recalled Kostas's certainty that it had been one of the waiters who had lifted the Louis Vuitton. It still nagged as to why the discarded bag hadn't been put in one of the bins.

She looked around the empty street, then back at the bins and then started towards them, walking on tiptoes to keep her low heels from striking the stone. There was a closed wooden door and a wide window on the back wall of the restaurant. An archaic extractor fan set high in the window emitted a repetitive tick-tick-tick like a macabre timer counting down towards some apocalyptic event, ramping up the tension in her already tight nerves. She veered wide of the window, hugging the shadows on the wall opposite. The fan was clearly as ineffective as it was irritating given the window was in fact open. The sound of voices, snatches of conversation, drifted out, smothered under the clattering of pots and pans. A mosquito net stapled crudely to the frame kept the kitchen clear of critters but allowed busy post-service sounds to escape.

Cat recognised Ethan's Californian drawl. She paused and stood for a moment, eavesdropping. Kostas's deep bass voice boomed out into the quiet night. He made some comment about supply and demand. Cat recalled Phil's comments about Ethan: he'd been right on the money—still talking business. She started to tiptoe away.

'What if she still says no?' Kostas said.

Cat froze, poised for Ethan's reply. Suddenly water erupted from a low-level drain underneath the kitchen window. Suds flooded across the road. Someone was emptying the kitchen sink or perhaps the dishwasher was ending its cycle. The gurgle of water blotted out the conversation from inside the kitchen. When she next heard Ethan speak, he appeared to be complaining about something. A sharp edge spiked his normally seductively smooth accent. But there was too much background noise now and she couldn't make out what was being said.

She started towards the bins but a sound from behind caused her to turn and look. The door to the kitchen stood ajar; thankfully it opened away from her, giving her some cover.

'I unlock the stockroom door and then we continue to talk,' Kostas said.

Cat's heart quickened. She ran to the back wall and squeezed behind the furthest bin. Footsteps approached. Her stomach lurched as she realised they were coming directly at her and not to the store as she'd expected. She sank further down. The groan of a hefty lid being lifted was followed by a muffled thud and then an almighty boom as the lid crashed down. Cat rushed to put her fingers to her ears but she was too late. Temporarily deafened and unable to make out the sound of retreating footsteps, she waited a couple of minutes before slowly rising. The kitchen door was once again closed and the alley empty. Her chest heaved and her heart raced. She looked at the bins—unremarkable in every way—and shook her head, realising the stupidity of her actions, sniffing around the scene of a two-bit crime like an amateur sleuth.

She started back towards the cobbled lane, but paused on hearing a strange thrumming sound. It was coming from the end of the alley. She frowned, trying to place it. Just then the corner of the restaurant lit up. The thrumming grew louder—tyres on a cobbled road—a car was approaching! The headlights started to track towards her. Seized by a sudden panic, Cat rushed to a door in the wall in front of her. It opened easily and she burst into what she assumed was the stock room. Trading the brightness of the alley for the unlit room, she closed the door behind her and stood blinking, waiting for her eyes to adapt to the relative darkness.

Outside a car door slammed.

The moon shone through a large skylight in the roof above, casting just enough light for Cat to see by. A long counter ran along the wall to her right. Its surface was littered with bottles and jars. She heard the handle turn and scrambled under the counter, pressing herself as far back against the wall as she could.

The door opened.

Long shadows stretched across the floor, moving and morphing to the sound of shuffling shoes. She heard the soft ping of a pullcord followed by the ticking and buzzing of the tube light as it sprang into life. Two pairs of legs came into view, wearing jeans and heavy boots. Her heart was pounding so heavily it was as though her fear itself were demanding to be let out. The legs strode purposefully to the back of the room.

Peering out of her hiding place, Cat looked down the length of the room. There was no sign of the two men. She looked back to the door, only a few feet away. She clasped a hand tightly around the strap of her handbag and set a foot forward, ready to make a run for it, but, just then, footsteps rang out from the back of the room, heading her way. Once again, she ducked under the counter and watched one of the men walk outside. She waited for a minute, when he still hadn't reappeared, she crawled forward and squinted into the gloom shrouding the back of the store. The room must have turned a corner as there was no sign of the second man. Cat looked back at the door and was wondering whether to chance making a run for it when an ear-piercing screech filled the small space. She clambered back under the counter, her heart banging in her chest, as, out of the dark, a forklift truck emerged. It moved menacingly forward, coming to a stop just feet away from where Cat was cowering. The hydraulics engaged, lowering its load to the ground. Cat slumped against the wall, all hope of a quick escape evaporating.

The driver cut the engine and shouted something to the other man who had reappeared from outside, pulling a hand-trolley laden with half-gallon jars brimming with pickled birds. Cat felt the bile rise, yet she couldn't tear her eyes away. It was a grisly display. Lifeless, pallid flesh on fragile limbs pressed tight against the glass walls; the pickling liquid that preserved them magnifying the horror. To Cat they looked more like specimens from Frankenstein's laboratory than a dinner table delicacy.

The man abandoned the trolley and went to join the driver who was busy unloading the forklift. Its cargo looked heavy and progress was slow, eventually though, all of the crates were laid out on the floor. The men approached a crate and prised open its lid. They lifted out the top row of contents, setting the jars to one side. In their place, they put a row of jars containing the pickled birds before putting the jars they'd taken out back on top. Finally, they fastened down the lid and loaded the box back onto the forklift. Then they turned to the next crate. Cat watched, aghast, as they repeated the process with box after box; lifting out legitimate produce with contents similar to those found in Tony's briefcase—sundried tomatoes, olives and artichokes amongst them—and concealing the contraband underneath.

For the most part the men had worked in silence but as their task drew to a close, they noticeably slowed and the conversation picked up. Cat listened intently, recognising a word or two from her rudimentary holiday Greek: words like bira, which she'd drunk enough of to recognise instantly, and kleftiko and kalamarakia, lamb and calamari dishes that regularly featured on the hotel's menu. Twice, at least, she thought they mentioned Americanos. She stopped herself from indulging in an audible sigh as she grew tired and wondered how long it would be before they left and gave her a chance to make her escape, praying it would be soon.

Eventually though, to her relief, they lifted the last crate back onto the forklift; every single one of them containing, hidden within, a layer of the ambelopoulia. A single jar of the featherless forms remained on the trolley. One of the men picked it up and started towards her. Cat tensed. She heard the jar bang down on the counter above her head, then watched the man's feet walk away, back to the trolley. While one man wheeled the empty trolley back outside, the other returned the full forklift into the dark depths of the storeroom. Finally, they left, turning the light off on their way out.

Despite the discomfort, Cat remained tucked tight under the counter, deliberating as to how long to wait before attempting to leave. Too long and she could get locked in. Too short and she might get caught, especially if they hadn't quite finished outside. On balance she decided that with the light out, it was more than likely they were finished for the night. And if she was right about their conversation, there was a reasonable chance they were already comfortably ensconced in the restaurant enjoying a much-awaited meal.

Slowly she emerged from her hiding place, stretching like a wakening cat. Standing tall she rolled her shoulders and indulged in a loud sigh, relishing its sound, as though it confirmed her very existence in that black velvety darkness. But the anticipation of freedom was short lived. Approaching footsteps and lively conversation once again sent her scurrying for cover.

Talking loudly in his native Greek, Kostas entered the store accompanied by one of the two men. Cat heard the light pull being yanked and watched two pairs of legs march to the rear of the room. They disappeared around the same corner that the crates had been despatched to. She looked towards the open door but the sound of a match striking put paid to any idea of escape. A faint smell of sulphur drifted in on the balmy night air.

Kostas was already making his way back across the room. He paused at the counter, close to Cat's legs. She pulled them to her tightly. She heard him drag something heavy over the surface above her head. He made some comment to the other man, who had followed him. Then, to her relief, the two of them made straight for the door, the jar of pickled birds dangling from Kostas's grip.

Again, she waited.

After what seemed like an age, the voices of the three men died away, replaced by the sound of an engine revving and the grating of metal on metal as the reverse gear was engaged, badly. Before Cat could even think about escaping, the door opened again. Kostas leaned in and turned off the light, subjecting her to a sudden sensory deprivation, the only interruption to which was the sound of the key turning in the lock.

Twenty-three

Cat blinked. Out of the blackness, shapes slowly emerged, picked out by the gentle wash of soft moonlight from the skylight above. She stepped tentatively towards the door, desperately hoping the evening's activity was over and no one was waiting outside.

Just then a cloud conspired against her, blanking out the moon's glow.

Undeterred, she moved blindly onward, groping about in the dark until her outstretched hands hit the wall and solid wood door. She let her fingers roam its surface until she found the cold metal of the handle. She pressed it down. It was no surprise when it refused to yield. She knew what she'd heard, but it paid to be sure.

She dismissed the idea of banging on the door to attract the attention of a passer-by. The last thing she wanted was to attract the wrong sort of attention. Instead, using her phone as a torch, she quickly located the light switch. She listened for a moment, reassuring herself that the coast was clear, pulled on the cord and waited for the light to breathe life into the unfamiliar space. There was no sign of the forklift. She walked towards the end wall, where the room opened out to the right. It was a cavernous space, filled floor to ceiling with crates. There appeared to be no windows and no doors other than the locked one. No obvious way out. The forklift loomed in the far corner.

Fighting a rising sense of panic, she tried to stay focussed on the practicalities of her escape, starting with looking for a spare key. It wouldn't be the first time she'd lost valuable minutes and wasted effort only to discover a key within arm's reach of a busted-open door. She retraced her steps and conducted a search of the area around the door, checking the wall for hooks and scouring the surface of the counter she'd hidden under. This time, though, luck was not on her side and after a hurried hunt she remained empty handed.

Okay, so there was no key. Maybe she could force the door open? Cat worked her way back to the rear of the store, looking for anything that could be used to jemmy the door with. At the point where the room turned a corner, the light diminished and the shadows became heavier with every step she took. She spotted a bucket. If there was a bucket, there was a chance there was a mop. A mop with a long handle could prove useful. With her phone helping to illuminate the way, she walked over to the forklift parked in the far corner, and peered into the gap between it and the wall. There was no sign of a mop, or anything else that might be of use. She was about to continue her search when her attention was caught by the slips of paper attached to each of the crates. Dispatch notes. Leaning in as far as she could, Cat started to photograph the ones in reach. Once satisfied the images were clear enough to read, she turned her attention back to her escape.

As she walked away, her foot hit something solid. It skittered noisily across the floor. She looked down and saw a chunky brush—course bassine bristles poked out from a solid slipper-shaped wooden base. She picked it up and turned it over. There was no predrilled hole for a handle. She flung the brush into the darkness and heard it clatter as it landed somewhere in the shadows ahead. Just then, it reappeared, illuminated by a wide shaft of light. She gazed skyward and spied a second skylight. Moonlight spilled through the glass and washed gently over the room. A passing cloud once more cast a dark blanket over the window but it soon continued on its way and the light bled back in and shapes grew out of the shadows.

Cat's hopes suddenly lifted. A rope, attached to the skylight, ran diagonally down to a metal bracket on the wall. She reached up and started to unwind it from its tether. As she released the tension, the window in the roof above swung open. She pulled on the rope and the window closed. A simple yet effective pulley. She let go of the rope; its end hung a little higher than her waist. Tantalisingly close. She felt the cool evening air roll in through the open window, a welcome relief to the room's stagnant atmosphere. She didn't need any sort of divine intervention to recognise an opportunity when she saw one. She could literally smell freedom.

Once again, she pulled the rope and the window closed. She chewed on her bottom lip as she considered the logistics of her escape. Even if it was strong enough to carry her weight, and she in turn strong enough to climb it, what she couldn't quite figure out was how the hell she was going to get onto the roof given the window closed as soon as there was any weight on it.

She looked around, scanning the dimly lit space for inspiration. Nearby, the forklift loomed. She felt a tremor of excitement. She'd never used one before, but there was a first time for everything. She rushed over and climbed onto the footplate. Peering into the cab her heart sank.

No keys.

Perhaps she could hot-wire it? She'd need to get the panel off the front first and, assuming she managed that, she hadn't a clue what to do next, but she'd cross that bridge when she came to it.

She slipped a hand inside her bag and felt for anything that might be remotely useful. In many other circumstances, a mobile phone, a pen, a purse or at least the money it contained, might have had some merit. None were any use in her current dilemma. The cubby hole in the vehicle's dash yielded nothing more than a dirty rag and an empty cigarette box and, apart from the scrubbing brush, the floor nearby was clear. She even returned to the counter by the front door and scoured its contents, again coming up with nothing. As she walked back to the forklift, she looked again at the dangling rope, the germ of an idea forming in her mind. She headed over and picked up the scrubbing brush, measuring it against her handbag.

Maybe? It might just work.

She emptied the contents of her bag into her coat pockets and slipped the hard-bristled brush in their place. With the bag slung over her head, nestled against her back, she pulled down on the rope. The window clunked closed.

She looked up. It seemed so far away.

A deep breath, and she grabbed the rope high above her head and jumped. She threw her other hand up and held on tight while, at the same time, clamping the rope tightly between her knees.

She slipped down with a sinking feeling.

Undeterred she tried again, jumping harder and reaching higher, but again the rope slipped from her grasp. She let go and dropped the short distance to the floor with a feeling of mounting anxiety. She needed to get higher—high enough to be able to wrap the rope around her feet and lock it in position, and give her something to push up from. If she couldn't, then the window may as well be on the moon as on the roof above her head.

Having seen the two men struggle, she ruled out using a loaded crate and walked around the room, pushing gently on the boxes. She soon found an empty one. Although awkward, it was light enough to carry. She set it down below the end of the rope. The lid was a flimsy thing made of thin plywood but she took some comfort in that both it and the box were edged in steel. She put the lid on, gave it a push. The plywood creaked as the lid flexed and strained. It looked as though her foot would go through it with the slightest pressure. Turning the box onto its side, she pushed from the top, then repeated the exercise with the box upside down. It seemed to offer no greater resistance whichever way she did it.

After a few minutes spent thinking through the options, Cat returned the box to an upright position and lifted its lid. Keeping it flat she turned it forty-five degrees to create an eight-pointed star. Physics wasn't exactly her forte but she knew enough to realise she needed to spread the load.

With the box in position, she grasped the rope as high as she could above her head and lifted a leg, placing her foot carefully on the edge of the lid where it overlaid the corner of the box below. She eased herself up cautiously. When nothing disastrous happened she let herself down, only daring to breathe once both feet were back on the ground. Without hesitating, she returned her right foot to the box and once again pushed herself upwards. This time she brought her left foot up and set it down on the opposite side of the lid. For a heart-stopping moment she waited. The box appeared to be holding.

She looked up, readying herself for the journey skywards and took a deep breath. It had been a long time since she'd done a rope climb—a very long time—and yet she still harboured black memories of gym class where a room full of unwilling school kids, herself included, would moan and groan throughout the ordeal that was circuit training—the PE teacher's idea of good wholesome exercise, the kids' idea of hell. Almost twenty years on and it hadn't improved any in her estimation.

She gripped the rope as high as possible and jumped. Quickly, she clenched her knees, trapping the rope between them as she twisted her foot around its end to create a makeshift stirrup. She spent a second just hanging there. When she could put it off no longer, she started the slow hitch up the rope's long length. All the while a voice deep within coaxed and cajoled, and at times cursed her to keep going, until her hands were only inches away from the glass. Again, she wound a foot around the rope beneath her, forming a strap to rest upon, and gazed upward.

Hardly daring to look, she inspected the window and blew out a long breath. About halfway up it had occurred to her it might be reinforced, but as far as she could tell, it was just normal glass.

With the rope gripped tightly in one hand, she reached for her bag. She slipped a hand inside and gripped the brush. She lifted the whole thing above her head and started to jab at the glass, using the bag to protect her hand. Soon the muscles in her arm began to burn and her optimism started to fade. She let her arm drop to her side and took a much-needed rest. She looked down at the ground far below and then back up at the skylight—her only hope of escape. She grabbed the brush with a renewed determination, barely noticing the sharp bristles sticking into her skin, and punched upwards, giving it everything she had.

The glass gave a loud crack and a shard fell away, smashing satisfyingly on the floor below. Soon dagger-like pieces of glass were falling like barbed icicles in a game of Tomb Raider until eventually the frame was clear of glass. Close to exhaustion she released her grip on the brush and returned the bag to rest against her back. She looked up at the opening and felt a wash of dread. It was only just in reach with an outstretched arm—how the hell was she going to get through it?

'Dig deep,' her brother had once said to her when she'd joined him on one of his training rides. They had been half way up what she'd considered to be the mother of all hills and all she'd wanted to do was get off and push. He'd laughed at the suggestion. Dig deep. As though that was all there was to it. She remembered the burst of pride she'd felt on reaching the crown of the hill, her legs and lungs burning and her breath rasping in her chest. She remembered the smile that had brought Pete's face to life, a big brother grin she missed so much it made her heart ache. That day... that grin... it was one of the last times she'd seen him alive. She knew what she had to do.

Freedom suddenly seemed that much closer.

Using the same technique as before, she lifted her free foot as high as she could and tethered it to the rope. From her new anchor point, she thrust upwards. A surge of adrenalin spiked through her veins as she let go with her hands and threw herself over the empty window frame. Her chest and arms slammed down on the roof and her chin banged down so hard it felt like she'd been kicked in the face by a mule. Terrified of slipping back through the window frame and falling to the floor below, she mustered the last of her reserves and gave an enormous heave, hooked a leg up through the frame and squirmed forward, pushing and wriggling along the roof until her entire weight was safely supported. Exhausted, she rolled on to her back and stared up into the starlit sky, her chest heaving.

She was absolutely spent.

Ten minutes passed before she was sufficiently recovered to continue. Carefully, she stood up and looked down the length of the red-tiled roof. Diamond bright, the stars cut through the blackness and cast a magical glow over the landscape. Pretty and peaceful, the scene was totally at odds with her pounding heart, and tired and bruised body.

Keeping low, she scuttled over to where the warehouse and restaurant buildings joined and looked down to the alley below. There were no vehicles by the storeroom entrance and no light cascading out from the kitchen window. Nor was there any obvious way down.

She clambered up to the ridge-line of the roof and then down the other side. It was exactly how she remembered: a porch extended out from the front of the single-storey restaurant building leading to the open-air dining area. She inched her way to the edge and peered over. There was no light spilling out from any of the windows here either and she prayed it was a sign that the restaurant staff had long since left. Illuminated by the moon and the stars, she scanned the side of the building, looking for a drainpipe to shimmy down but was once again out of luck. The only thing she could see between her and the cobbled floor below was a clutch of cream umbrellas left open overnight, looking like a fleet of capsized small-sail skiffs. She recalled sitting underneath one when she and Amy had lunched with Ethan. She could barely believe that was only the day before. The recollection of Amy made her stomach lurch but she pushed her feelings to one side, determined not to succumb to such untimely sentimentality.

So, there it was. There was only one way down. And before her nerves could fail her, she squatted low on the edge, took a deep breath and launched forward, crowd-surfing onto the open canopies. But unlike a sea of open hands carrying her to safety, the taut canvas resisted and sent her breath exploding from her chest. A stiff wire spoke jabbed her hard in the side, bruising her liver and a couple of ribs. The umbrella swayed precariously but it held. Balancing on top, she waited to get her breath back. The umbrellas hadn't seemed that high when she'd been sitting beneath them, only seven feet or so, no distance at all, but now...

She shifted her weight to one side, intending to slowly slide down the canopy to where it touched a neighbouring umbrella. She had hoped it would buffer her descent, enabling her to drop gently onto the pavement below. Instead the umbrella suddenly tilted and sent her into an immediate spin. She burst out from between the canvas panels and fell into the arms of a not-so-welcoming wrought iron chair. Twisted, winded and in pain, she bit back her groans and started the agonising struggle to extricate herself from the furniture that had broken her fall and possibly even a bone or two. As soon as she was divorced from the fixtures, and the scraping sounds of metal on rough stone had stopped, she cocked her head, listening hard, but the square was silent.

She forced herself to stand, the slightest pressure on her injured ankle causing her to yelp. And with her ankle throbbing and enough pain to make her nauseous, she gritted her teeth and hopped and hobbled back through the town, and to her waiting car.

Thirty minutes later—more than twice as long as it had taken to walk to the restaurant at the start of the evening—Cat clambered into the driver's seat. She started the engine, thanking whatever power it had been that had let Amy persuade her to take an automatic, slipped the transmission into drive and began the journey back to the hotel.

Twenty-four

Their lips touched, gently at first and then with mounting pressure. She felt his tongue, tentatively feeling its way. With its movement growing more urgent, she felt his hand brush against her breast. Moving to rise towards him she realised he had her pinned down, her legs restrained by the grip of his powerful thighs. Her heart quickened as the realisation of her vulnerability hit home.

Cat awoke with a start.

The last remnants of the dream rapidly evaporated, the details of the faceless man already dissolved, his name never to be known.

Slowly her heart rate calmed and her gasping breath grew quiet. She let out a sigh, only it came out as more of a groan, a manifestation of her pain. She eased herself up and untangled the knot of sheets around her legs. The simple action of kicking away the bedclothes set her ankle throbbing anew.

Morning was pouring in through wide gaps in the curtains. Cat looked at her watch: eight forty-five. Over nine hours since she had said goodbye to Ethan, five since she had escaped incarceration and enough close shaves to last her a lifetime. Her heart fluttered fretfully as she recalled her nocturnal exploits.

The drive back to the hotel had been uneventful and, as far as she could tell, she'd made it to her room without anyone other than the night clerk catching sight of her. Once there, she had been way too wired to contemplate sleep, despite her physical exhaustion. And so, to the sounds of Gomez playing quietly in the background, she had turned her attention to her notes, updating them with the few new facts she'd managed to extract from the day. Then, in gentle strokes drawn soft enough to be easily erased, she had sketched out her emerging ideas, tying them, like a delicate climber onto a trellis, to what little she knew to be true. Eventually though, her thoughts had clouded and the pencil slipped from her limp hand as her body's need for rest won out.

Cat swung her legs out of bed. She bent over and picked up the pad and pencil from the floor nearby and placed them on the bedside cabinet before making a slow and painful path to the bathroom, to get ready for whatever the new day would bring.

The taxi driver jumped out of his seat and rushed around the bonnet to open the door. His haste, though, was somewhat premature and he was forced to wait while Cat covered the short distance at a pitifully slow pace. She did her best to get comfortable, easing her leg up on the seat, and spent the half an hour journey watching the passing scenery in a daze. She roused herself as the car slowed and pulled up outside the police station: constructed in pristine sandstone, it was a large, striking building, which oozed colonial charm. A wide concourse led to it from the road.

Cat slid out of her seat and squinted in the bright sunlight. She had the beginnings of a headache to go with her throbbing ankle, owing to the God-awful wailing racket—there was nothing musical about it—that had blasted out of the surround-sound speakers for the entire journey. She politely declined the driver's offer of an arm to lean on and hobbled into the station. Pushing the door open, a stew of familiar smells, sweat, coffee, and junk food, accosted her, giving a sudden reminder of her office and life back home. Ignoring the tug of her emotions, she stepped around a woman rowing noisily with a shamefaced teenager and headed for the desk where a uniformed man with a heavy jaw and pock-marked skin looked at her blankly.

'Hello. Do you speak English?' she said, articulating her words carefully.

Two eyebrows, each the size of a small mouse, lifted.

'A little,' he said in a gravelly baritone.

'I'd like to talk to somebody about the death of Amy Reynolds, the English woman who drowned on Friday night.'

The mice dropped and huddled together over heavy lids. He picked up the phone and pressed a quick-dial key. After a short burst of rapid tongue-twisting dialogue he looked back at Cat.

'What is your business here?'

'I'd like to speak to whoever is dealing with the death of Amy Reynolds, the woman who drowned,' she repeated patiently.

'But why?'

'Because I am... I mean, I was her friend, and I... To be honest, I'd rather save that for the detective in charge.' It was a struggle to keep the emotion from her voice.

More garbled lingo as the uniformed man relayed the information back down the line. He put the phone down and gestured to a row of chairs that lined the wall opposite.

'Please wait.'

Cat sat down. She wondered whether Glafcos had told them about her being a detective. She wondered whether it would actually be Glafcos who would come and see her. And then she remembered Alex's words of warning.

She looked up at the clock on the wall and watched the second hand jerk its way around the dial. Five minutes passed before the sound of a door opening interrupted her thoughts. She turned and watched a smallish, tired-looking man approach from the far end of the room. He may have looked a little weather-beaten but he walked with a sure step and held her gaze steadily, maintaining eye contact for the whole length of the room.

He came to a stop a few feet in front of her.

'Miss McKenzie?'

Cat nodded. She was impressed—she hadn't given the sergeant her name.

'I'm Detective Chief Inspector Haralambopulous. Please, if you will come with me.'

He led her to a small interview room. Sparsely furnished, with only a table and four chairs, the lack of recording equipment or mirrors suggested it was used for nothing more than preliminary interviews and statement drafting.

Cat came close to walking around the table, to the seat that would normally be reserved for the investigating officer, but then she remembered her role in this theatre and took the seat nearest to the door. The detective walked around the desk and sat opposite.

He leaned back in his chair. For a moment he appeared to be studying her, and then abruptly, he sat upright and clasped his hands on the desk in front of him.

'Miss McKenzie—'

'Please, call me Cat.'

He looked at her blankly.

'Miss McKenzie, you asked to speak to someone about your friend.'

'Yes. Are you leading the investigation into Amy's death?'

He paused.

'I am in charge of the detective squad, yes.'

Cat frowned.

'But not the investigation?' After a moment adding, 'There is an investigation, isn't there? Surely you're treating her death as suspicious?'

A lean eyebrow arched.

'Should it be?'

She clenched a fist. She couldn't believe it. Thank God she'd taken the trouble to check what the police were doing.

'Absolutely. Amy was murdered. I'm sure of it. I don't know how, but I believe it's related to the death of another guest at the hotel. Tony Vostanis?'

The detective remained stony-faced. He reminded Cat of Al Pacino, from one of his older films, Scarface maybe, only he had no scar, just the same dog-day expression and eyes that looked as though they could switch from smouldering to steel in an instant.

'I think it may have something to do with the practice of ambelopoulia,' she added. 'I know there's an ongoing investigation into arson attacks targeted on ambelopoulia suppliers. I think Tony Vostanis was killed because he was somehow involved. Amy must have said or done something that posed a threat to whoever killed Tony. I think she was killed to keep her quiet.'

The detective dropped the stony look as surprise registered on his face.

'You think Mr Vostanis was killed because he was involved in the arson attacks?'

'No. I think this is about the illegal trade in ambelopoulia. I believe Mr Vostanis was either involved in it or knew something about it. Perhaps Mr Vostanis threatened to report one of his suppliers trading in it?' Cat was starting to get on a roll. It felt good to have someone to bounce ideas off. 'I don't know for sure but—'

Scarface held up an index finger; a simple but effective move. Cat shut up.

'Miss McKenzie, if you can put aside for a moment the things you *don't know for sure*,' he said, not bothering to hide his sarcasm. 'What do you actually know that is pertinent to the deaths of Mr Vostanis or Miss Reynolds?'

Cat looked into his black eyes, waiting for some warmth of pity to seep out and touch her. But like a shark's they remained dead and emotionless.

And then he opened his combative jaws and took a bite.

'What about this scenario… Mr Vostanis was prone to health problems as a result of his diabetes. He over-indulged and failing to manage his condition passed away prematurely. A tragedy, no doubt. As are the deaths of the four million people who die of diabetes each and every year.' He paused a beat before continuing, 'That's right, four million a year.' He held eye contact, watching as she considered whether it was worth the fight.

She mentally kicked herself. She was too used to being part of the investigating team where speculating about what might have been was par for the course. Adding to that the few things she did know but wasn't able to share, her heart sank as reality struck home. Alex had been right. There was nothing she could actually tell them without it coming across as idiotic or getting herself into serious trouble.

'What about Amy?' she asked, her voice sounding feeble, even to her own ears.

'What about her? There were no similarities between the two deaths.'

'But there were similarities in the circumstances,' she parried. 'Both Tony and Amy ate at the same restaurant on the day they died. The same place I know is supplying pickled birds. The same place where Tony's wife had her bag stolen the day he died. The bag that contained his syringes. It's possible that—'

'We tested his syringes,' Scarface interrupted. They only contained what they were supposed to. But please tell me, you say that you know that this place supplies ambelopoulia?'

'Yes,' she said, cautiously.

'How do you know this?'

236

Cat stalled, trying to think of a suitably non-incriminating answer.

'Somebody I trust told me they've seen jars of the birds in there. I think if you were to raid their storeroom and look inside some of the crates prepared for shipping to America, you'll find plenty of evidence.'

He didn't look impressed.

'Let me rephrase my question. How do *you* know that is true?'

Cat looked away from his direct gaze.

'That is my point. We cannot run a murder investigation based on hunches and hearsay. You more than most must realise that.'

Cat's eyes widened and he nodded.

'Yes. I know that you are a member of the British Police Force. That is the only reason I was prepared to meet with you.'

'But what about Amy? She'd been to the same restaurant the night she died. Surely you can't think her death was just a coincidence?'

Suddenly the hard man's features softened and a small sympathetic smile flitted across his features, only to disappear just as quickly.

'What I think is that you have let the death of your friend colour your judgement. That, and the fact that perhaps as a detective you see murder where it doesn't exist?'

Cat felt the heat flush across her face as sure as if he'd slapped her.

'That's not the case at all,' she snapped. 'A second death, of anyone, would have had me asking the same questions. Look, at least take the details of the restaurant.' She began to rummage in her bag for the small promotional cards sporting the restaurant's picture.

'Oh, where the hell are they? I put two of the bloody things in here last night. It's a place called Kostas in Paphos.' She tipped the contents of the bag on the desk and started to sift through. She sighed and closed her eyes. 'They must have fallen out last night.' She could just imagine them lying somewhere amidst the dirt and dust on the floor of Kostas's storeroom.

Unexpectedly, the detective pushed his chair back and stood up.

'Wait!' She hurriedly threw her belongings back in her bag. 'Aren't you even going to try to see if there's a link?'

He paused, already at the door.

'No. There is no evidence of any wrong doing.'

Cat jumped up out of her seat.

'What if he was the arsonist? Tony, I mean.' She knew she sounded desperate. Hell, she was desperate.

Scarface curled his mouth upwards, although his eyes remained cold and unsmiling.

'I suggest you see if your hotel has a copy of a local newspaper when you return, Miss McKenzie. You are, I think, behind the times.'

Cat thought about it for a second before realisation dawned.

'There's been another arson attack?'

'The night your friend died. Even you must not believe in ghosts?'

Cat looked at him through narrowed eyes. He was seriously starting to piss her off.

'I didn't know that and there's no need to belittle me,' she said with clipped words squeezed out through gritted teeth. 'I came here to try to help.'

Her thoughts wrestled with the new information. Could it somehow be relevant to Amy's death?

'What time?'

'I'm sorry?'

'What time do you think the arsonist hit? Was it before Amy was found or after?'

238

He gave a slow shake of his head, a pitiful gesture.

Stalemate.

She forced the frown from her face, knowing she somehow needed to appeal to his less ruthless side.

'Look, I'm there in the hotel and I *know* something's not right. What if I can find out what caused Mr Vostanis's hypoglycaemia? There are things that can induce it, toxins that can simulate the effect of excess insulin. It could have been mixed with something he ate.'

'Which would have shown up in the contents of his stomach and most likely would have caused—'

'What about any irritation to his digestive system?' Cat jumped in. 'Was there—'

Scarface held up a warning finger again and continued talking.

'There is no evidence that it was anything he ate.' He paused. 'Miss McKenzie, we know that Mr Vostanis died of hypoglycaemia and your friend drowned, after having too much to drink. Two sad and tragic accidents. Sometimes you have to accept the most obvious answer is the correct answer. Both deaths had one thing in common: the two people who died did what thousands of people do on holiday every year. They ate too much and drank too much and unfortunately as a result they became just another statistic.'

But Cat wasn't to be deterred.

'Okay, okay. I accept what I've got is not enough, that you need some hard evidence. But what if I can get you something solid, something other than just my speculations, would you listen then?'

For a moment he looked at her, saying nothing. Cat waited. In an uncharacteristic display of superstition, she hid her hands under the desk and crossed her fingers. Eventually he shook his head and opened the door.

'I'm sorry Miss McKenzie but you need to come to terms with what has happened.' He walked away with a purposeful stride.

Cat hurried after him.

'Miss McKenzie is just leaving,' he said loudly, as he passed through the security gate that barred entry into the offices.

Cat stood and watched, until he disappeared through the door at the end of the corridor. She looked back at the desk sergeant. He gestured towards the door, his face devoid of expression. With a leaden tread she left the cold artificial light of the station and stepped out onto a street radiant under a bright sunlit sky. She leaned against the wall, the warm bricks doing little to soothe the anger that was beginning to bubble away inside her. The meeting had been a disaster. Not only had she managed to antagonise the lead detective but she had learnt virtually nothing new. And with a sinking realisation, it dawned on her she hadn't even thought to ask about the missing notepad.

She eased herself off the wall and started down the concourse towards the taxi rank. Sensing she might just have got lucky and been gifted a second chance, a small smile curved her lips. Glafcos was standing, leaning on an idling taxi, directly in front of her. She was about to make her way over to him, when he shifted slightly, revealing a familiar figure. Cat shuffled to a nearby sycamore, as quick as her ankle would allow, and peered past the mottled, peeling bark, the tree's vast trunk proving more than adequate cover. She watched the two men chat, until shortly, Phil climbed into the back of the cab. Glafcos pushed the door closed and brought a hand down onto the roof, tapping it briskly to initiate the taxi's departure.

She slipped behind the tree and waited until Glafcos drew level before stepping out.

'Hello Glafcos.'

A rush of surprise crossed his face.

'Cat! Where did you come from?'

'I came to see if there was any sign of a notepad amongst Amy's belongings.'

'A notepad?'

'A small thin pad, the sort the hotel provides in the room for guests. I think Amy may have taken it without realising I'd already written some personal information in it.' The lies were growing easier by the minute.

The big man shook his taurine head.

'No, I'm sorry. I don't think we found anything like that. Only the towels and her clothes.'

'Folded neatly,' Cat said, repeating Glafcos's own choice of words from that night.

'That's right.'

'Were they dry?'

Glafcos appeared to give the question some thought.

'I don't know,' he said eventually. 'I'd have to check. I think perhaps the towels were a little wet.'

'One or both?'

Glafcos gave her a curious look.

'As I said, I don't know. I would need to check.'

'Was that because of the incoming tide?'

'No. They were on a lounger.'

'How come no one saw her clothes and the towels sooner?' she asked.

'They were at the far end of the beach. The lounger was not visible from where your friend was found.'

Cat's forehead puckered into a frown.

'But I walked across from that end. There aren't any sunbeds that far down.'

'Perhaps you did not see it in the dark. Look Cat, what are you thinking? If you tell me perhaps I can help.' Glafcos put a gentle arm around her shoulder. 'It is a great shock to you, the death of your friend. Do not underestimate that.'

She looked at her watch.

'I should get going.'

Glafcos paused, as though he wanted to say something more, but then simply nodded.

'Take care, Cat. You have my number, if you want to talk?'

'Yes, thank you. If you do manage to find that notepad, you will let me know, won't you?'

'I will check. You are sure she had it with her?'

Cat shrugged.

'Not a hundred percent. I just couldn't find it in our room.'

'Perhaps it was in her handbag? There wasn't one amongst her things on the beach.'

Cat couldn't remember seeing Amy's bag when she'd packed her things away.

Maybe she really was losing it?

No. She might be tired, and okay, a little over-wrought, but she knew her instincts were as good as ever. Regardless of what anyone else might be thinking.

Twenty-five

The dust-ridden scenery passed by in a blur. Mesmerised by her reflection, Cat watched with a strange detachment as a rogue tear rolled out of her eye as though specially expressed to feed the maudlin she had created. The solitary drop made its way down her cheek. She sniffed and wiped it away with the heel of her hand.

The taxi was making good progress and after a few minutes the rows of white stucco buildings, all angles and squares—a celebration of modern geometry—were traded for a landmark-free horizon, its sparseness softened by random outbreaks of scrub, dotted about like dandelions on a grey pavement.

Cat looked at her watch: it would be at least another ten minutes until they got to the hotel. She reached for her bag and felt for her mobile.

'For fuck's sake,' she said, pulling items out onto her lap. The taxi driver shot her a look over his shoulder. She found the phone and hit a quick dial key as she piled the rest of the contents back into the bag.

'Hi Cat. How are you doing?'

'Oh Alex, I don't know where to start,' she said, staring out of the window, yet seeing none of the passing scenery.

'Have they got any more of an idea what happened?'

'They're treating it as an accident.'

'And you're not happy with that.' It was a statement not a question.

'No I'm bloody well not, which is why I called. I need you to—'

'Cat, we've had this conversation. You've got no jurisdiction and no right to be informed. They could be doing everything possible but you're the last person they'd tell. Look, it's only a couple of days before you come home, can't you find something to take your mind off it?'

Silence.

'Cat...?'

'Alex, you don't understand. I don't know what's going on but something's not right. I need you to—'

'Cat. Stop!' Alex said sharply. 'You're—'

'This isn't about me,' she snapped back. She could feel her chest grow tight and her heart thump heavily, a tribal drumbeat girding her resolve. She took a breath, and forcing her words to come out calmly and evenly, continued, 'Look, I just need you to do one thing for me.'

She waited and heard Alex take a deep breath.

'Please...?'

'What is it?'

'Just a background check.'

Alex remained quiet, which Cat took as a sign to continue. She could picture him looking around on his desk for a pen and pad.

'The name's Phil Rogers. As far as I'm aware he's got one kid, Bethany, and an ex-wife called Penny. He lives in London somewhere. I haven't got an address but if you draw a blank I can try to get hold of one. Says he works in security, but he's never said who for.'

'And why you want the low-down on him?'

'On the night Amy died, I swear I saw him leave the hotel and head for the beach in the same direction as where Amy's things were found. That was much earlier than when he said he went out. And he was the one who later found her body.'

'And you're sure it was him you saw earlier?'

244

'Well it was dark but I was pretty convinced it was him at the time.'

'That's it? That's all that you've got?'

'My instincts tell me he's not being entirely honest.'

'Who is?' Alex said.

'Look, you were the one who told me I had nothing of any substance, no evidence to show for my theories. A fact that is painfully obvious to me now.' Her voice ratcheted up an octave. 'So please don't stop me doing what I can to find some fucking evidence because if I don't get something soon, I will go fucking mad.'

'But Cat...'

Although he sounded more concerned than angry at her outburst, she just knew he'd try to talk her out of it again.

'Alex I've got to go. The taxi's just pulled up at the hotel,' she lied. 'Will you do the check for me or not?'

The line fell quiet.

'Alex?'

Another deep breath.

'I'll see what I can find out. I doubt it'll be much. I don't have any authority to do this. But if I do manage to get something, you've got to promise me you'll just let the local police know and leave it to them.'

'I promise.'

She hung up and spent the rest of the journey staring out of the window, considering her options. All she wanted to do was to get back to her room and look again at her notes. News of the latest arson attack cast a different light on things. Or did it? She needed time, and some peace and quiet, to think things through.

The cab dropped her back at the hotel. She was crossing the lobby, on her way to the lift when she heard a voice.

'Cat!'

She turned full circle, looking around the deserted space.

'Tom, is that you?'

'Yes. Over here.'

She spotted him waving at her through the large glossy fenestrated leaves of an enormous Swiss Cheese Plant. He was sitting on his own in an easy chair tucked away in a corner.

'What are you doing hiding back here?' she asked, skirting around the living screen.

'Thought I'd see what's going on in the world.' He held up a folded newspaper and gave her a comforting smile, radiating good intent mixed with a little paternal concern. 'How are you?'

'Okay I guess.'

'Why don't you join me? I could do with the company.'

Cat deliberated for all of two seconds and then flopped down into the facing armchair.

'Where's Rose?'

'She's gone gallivanting off to yet another market. They run a mini-bus every Sunday. We've done it every week. I couldn't face it again. I don't know how you ladies do it. There are only so many times I can be wowed by local cheeses, and olives, and breads... Well you get my gist. It's not as though we don't have all that at home.'

Cat shrugged. Ordinarily she'd have come up with some small talk but not today.

'With everything that's happened Rose almost gave it a miss herself,' he went on. 'She was going to call in on you this morning. To see if you wanted some company. I hope you don't mind, I persuaded her to leave it till later. I thought you might prefer to be on your own for a while. I said Cat knows where we are if she wants someone to talk to.' He looked at her. 'That is right, isn't it love, you do know where we are if you need us?'

Without warning Cat was filled with an overwhelming need to cry.

She quickly stood up.

'I'm sorry Tom, I've got to go.'

The wobble in her voice was nowhere near as obvious as the wobble of her ankle, which gave way under the pressure, thwarting any attempt at a swift exit. She put out a hand to the back of her chair and steadied herself just as Jaclyn came rushing through the reception. Ethan followed, looking notably more relaxed with his long, loping stride.

'What can I say? I warned you Kostas wouldn't release you from the contract without full payment,' he said. 'You should have taken my first offer. It was a good price. You'd hardly have been out of pocket. But now that the wholesale price has dropped, you'll be lucky to get a fraction of what you've paid. That's if you can find anyone who wants to buy it other than me. Tell you what. I'll make it easy for you. I'll make you a new offer.'

'You can stick your offer!' Jaclyn shouted over her shoulder. 'I'm not being held to ransom by you or anyone else.'

'Why don't you sleep on it? Or consult a friend. I'm sure David will be happy to advise.'

The pair of them hustled past Cat, who was hidden from view behind the foliage, and the reception once again fell quiet.

With her ankle objecting to anything but the lightest load, Cat shuffled across the lobby and through the double doors out onto the terrace.

Bethany was playing in the shade of a small myrtle tree. As soon as she spotted Cat, she broke into a big grin and came running, her sandals slapping across the floor with a familiar flick-flack. Cat reached down and gave the little girl a hug, deliberately avoiding looking at Phil, who was reclining in a solitary chair under the tree.

'Hi,' he said, too loud to ignore. Out of the corner of her eye she saw him jump up. 'Here, have a seat.'

Cat stalled. She hadn't intended on staying.

He pointed at her injured ankle.

'Your foot, I noticed you limping.'

Seeing it as an opportunity to do more digging, she lowered herself gingerly onto the chair as Phil settled on a patch of grass nearby.

'Thanks,' she said.

'That looks painful.'

'It's okay. It's only twisted.'

'How did you do it?'

'I turned it on some cobblestones last night. I didn't think it was that bad at first but it seems to be getting worse.'

'I've got some anti-inflammatories if you need any.'

'I took some earlier. Though I'm not sure they've made much difference.'

'You should see if you can get some ice from the kitchen. If you keep it elevated with ice on it, it should help.'

Cat nodded.

They both fell quiet for a moment. Phil sat watching Bethany play with her doll. Cat, meanwhile, watched Phil.

'I was at the police station earlier today,' she said shortly.

'Any news?'

'News?'

'About Amy.'

'No. Nothing. How about you? Did you learn anything when you were there?'

A look of surprise flashed across his face.

'They asked me to go in,' he said. 'For a statement. Well I say statement, it was more of an account of what had happened.'

Cat waited, saying nothing, hoping Phil would fill the void, but it wasn't to be; only the remonstrations of one little girl, starved of attention, broke the silence that hung between them.

Twenty-six

'Hello?'

'It's me. Things are moving fast.'

'What is it? I can't really talk; I might be overheard. Has something happened?'

'Events are overtaking us. We need to rethink our plan.'

'What do you suggest?'

'I think we make a move now. Go in hard before it's too late.'

'What's brought this on?'

'What do you think? Somebody has been prying where they shouldn't.'

'Do you need me now?'

'No, not yet. Soon. I'll call you. Just be ready.'

The phone line went dead.

Twenty-seven

Cat set the mug down on the table and eased her leg onto the couch. The reception staff had rallied into action, bringing a bag of ice and a towel to wrap around her swollen ankle. They'd even been kind enough to make her a coffee.

After taking a drink, she leaned back and watched the ceiling fan turn about its locus, oscillating slowly, strangely redundant in the expansive air-conditioned reception.

After a minute she sat forward, grabbed her tablet from her bag and attached the keyboard. She typed in the wi-fi password and was connected to the rest of the world in an instant.

Her first search drew a blank. She could find nothing on diabetes-specific toxins or poisons and although the key words 'diabetes' and 'toxic' returned several hundred thousand entries she found nothing of any real interest in the first few pages. Likewise, her search for insulin, insulin simulation as well as insulin stimulation, got her nowhere. The layman's explanations were in short supply compared to the myriad of biochemical and pharmacological terms that left her guessing and she found her intellect being stretched despite her once scientific background.

She paused and set the tablet down. Reaching down to her ankle, she loosened the towel securing the bag of ice. She'd tried to knot it tight enough to act as a compress, only it was too tight and the ice was digging in. A minute later, with it repositioned, she eased herself back and reached for her drink. But the coffee was cold. She grimaced and returned the half-empty mug to the table. She thought fleetingly of ordering a beer but quickly dispelled the idea. It was hard enough to make sense of everything as it was without having her intellect dulled by alcohol.

She picked the tablet up and cast her mind back to the evening of Tony's death. She thought of his lumbering walk and agitated state and recalled from her earlier internet session it was possible the hypoglycaemia, rather than too much alcohol, had made him appear drunk.

She drummed her fingers restlessly on the clip-on keyboard. What she really wanted to know was how did a diabetic, who by all accounts had taken the correct dose of insulin at the right time, get to be hypoglycaemic in the first place? If Andreas was right and Tony hadn't over-indulged that night then alcohol wasn't the answer, but something must have caused it.

'It must have been something he ate?' Cat said under her breath.

She cast her mind back to that first night and to the food that had been served, a veritable smorgasbord of Greek delights. But surely there was nothing there he wouldn't have tried before. There had been nothing there that was new to her and she wasn't a gourmet food buyer.

Despite logic telling her otherwise, she couldn't shake the feeling that she was on the right lines. Food featured at every turn. She remembered the intruder in Jaclyn's room and the bag of samples. What if the purpose of the break-in was to remove whatever it was that had caused Tony's death? Without the results of the post-mortem and the toxicology tests it was an impossible task. All she could do in their absence was make wild guesses. Not for the first time, she wondered why she was even bothering. If she was going to try to figure out what happened to anyone it should be Amy, not some well-heeled businessman whose own family appeared not to care. Suddenly, a gut-wrenching knot twisted in the pit of her stomach as an image of her friend's lifeless body, cast down and left for the tide to take, flashed through her mind. If Amy had been guilty of anything, it could only have been engaging in idle speculation. It followed that whoever had killed Tony had also taken her friend. Whether she liked it or not, her hunt for answers had to start with the American.

With a fresh determination and her mind open to new possibilities she resumed her search. Every so often she would stop and make a note or, remembering something, go back over her scribbled jottings, hoping to find something to help her clear up those 'loose ends' she'd set out on the cheap grainy paper.

One such loose end was the missing notepad.

Despite looking high and low for it, Cat's original notepad continued to evade her. Glafcos's suggestion of looking in Amy's bag, which had been found hanging on the back of the bedroom door, proved to be fruitless. And she didn't hold out any hope that Glafcos would find it amongst Amy's belongings left on the beach either.

And then there was Jaclyn's bag. Why was it taken? Could it really have just been some hapless opportunistic thief? Cat felt sure there was more to it than that. Only a few bank notes were missing and hiding it behind the bins, well, that was just sloppy. If the thief hadn't wanted to be seen with the large tote bag, if all they were after was the cash, then surely, they would have simply pocketed the much smaller purse that was inside and binned the bag. As for the suggestion it was a dishonest member of staff, it was feasible, Cat admitted, but highly unlikely. What were the chances that a waiter could smuggle a woman's tote bag the full length of a bustling restaurant without anyone noticing? Now, if it was one of the other diners, or even one of the American's own party, that was a different proposition, especially if it was a woman. In fact, Jaclyn could have even set it up herself.

But what did it matter? The syringes only contained what was expected.

Perhaps she'd been looking at everything from the wrong perspective all along. She closed her eyes and let her mind roam over the few facts she did know.

A glimmer of an idea hit her, small and possibly insignificant, but it made itself felt like a piece of grit in the eye. She jumped up, ignoring the pain in her ankle, and made her way towards the junior suites, praying Jaclyn was still showing reclusive tendencies. As Cat opened the door into the corridor, the door to Jaclyn's room swung open and Ethan hurried out. He pulled the door closed behind him and covered the short distance to his own neighbouring room without so much as a backward glance. Cat limped towards Jaclyn's room. She gave a firm knock.

The door immediately jerked open. Jaclyn, sporting a mean scowl, stepped forward and glanced up and down the corridor. She looked back at Cat.

'Yes?' She sounded as tired as she looked, her previously perfect skin appearing tight and pinched.

'I'm one of the women who—'

'I know who you are. What do you want?' She stood there, waiting.

'I just wondered if I could ask you a couple of...' Cat paused. 'I don't mean to intrude but could I perhaps come in, just for a moment?'

Jaclyn retreated into the room. Cat followed, closing the door behind her. When she turned around, Jaclyn was leaning against the dressing table, arms crossed, a stony expression on her face.

'Well?'

Cat wondered where the animosity was coming from.

'First, please accept my condolences on the death of your husband. I'm sure you've heard, my friend Amy, she's been... well, she was also found dead. I realise it's not the same as losing a husband but I just wanted you to know, I do have some sense of what you're going through.'

Jaclyn looked at her, her expression softening, only a little though. She gave a small nod.

Cat continued, 'I travel back to the UK tomorrow so this might be the last chance I have to talk to you. I was really hoping you would be kind enough to give me some information. It might be relevant to both your husband's death and that of my friend.'

Jaclyn slowly uncrossed her arms.

'What information?'

'I was told that on the day your husband died, your handbag was stolen while you were at lunch.'

'That's right.'

'Before you realised the bag was missing, was there anything that with hindsight seems suspicious? Anyone brush past your chair or come over to talk to you unexpectedly?'

Jaclyn shrugged her skinny shoulders.

'There were a lot of people walking backwards and forwards. It was a hot day; people had their jackets thrown over their arms. It wouldn't have been too difficult for someone to have taken it on their way past.'

'Do you have any idea what time it might have happened?' Cat asked.

Jaclyn cocked her head and gave Cat a searching look.

Shortly, she replied, 'No idea. I only realised it had gone when we went to leave.'

'You didn't get anything out of your bag while you were in the restaurant?'

'No.'

'No lipstick or face powder?'

'No. Well not until Tony asked for the check. I was going to go to the restroom to freshen up. That's when I noticed it was missing.'

'What about your husband? Did he get anything out of it during lunch?'

Jaclyn started to shake her head, but then she frowned and the movement slowed to a stop.

'Actually, I did get something out. Tony's insulin. I passed him his syringe straight after he'd finished eating. He took it to the restroom with him. He gave it back to me afterwards and I put it straight back in the bag.'

'So, the bag was taken after he'd had his meds.' Cat gave a curious smile.

'Look, what's this all about?' Jaclyn asked.

'I'm just trying to narrow down when the bag might have been taken. It's interesting it went missing after your husband had taken his insulin.'

Jaclyn appeared to give Cat's comment some thought. Slowly a scowl screwed up her features. 'I don't think I like what you're insinuating.'

Cat quickly put up her hands hoping to appease but Jaclyn was walking over to the door and didn't appear to notice.

'I'm sorry. I'm not insinuating anything,' Cat said urgently. 'I was just—'

Jaclyn yanked the door open.

'You can go now.'

Cat took one look at the determined set of the other woman's jaw and nodded.

'Thank you for talking to me. You've been a great help.'

With a new-found spring in her step, figuratively if not literally, Cat went to her room and settled on the balcony with her notepad. She'd barely been there five minutes when she thought she could hear knocking. Out on the balcony it was difficult to make anything out over the quiet rumblings of activity and carried conversations from the pool and terrace below. She leaned back in her chair, straining to hear. There it was again, only louder this time. She stood up and limped across the room, throwing the notepad into the dresser drawer on the way through.

'Okay, okay, I'm coming.'

She pulled the door open. Ethan flashed his charismatic smile before glancing down.

'Wow, what happened to you?'

She lifted her bandaged ankle and looked down at it, inspecting the duck-egg sized swelling.

'It looks worse than it is. It's only a sprain. I've had ice on it, thought it might help it recover a bit faster, but it's still sore.' She looked back up at him and gave a weak smile.

'I came to see if you would like to join me for lunch. That is, if you haven't already eaten... though you might not want to, now, what with your injury and all.'

Cat looked over at the clock on her bedside table. It was just approaching one.

'Nothing too fancy,' he went on. 'I thought it might be nice to get out for a couple of hours. What do you think? Feel free to say no.'

'It's really nice of you to ask. I'd love to. Give me a minute to get changed.'

'You're fine as you are.'

Cat looked down at her beach shorts and t-shirt and screwed up her face.

'Okay,' he said. 'How about I meet you in reception, say in ten minutes? But don't go to any trouble. Like I said, nothing fancy.'

'Right,' she said, unsure what his definition of fancy was. From what she'd seen, the American women wore outfits to the pool that Cat would have considered dressy even for an awards ceremony.

As soon as Ethan left, she rummaged desperately through her wardrobe discarding everything until all that was left was a turquoise and white patterned maxi dress. The two side pockets were a little large and gave it a shape that didn't exactly flatter her figure but it was loose and at least the colour suited her. She slipped it on.

If Ethan considered her outfit too fancy he didn't remark.

'Have you booked somewhere?' she asked.

'Uh-hu.'

She waited for him to elaborate. Only he didn't.

They set off along the coastal road, which led to a string of small fishing villages that dotted the western peninsula. Ethan drove quickly, handling the powerful sports car with confidence.

A few minutes into the journey he glanced over to her.

'You seem quiet today. Everything alright?'

Cat stopped staring out of the passenger window and turned to him, smiling.

'Sorry, I was miles away.'

'Thinking about anything in particular?'

'Actually, yes. I've decided I'm going to do things a little differently when I get back home.'

'Like what?'

'Well, for one thing, I'm going to make more of an effort to enjoy life for a change. If Amy's death has taught me anything, it's that you never know how long you've got.'

'That is very true. But why wait until you get home? You could start enjoying yourself now.'

Cat sensed he was about to say something else when his mobile started to ring. He reached into his jacket pocket and pulled out the phone. A small card fell into his lap.

'Hello... Hello...' Ethan looked at the phone and hit the red 'end call' icon. 'No signal.' He discarded the phone into the storage bin in the central console.

'You dropped something,' Cat said, carefully picking up the small promotional card from the side of his seat.

She turned it over at the same time as Ethan looked across. He took it from her fingers and reached over and threw it into the glove box.

'I should throw those things away. They get everywhere.' A smile returned to his face. 'Anyway, we're not going to Kostas today. I thought it would be fun to do something a little different. Hope you like surprises.'

The next few miles were spent in silence. Ethan watched the road and Cat the passing scenery, every so often catching sight of the pristine turquoise sea, with its soft meringue-like peaks that marked the edge of the breaking waves. It mirrored the blue of the sky and the little whipped cream clouds that lined the distant horizon. It was a beautiful sight that should have filled Cat with warm contentment but the memory of Amy cast a dark shadow.

Advertising hoardings started to spring up at the road's edge, promoting restaurants and superstores, all soon to be in reach, if the simple directions and line maps posted at every junction were to be believed. Then came pretty villas, in summery pastels, all sitting in expansive grounds filled with tropical-looking greenery. As they drew closer to the heart of the town, the properties began to increase in number and diminish in size; terrace houses stood shoulder to shoulder with shops, garages, surgeries and schools.

Soon they were navigating a maze of narrow cobbled streets. People strolled casually along the pavements, creating pinch-points that forced others into the road as they stopped to browse window displays and menu boards of chic shops and busy bistros. Ethan slowed the car to a crawl, steering a course around the chilled-out holiday-makers as they wandered carefree and carelessly into their path. Soon they left the shops and eateries behind.

'Nearly there,' Ethan said as they rounded a corner, the sea popping into view like the surprise guest at a party.

He pulled into a small car park at the end of a jetty and turned the engine off.

'Here we are.' He pointed towards a small group of fishing boats. 'What do you think?'

Cat looked at the boats and felt a momentary grip of panic.

'We're going sailing?'

'Uh-hu. You do sail, don't you? I mean, I assumed that in the Maldives...'

'Well yes, but not for years, and I'm not sure I'm exactly dressed for it.' She glanced down at her long dress and bandaged ankle.

When she looked back, Ethan was laughing.

'What?' Cat asked.

'Stop worrying. You won't need to do a thing. Look over there, to the left of those four fishing boats.' Cat followed his pointing finger to a small motor launch. 'That's ours. Well for the next couple of hours it is. We're going to a beautiful little bay nearby. I've packed a picnic. You might want to ditch the sandals but otherwise I think you're good to go.'

As promised, Ethan steered a course for a small sandy cove where he secured the boat, before carrying a shoeless Cat ashore.

The setting was idyllic. The beach—a crescent moon of camel-coloured sand that caressed the soles of Cat's feet like satin-lined slippers—melted away into a kingfisher blue sea, so flat it could have been made of glass. Even the fluffy clouds had deserted their post, giving way to a clear, azure sky.

Ethan spread a white linen tablecloth in place of a picnic rug and set down a substantial wicker hamper. He lifted the lid to reveal what appeared to be a complete wedding list of tableware alongside an array of packets and jars and foil-wrapped parcels.

Having grown up believing picnics to be synonymous with tartan-patterned vacuum flasks, a rug that smelled of dog and

259

warm salmon sandwiches whose edges curled up as soon as the cellophane came off, Cat was impressed.

'This is amazing. I can't believe you've gone to so much trouble.'

'Don't thank me, thank David. Believe it or not it was his idea. Though call me a cynic, I think he might have just wanted me out of Jaclyn's way. We don't seem to be getting on too well at the moment.'

'But all the same, this is one hell of a spread,' Cat said, awestruck by the banquet-like feast that was emerging from the basket.

'Ahh, again, can't take all of the credit. Michael jumped at the chance to help pull this together. Any excuse to spend a morning playing around in a commercial kitchen.'

He passed Cat a plate and cutlery while she grabbed a linen napkin from the basket.

'Can I tempt you with an olive?' he asked, as he wrestled the lid off a jar.

'So how are your plans progressing, have you managed to get anything sorted?' Cat asked, taking a bite of a large kalamata.

'No. I think it's a bit too soon. It seems, well I don't know, disrespectful to be thinking of myself just now.' He helped himself to a squid ring marinated in some sort of dressing from a small plastic pot. 'How about you?'

'Actually, I have made some plans. I'm feeling a lot more confident about things than I was,' Cat said.

'That's excellent news. So, tell me about these plans.'

'I'm going to finish off a project that I've already started. Only this time I'm going to do it properly.'

'Another whale shark project?'

'Not this time. A different type of shark.'

'Sounds dangerous.'

'Oh, I'll be careful, don't worry.'

'Well then, I think a toast is in order. Champagne?' He pulled out a bottle from a cooler bag.

'You really have thought of everything, haven't you?'

'Thank you.' He poured the champagne into a couple of cut crystal flutes. 'Cheers. Here's to whatever the future may bring.'

They touched glasses and after taking a drink of the vintage bubbly, Cat leaned forward and peered into the hamper. She spotted a box of breadsticks. 'Is there a dip to go with these?'

'Sure, there's hummus in that one, there,' Ethan pointed to a small glass jar with its familiar golden grainy contents.

Cat leaned over to reach into the hamper, wincing as she twisted her foot.

'Here,' Ethan said, passing her the jar. 'Ankle still hurting?' he said, a look of concern on his face. 'You could use one of these ice packs if it helps?'

'It's fine,' she lied.

'How did you do it?'

'It was the stupidest thing. I just turned it on the cobblestones when I left the restaurant last night.'

'I knew I should have walked you back to your car. I feel terrible now.'

'Don't. It would have happened whether you'd been with me or not.'

'I bet it wouldn't. Anyway, it sounds like you're in need of a special treat. Here, look what I managed to get hold of.' He passed Cat a small ceramic pot sealed with a tinfoil lid.

Cat took the offering.

'What is it?'

'Take a look.'

She lifted off the lid.

'Mushroom pâté. Is this from Kostas?'

'Sure is. I called by earlier and they were kind enough to let me steal some from today's lunch service. I thought it would be

261

perfect. I know how much you enjoyed it. Here...' He passed Cat a brown paper parcel. 'They also gave me some crostini to go with it.'

Cat propped her glass against the hamper at her knees and reached for her knife. She began to spread a generous helping of pâté on a miniature toast and lifted it to her lips but just then her champagne glass slipped from its spot sending its contents all over the skirt of her dress. She jumped up and began to wring out the fabric, which was dripping with champagne.

'I'm so sorry,' she said as Ethan set about mopping up the spilled drink with his napkin.

'Don't worry about it. It hasn't done any damage and there's plenty more champagne.'

Cat sat back down, fussing with her dress to avoid sitting on the wet patch.

'What happened to your pâté and toast?' Ethan asked, looking around for the abandoned canapé.

'I managed to eat it before champagne-gate happened. It was just as delicious as last night's.'

'Please, have another.' He offered her the paper parcel containing the crostini.

Cat reached in.

'Oh no, they're ruined.'

'All of them?' Ethan peered into the soggy mess.

'It looks like it. And the pâté. It's swimming with champagne. I'm sorry.'

'I'll just tip it out,' he said, tilting it on its side. 'Look, it's fine.'

Cat took the pot from him and set it down nearby.

'I'll try some with a breadstick in a minute,' she said, as she scanned the contents of the hamper, considering her next mouthful. 'Let's see. What other delights are hidden in here?'

She had just popped another olive in her mouth when Ethan's mobile rang again. He checked the caller display.

'Excuse me,' he said, climbing to his feet. 'This had better be important,' Cat heard him say as he walked away.

He glanced over to her and gave a tight humourless smile when he spotted her looking. Cat picked up a breadstick and dipped it into the mushroom pâté. Scooping up a generous helping.

Ethan turned his back to her. She watched him grow rigid. He appeared to say very little and after a few minutes the call ended. He let his hand drop to his side. Eventually he turned around, his expressionless face appearing to mask a world of worry.

'I'm sorry,' he said, walking back over. 'Something's come up. I'm afraid I'm going to have to cut lunch short.'

'Don't worry about it. These things happen.' Cat began to replace lids and re-seal packets as she returned the remains of lunch back into the hamper.

Ethan rushed to assist.

'Here, let me,' he said, taking everything back out and throwing them into a large black refuse sack.

'You're throwing it away?' Cat asked, astonished.

'Sorry, did you want some more? I can put anything you want on a plate. You can eat it while we make our way back. In fact, why don't you just take the breadsticks, the tub of hummus and the pâté? You won't need any silverware then.'

'Honestly, I'm fine,' Cat said.

The return journey passed in silence. Ethan drove hard and fast, stopping only to drop off the bag of rubbish by a parade of shops on the outskirts of the town. He was clearly agitated and seemed disinclined to disguise it. Tight lipped, his restless eyes flitted across the landscape and Cat could visualise his mind racing almost as fast as the speeding car. Though she remained in the dark as to what had caused such a reaction.

He pulled away the second she alighted from the car, leaving her standing at the hotel's entrance. With a plan clear in mind, she returned to her room armed with a full ice bucket and a handful of plastic food bags, gleaned from a young commis chef who had been happy to help the pretty English lady. After putting everything away, she changed out of her lunchtime outfit, and was on her way out of the door when she heard her phone signal the arrival of a text message.

So far no joy. Will keep looking. A

She started to draft a reply but immediately abandoned it. There wasn't time.

The road to Paphos was straight and wide and the traffic relatively light, unlike in the opposite lane, which was jammed full of tired tourists and city workers returning to the rural resorts. She hit a fast-dial key on her phone and held it to her ear. Usually a stickler for the rules, she thought if ever the circumstances justified a misdemeanour it was now. She set the cruise control a few kilometres per hour under the speed limit and kept a watchful eye on the road, scanning for police patrols as she listened first to the ring tone and then the phone network voicemail message. She was on the verge of hanging up when she thought better of it.

'Hi Glafcos. It's Cat. I know you and your colleague think I'm on some sort of personal crusade but I've finally got evidence I'm sure will prove Tony and Amy's deaths were anything but accidental. You might want to think about searching Jaclyn Vostanis' room. You should find a leather bag containing a whole load of food samples. I suggest you get them tested, especially the mushrooms. You might be too late but it's worth a try. I'm on my way into Paphos now, where, if I'm right, I should be able to get even more evidence and put the final pieces of the jigsaw together. I'll call and explain later. Bye.'

264

She tossed her phone onto the passenger seat. It was anybody's guess whether her call would pay off but she prayed Glafcos was a good enough detective to recognise a bona fide tip-off when he got one.

She spent the rest of the journey thinking about her approach. It was going to be difficult to do what she wanted in broad daylight but she couldn't afford to leave it any longer. She thought back to her covert operations training and used it to develop her plan of attack and an accompanying narrative if things didn't go quite as intended.

It should be simple. She only had two objectives. If things went smoothly, she should be in and out in less than an hour. If they didn't, well, then...?

Twenty-eight

In the midst of a throng of sightseers Cat limped along the cobbled lane towards Kostas' restaurant. At the entrance of the alley, which led to the storeroom and the bins beyond she stopped and pulled out her phone. She stepped to one side, out of the crowd, and leaned against the wall, faking a phone call.

She turned and appraised the scene. The kitchen door was closed and there were no cars parked outside the storeroom. So far, so good. Now for the not so easy bit.

She put a finger in one ear, pretending to chat, and wandered towards the kitchen window. She walked until she was close enough to hear the sounds of a busy kitchen in full service. Close up she noticed the kitchen door was actually ajar. An insect screen on the inside reduced her view of the kitchen to a blur.

She put the phone back in her bag and re-joined the footpath, making her way to the front of the restaurant, stopping to make a show of studying the menu posted at the entrance. Already clear on what she was going to say if approached by the maître d' she took her time, checking the restaurant was as busy as she'd hoped it would be. And it was. All of the outside tables were occupied. She should have turned around then and continued with her plan, but instead she remained standing at the entrance, watching a solitary waiter as he tried to appease diners at a half a dozen tables, all demanding his attention. He rushed from table to table, darting the occasional look towards the restaurant. Cat took a step forward and, following his gaze, spotted a knot of black and white attired staff just beyond the door, huddled together like penguins defending themselves from an artic storm. They appeared deep in conversation.

Thinking her timing couldn't be better, Cat retraced her steps. She turned into the alley, took a deep breath and walked up to the storeroom. She prayed it was open. The handle turned easily in her hand and she entered with a brisk business-like demeanour, just in case she needed to convince anyone who might be inside of her entitlement to be there. Then she froze, dumbfounded.

All of the crates had gone.

She advanced into the room and took a look around, taking in the detail of the few items that remained. Brushes and buckets, trolleys and jacks as well as the forklift—keys now in the ignition—were sitting amongst the usual detritus of dirt and dust and scraps of paper that littered the floor. It looked like only the stock had been removed. But all of it? She ventured further into the room and began to scour the floor and surfaces. Not a single despatch slip remained. She took one last look around and left the building, grateful to be exiting through its single door. Unlike the last time.

Outside, she moved quickly to the industrial bins, lifted the lid on the first and peered in.

'You're kidding me!'

She checked the adjacent bin. It was also empty.

She gave a puzzled shake of her head, and started towards the cobbled lane, wondering what it all meant. Had her visit somehow been anticipated and prepared for? She was nearing the end of the alley when she spotted him, standing stock-still in the middle of the path, crowds of pedestrians flowing around him. He was talking animatedly into a mobile phone. Cat was sure he hadn't seen her and, anxious that he didn't, sought refuge in the closest place to hand.

The metal gauze screen creaked and then slammed shut behind her, the humid heat of the kitchen a stark contrast to the warm dry air of the street.

The chef stopped, knife poised. He looked at Cat, a deep crimp appearing above his nose. He laid his cleaver on the table next to a partially butchered rabbit.

'I'm very sorry,' Cat said. 'I didn't mean to interrupt but there was no one out at the front entrance. I was walking past and saw the door and thought maybe...?' Despite starting confidently, her words slowed to a stop. The chef's furrowed brow remained. For the first time, she wondered whether he actually spoke any English. She continued, 'I was here last night. I lost my bracelet. I wondered if anyone had handed it in?' She looked towards the door to the dining room. 'Is there someone I can talk to? A manager, perhaps?'

The chef nodded in the direction of the door.

'I'll just go and look then, shall I?' Cat said, but before she could move, the door swung open and Ethan walked in. His eyes shot wide with surprise.

'Cat! What are you doing here?'

'I lost my bracelet last night. Thought it might have been handed in.'

'In the kitchen?'

'I was trying to find the manager.'

'Oh. Me too.'

Cat heard a harrumph from behind. She turned. The chef was staring at them. Ethan rattled off something in Greek, while crossing the kitchen floor and peering around a corner, into an adjacent room. The chef replied in his native tongue. Cat heard the name Kostas a couple of times. Eventually Ethan turned back to her.

'Come with me. I'll get someone to see about your necklace.'

'Bracelet,' she corrected.

'Yeah, whatever.'

Ethan steered her through the door. He paused and said a few words in Greek over his shoulder to the chef, who muttered something in response. Ethan let out a few more garbled sentences, each one sounding more heated. Cat cast a sidelong look at the chef, who just shrugged and returned to the task of dissecting the rabbit.

Ethan ushered Cat toward the front of the dining room.

In the main restaurant, the huddle of waiters had disbanded and were busy clearing away the lunch service. Ethan put out a hand to stop one of them as he rushed toward the kitchen, his hands full of dirty plates.

'Alexander, this lady thinks she may have lost her bracelet here last night. Do you know whether one was handed in?'

The waiter glanced at Cat, who gave him a hopeful smile.

'I will look,' he said and continued in the direction of the kitchen. A minute later he returned with a stiff cardboard box which he opened and presented for Cat to inspect. She cast her eye over the eclectic collection: a silk scarf, a set of false teeth, a smart looking digital camera and a single diamante stud earring. No bracelet.

'It's not here,' she said, adopting what she hoped was a suitably disappointed expression. She passed the box back to the waiter.

'I don't remember seeing it on you last night,' Ethan said. 'Perhaps you lost it someplace else. Was it valuable?'

The imaginary jewellery had served its purpose. It was time to let it go.

'Only sentimental value. It was just a small chain. The clasp had broken before so I suppose I shouldn't be surprised. I'll have another look in my room when I get back.'

'Well, good luck. I hope you find it.'

Ethan started towards the kitchen.

'Good luck finding the manager,' Cat called after his retreating back.

'You are looking for Mr Constantinopulos?' the waiter said.

Ethan stopped.

'Yes. Do you know where he is?'

'He left, for his house. He was to meet you there.'

Ethan glowered at him.

'What? Nobody told me. Are you sure?'

'Oh.' The waiter seemed genuinely at a loss. 'With all of this upset I do not know.'

'Well, if he's not here then someone else will have to sort out my order. There's a mistake with the address. I don't intend on leaving until I see the order book corrected.'

'But only Mr Constantinopulos...'

Ethan shook his head.

'As Kostas isn't here, someone else will have to do it. I can't wait all day.'

'I will see what I can find out.' The waiter looked down to the lost property box in his hands. For a second Cat thought he was about to hand it to Ethan, but then appeared to have a change of heart. 'I will come back soon.'

Ethan rubbed his hands over his face. He took a deep breath and let his fingers slide from his eyes. He caught Cat staring.

'I think we've established that your bracelet isn't here.'

'Yes. I was just leaving. I thought... do you need a lift?'

'No. I've got my car.'

'Of course. You dropped me off earlier.'

But Ethan had already turned away from her and was watching Alexander the waiter as he consulted another member of staff.

'Well, okay then...' Cat said. 'Maybe I'll see you later?'

Ethan nodded absentmindedly. She was just about to leave when, for a second time, she was stopped in her tracks.

'Miss McKenzie, what a surprise,' Scarface said, with an impenetrable expression.

Cat kicked herself for having forgotten why she'd sneaked in through the back door in the first place.

'Chief Inspector,' she said, drawing a blank at the detective's name and not sure she'd pronounce it properly, even if she could remember it.

The detective fixed his cold black eyes on Ethan

'Mr Garrett. I was hoping to find you here. I'm Detective Chief Inspector Haralambopulous. I believe you can help us with our enquiries.'

'A detective?' A wide, warm smile broke across the American's face, bringing his handsome features to life. 'How can I help?'

'You are aware that the goods in the warehouse, some of which are yours, have been found to contain prohibited items. Yes?' Scarface said.

Ethan's expression hardened around the edges.

'No. I heard there was a problem with the shipping address, which was delaying deliveries, but nothing about prohibited items. What does that mean anyway?'

'Items that are banned both in Europe and the US.'

'I don't know anything about that. All I know is when I checked the stock the other night, I noticed the crates had got the wrong delivery address on. I came to see if Kostas had sorted it out.'

Scarface turned to Cat.

'And let me guess, you're here to keep him company?'

'No. My being here is purely coincidence. I lost my bracelet last night and came to see if anyone had handed it in.'

'But they haven't.' It was a statement not a question.

'No.'

271

'Then please feel free to leave.' He turned his back on her. 'If you would come with me Mr Garrett, we can carry on our conversation at the station.'

'I don't think that will be necessary,' Ethan said. 'I can find us somewhere private to talk here. I'm sure whatever confusion there is can be quickly cleared up.'

Scarface pointed towards the front of the restaurant.

'The car, please, Mr Garrett.'

Cat looked out through the restaurant and spotted a waiting marked car.

'This is ridiculous,' Ethan said. 'I haven't done anything wrong. I've already explained what's happened. If you're saying someone has been using our order as a cover then I'm as much a victim as anyone else.'

A spark of interest ignited in the detective's features.

'Our order? Who is this "our" you refer to?'

'I worked for someone called Mr Vostanis. The order was placed in the name of his business.'

The spark died out and once again the detective's face was a flat mask.

'It was, but it has since been changed into your name. Correct?'

'Yes, but that's irrelevant,' Ethan said. 'The mistake in the delivery address was made long before that. It would have been the case regardless of whether or not I took over the order.'

'Mr Garrett, I am not prepared to debate this now. Please come with me.'

'I'm a US citizen and I'm going nowhere until you tell me what I'm supposed to have done.' He opened his hands, appealing to the detective. 'Look I've already explained. You should be talking to Kostas, not me. I can show you what I ordered, what I was expecting to be delivered, and it certainly wasn't anything dodgy. And the thing about the address, well that was Kostas's

272

error. Why don't I show you the paperwork? It will only take a minute. I'm sure I can find it.'

Without waiting for Scarface to reply Ethan walked briskly into the small room just off the side of the kitchen.

'Mr Garrett, stop! Now!' the Cypriot detective shouted. Cat was taken aback by the menace in his voice, though it didn't appear to have much of an effect on Ethan.

Scarface hurried after him. Cat followed close behind.

Ethan was rifling through a stack of paperwork piled untidily on a table in the corner of the room. 'It's got to be here somewhere. Just give me a minute...'

'Mr Garrett!'

'Wait... here. I've found it.'

Ethan returned to the kitchen carrying a hard-bound order book which he laid on the counter precariously close to the rabbit's remains. He reached into the breast pocket of his jacket and pulled out an envelope from which he retrieved a single sheet of paper.

'This is my copy of the order. It clearly shows the address of Tony's warehouse in Monterey. See, here...' He pointed to the typed purchase order. 'This is where they are supposed to be sending the goods.' He looked down and pointed to a line in the open order book. 'This address here is wrong.'

'You are saying the orders are going to a different address without your agreement?' Scarface said. His voice was flat and unreadable, like his face.

But Ethan was still looking down at the book. He flicked back through page after page of orders.

'I can't believe it. The devious bastard. None of these orders have got the correct delivery address. You say he's been smuggling contraband out with the legitimate shipments? He must drop off the illegal stuff first and then re-route the rest of the order to the correct address.'

'How do they know where to drop off your stuff if there's no record of your address in their paperwork?' Cat said.

Scarface looked over his shoulder at Cat and frowned. Evidently, he'd forgotten she was there.

'What?' Ethan said.

'Well if they were dropping off the illegal stuff at their secret location before taking the legitimate exports on to Tony's warehouse, why does their order book only give the address of their secret location?' Cat said. 'It would need both addresses wouldn't it?'

For the shortest of seconds Ethan looked stumped.

'I don't know. It must be recorded someplace else. The point is my order is completely legitimate.'

'May I?' Cat said, pulling the printed order out from between Ethan's fingers. Open mouthed, he watched as she started to compare it and the open order book.

She looked up at Ethan.

'Is this the same order that Tony was complaining about?' she asked. 'The one that Michael found a discrepancy with?'

More pieces of the puzzle were slowly falling into place.

Ethan pulled a sour face.

'What?'

'On the day that Tony died, he was upset about the prices on one of his orders. Was it this one?'

'I don't know what you're talking about.'

'I think you do. Isabella told me about it. And this morning I heard you tell Jaclyn that the value of the stock on this order has dropped. If Tony's quote also covered the cost of the illegal merchandise, that would bump the order price up quite a bit, I bet.'

Unexpectedly Ethan laughed.

'You don't know what you're talking about. I was just trying to get Jaclyn to sell her stock to me for a lot less than it costs. It was just a ruse.'

'So, if we compare the prices on this printed order to the prices in Kostas's records, or even to other suppliers, they wouldn't be a million miles apart?'

Ethan ran his hands through his hair.

'Look, you're deliberately missing the point. I'm the one who's been duped. Okay, Inspector, I can see the only way we'll get this sorted is if I come to the station with you.' He looked pointedly at Cat. 'She's just complicating matters. She hasn't got a clue what she's talking about. Any negotiations Jaclyn and I have had between us are totally irrelevant.'

'Wait a minute. Please,' Cat said quickly. 'I don't read Greek but look at these two documents.' She laid the hardback book open on the table and set the printed order next to it. She looked at Scarface, who was already studying the figures. 'You'll notice in Kostas's order book there are seven lines,' she went on. 'I assume these relate to seven different items that were ordered and the figures next to them are the quantity and price for each. But if you look, you'll see there are only six lines on this printed version of order, yet the figure at the bottom, which I take is the total order value, is the same on both.'

Scarface ran his eyes down the two lists. He jabbed a finger at the last line in the order book.

'What is this?' he asked Ethan

Ethan leaned forward.

'It says special delivery.'

'I know what it says,' the detective said. 'What does it mean?'

Even Ethan's tanned skin couldn't hide the flush of colour that flooded into his face.

'I guess that's how much the delivery charge is.'

'It's almost half as much as the rest of the whole order.' Scarface fixed Ethan with a stare that could reach in and touch your soul.

Ethan stayed silent.

'It's the cost of the birds, isn't it?' Cat said. 'In Tony's order the cost of the birds has been spread over the cost of all of the other items, which is why everything seemed so expensive when Michael did the comparisons.' She regarded Ethan coldly. 'It was *you* who was importing them to America. You had them delivered to a different address, where you unloaded the pickled birds before forwarding the rest of the order on to Tony's warehouse. He didn't know, did he? I bet if the authorities look back at the accounts, they'll find that Tony's been bankrolling your stock of ambelopoulia for years. It's a good business model. I bet you get a great price selling them on the black market to Cypriots and other Europeans living in the US. It is a common delicacy after all. Only it all started to go wrong when Tony announced his retirement.'

Ethan looked at her as though entertaining a child's fantasy.

'Tony started to get wise to you, didn't he?' Cat continued. 'He realised something wasn't right when Michael compared prices across suppliers. I heard you made out it was Michael who was incompetent but Tony knew both of you better than that. That's why you had to get rid of him, wasn't it?'

Ethan exhaled noisily.

'Detective, this is ridiculous. You can't expect me to just stand here and listen to these unfounded allegations. There isn't a shred of evidence to link me to Tony's death. In fact, as far as I'm aware, there's nothing to even suggest it was foul play.'

'Wrong,' Cat's voice rang out, drawing a perplexed look from both Ethan and Scarface. 'It took me a while to figure it out, because the symptoms aren't what you'd expect.' Cat turned to Ethan. 'I bet even you were surprised.' Her challenge caught him off-guard and for a second his eyes flared wide. 'I thought so,' she said. 'That's why you'd booked to go on the Cairo trip, wasn't it? To distance yourself from all the unpleasant stuff. You thought Tony would be taken ill while you were away.'

She stared at Ethan's stony face. His complexion had taken on a clammy sheen.

'You got hold of his syringe the morning of the day he died,' she said. 'I don't suppose it was difficult. Everyone's in and out of Jaclyn's room all the time. All you had to do was switch his lunchtime dose with a syringe you'd filled with a solution made from amanita. I have to take my hat off to you. It was all very clever. Tony actually administered the lethal injection himself after his lunch the day he died. Once the poisoned syringe was back in Jaclyn's bag, you waited until no one was watching and took the bag, switching the empty syringe back for one that had contained the correct dose of insulin.' Cat looked at Scarface. 'I imagine he ditched the poisoned syringe in one of the bins. Unlike the bag, which he dumped in clear view of anyone looking for it. It was important the bag was found. It removed suspicion from there being anything wrong with the insulin.'

Ethan started to clap, slow and sarcastic.

'Quite a teller of stories, aren't you?'

'But things didn't quite go as planned,' Cat continued and the clapping stopped. 'Tony acting like an old drunk at a wedding must have come as a bit of a shock. That's why you were worried and unable to settle. You should have done your homework. When amanita is injected it reduces the blood glucose levels, which is exactly what insulin does. It was no different to giving him a massive dose of insulin. Tony didn't die of amanita poisoning, he died of hypoglycaemia. That's why he appeared drunk even though he hadn't had much to drink and died quietly, falling asleep in the bar. I imagine once you'd got over the initial shock you couldn't believe your luck. If it had gone the way you intended, Tony would have died days later from organ failure after having been violently ill with suspected food poisoning. Smart choice, given that he was trying all sorts of different foods all the time he was over here.' Turning to Scarface, she said, 'I expect you'll find some dried amanita in amongst the packets of samples in Mrs Vostanis's room. I suspect Mr Garrett planted some, just in case. I dare say it would have just been put down to an unfortunate accident if it was discovered.'

'Amanita?' Scarface said slowly with a frown.

'Death cap mushroom,' Cat said. 'It should be easy enough to find traces of it in Tony's body, now you know what you're looking for. There's also the syringe he dumped out back. If you can find it. The only thing I haven't worked out is where he got the death cap from. It grows in Cyprus and California. I wouldn't be surprised if he brought it with him, as an insurance policy in the event things started to go wrong.'

Scarface turned to Ethan.

'What do you say to these allegations, Mr Garrett?'

'You can't take anything this woman says seriously. It's total fabrication. The guilt over her friend's death is obviously getting to her.'

'Guilt?' Scarface repeated.

'She knows if she'd been in her room when I went to look for Amy, her friend would be alive today.'

'That's bullshit!' Cat hissed. She jabbed a finger at Ethan. 'You killed her. Your hands pushed her under and held her down until she stopped struggling.'

'Why? What possible reason would I have?'

Cat gritted her teeth and tried to control the rage that was growing inside her. Shortly, she turned and addressed her reply to Scarface.

'Amy asked questions because she wanted to impress. She wanted him to think she was pretty and intelligent. She talked a lot about Tony's death. It probably sounded as though she knew something. To make it worse, I had found out a few bits and pieces and had stupidly made notes. I think Amy took my notepad and passed my thoughts off as her own. That notepad is now missing. I suspect Mr Garrett took it the night Amy died. I wouldn't be surprised if it's hidden somewhere in his room.'

'If you're talking about the childish scribbling in a tatty old notepad, you're right.' Ethan looked at Scarface, a confident tilt to his chin. 'Amy showed it to me. She forgot to take it with her, that's why I've got it. Nothing more sinister than that.'

'When?' Cat said sharply. 'When did she leave the notepad in your room?'

She knew it had been on the balcony table when she'd stormed out the evening Amy died.

'Before we went to dinner. I invited Amy to my room for a drink while we waited for the taxi.'

She shook her head, clearing her thoughts.

'The timing doesn't matter. What's important is he saw those notes and something in them made him think Amy might actually discover the truth about Tony's death. They say keep your friends close but your enemies closer, well that's exactly what he did.'

She looked at Ethan.

'Ever since that day when you broke into Jaclyn's room, planting the dried death cap in amongst the different samples in Tony's bag, you barely left Amy's side. I remember how you helped her to put some sun-cream on. You recognised the smell of it from Jaclyn's room. You thought Amy was the one who'd gone in after you, didn't you? Well you were wrong. It was me. I'd used Amy's sunscreen that morning.'

Ethan stared at her blankly.

'I don't understand. What is all this talk of sunscreen?' Scarface said.

Cat waved a hand.

'It doesn't matter. My point is, he thought Amy was getting a little too close for comfort. He knew she was a weak swimmer and after plying her with alcohol, drowning her would have been child's play. He only had to wade in to where it was deep enough to hold her under. I bet he didn't even get his hair wet. It would have been easy enough to run to the bar and pretend he'd just got back from the restaurant, striking up a conversation with Larissa while waiting to be served. Everyone knows how flirty she is. She would have kept him chatting long enough for him to seem to be late meeting Amy, when all along she was already dead. If you've got the towels your forensics guys should easily find a hair or traces of his skin, something to link Mr Garrett with the crime scene.' Cat turned back to Ethan. 'Amy didn't put the clothes and towels on the sun bed. You did. I imagine you put the lounger there too. Nicely out of the way. And the thing with the sandal, that was stupid.'

Scarface looked at her irritably.

'What sandal?'

'One of Amy's sandals had been left near the steps on the way to the pool. I know, because I left it there. If Amy had walked past, she would have recognised it and picked it up. My guess is that's exactly what she did, probably putting it with the rest of her clothes on the sunbed. I reckon Ethan took it up to our room to show he'd gone there looking for Amy.'

'I knocked on the door. If you'd been there you'd have known,' Ethan said.

'I bet you didn't knock. Even if I'd been in the room at the time it would have been easy enough to suggest I was already asleep and didn't hear you or was in the bathroom, or whatever. The important thing was to leave the sandal outside the door, showing you'd been up to the room.' Her eyes roamed over Ethan's composed features. 'That's what got me wondering. That

280

sandal. It seemed an odd thing to draw everyone's attention to, as though it was some sort of prop. It just felt fake. I started to think back over everything that I'd seen and heard, looking for other things that might have been stage-managed.'

Ethan turned to Scarface and flashed an unexpected smile.

'As I said, I'd be happy to continue this at the station.' He darted a look towards Cat. 'Anything to get away from this deluded woman.'

'Hoping to be someplace else when I suddenly fall ill?' she said. 'You don't think I actually ate it, do you? I must have been too distracted with all the champagne flying around. I think I accidentally put it in my pocket rather than in my mouth.' A scornful smile crept over her lips. 'I knew as soon as you asked me for Amy's address you were up to something. You just wanted a sample of my writing to see if they really were Amy's notes. Or whether, in fact, they were mine. Your suspicious little mind had me in its sights. Quite a merry little dance we've had. Well, it's over now. The police can take it from here. A sample of the pâté you brought at lunchtime is in my room, chilling on ice as we speak. That should help seal the case against you.'

Ethan turned to Scarface.

'I don't know what she's talking about. I got the pâté from here. It's not like I made it myself.' He gave Cat a disparaging glance. 'If there is something wrong with the pâté she must have done it. She's clearly deranged.'

Scarface reached out and seized Ethan by the elbow.

'Time to go now, Mr Garrett. Better to drop the charade. We know about your side-line in ambelopoulia. You've built up quite a business over the years and with all the evidence Miss McKenzie speaks of, things look very bad for you indeed.'

Ethan grew rigid.

'It's all rubbish. This is entrapment.'

The door from the dining room swung open and Alexander, the waiter who'd earlier helped Cat look for her imaginary bracelet, interrupted them. He walked over to Scarface and spoke to him in hushed whispers.

'Yes, let him through,' Scarface said.

The waiter hustled out of the room. Moments later a weary-looking Phil entered.

Cat frowned.

Scarface looked at Phil, who shook his head.

'Too late. Already dead by the time we got there,' he said.

Cat's jaw dropped. She didn't know who was dead, but she had a pretty good idea who might have been responsible. She took a step away from Ethan, sending a new pulse of pain shooting through her swollen ankle, and looked over at Phil, wondering who the hell he really was.

'A blow to the head,' Phil added, turning to look at Ethan.

'I don't know why you're looking at me like that,' Ethan said, pushing his fingers through his hair. A faint sheen of sweat had formed on his brow. 'I've been here all the time.'

'That's not true,' Cat said. 'I got here before him and I was at least half an hour at the hotel after he'd dropped me off.'

'We know you were at Mr Constantinopulos's home this afternoon Mr Garrett. There's CCTV at the house,' Phil said.

'And I know it's not working. Kostas was complaining about it only the other day.'

'Well he must have got it fixed because I watched the playback from this afternoon myself, less than half an hour ago,' Phil said.

Ethan opened his mouth but then closed it, his composure crumbling.

'Look, I admit, I went to the house and knocked but there was no one there. I got in the car and came straight here. That's the God's honest truth.'

282

Cat noticed Alexander slip through the door and stand next to the chef, who was standing motionless, staring at Ethan, open-mouthed.

'You'll need to do a little better than that. We know you entered the house. The back door has a camera on it.'

'This is ridiculous,' Ethan said, but his voice had lost its bravado.

Suddenly he paused. He looked Phil up and down, taking in the slim Londoner's attire of t-shirt and jeans. 'Who the hell are you anyway?'

'This is Detective Sergeant Phil Rogers of Interpol,' Scarface said. 'This is the man we have to thank for getting to the bottom of your not-so-innocent trading activities.'

Security...? Cat rolled her eyes.

While she was coming to terms with Phil's real identity, others in the kitchen were reeling from the shock of Kostas's murder. Alexander, the waiter, was slumped against the door frame, overtaken by grief at about the same time that the chef's face began to contort with rage. He clenched his jaw and looked at Ethan through pinched eyes. All of a sudden, he lowered his head and charged at Ethan in a move more fitting for the rugby pitch than the kitchen. Phil and Scarface surged forward and started to wrestle the big man away. Eventually the tangle of men unravelled. Ethan clambered to his feet and clung on to the kitchen table, clearly shaken by the ordeal, while the chef was being forcibly held back, red-faced and sweating. Scarface held on to him as he let rip a torrent of abuse at the American. As soon as he paused for breath Scarface grabbed him by the shoulders and turned the seething chef to face him. Looking him straight in the eye, he muttered a few words, barely audible to the rest of the room and entirely unintelligible to Cat, and the big man began to calm down. She could see the hurt in his eyes and remembered Kostas's comment to Alexander about joining his cousin in the

283

kitchen. Looking now she could see the similarity. The chef was Kostas's son.

Cat took a step towards him, intending to offer some comfort, when she felt a shock of pain as something snagged her hair, tugging her backward. Before she could steady herself, a second, more violent force yanked her head backwards. Confused by the sudden assault, she reached a hand up to her hair and froze as something sharp was pushed into the soft, open flesh of her throat. She remembered the knife on the kitchen table, next to the rabbit carcass.

'No need for any heroics,' Ethan said, his voice loud in her ear. 'Like they say in the movies, nobody move and she won't get hurt.'

Unbalanced on her feet, Cat tried to find a firmer footing. She felt the knife bear down even harder. With no warning, Ethan released her hair from his grip and in one smooth movement swung his left arm around her chest, pulling her into him. All the time the knife remained pressed against her throat.

Unbidden, the first thought to cross Cat's mind was Alex's reaction on hearing how she had been caught again so easily. She took a slow, calming breath in and registered the sharp and pungent scent of fear. But it wasn't her fear she could smell, it was Ethan's, and that worried her even more. Frightened men tend to act first and think later.

'The back door,' Ethan said, his lips so close to her ear she could feel his breath on her skin.

She knew it was only a few steps to the street, no distance at all, but then what?

Without letting up on the pressure at her neck, Ethan managed to manoeuvre Cat to one side and, with him at her side, forced her to side-step around the large table. Her ankle complained with every step.

'That's it,' Ethan said. 'Everyone stay nice and calm.' He didn't sound anywhere near as confident as his words suggested.

Cat let her eyes flick over to the two detectives. They looked tense and ready to pounce. She knew it would be killing them to stand by and watch. Out of the corner of her eye she saw Alexander wide-eyed. Next to him was the chef, hunched forward, his hands clenched into tight fists.

'Anyone does anything stupid and she gets it,' Ethan said. 'I mean it!' Cat gave a sharp intake of breath as the blade dug in even further.

She noticed the chef ease back a little.

After a moment's stand-off, the pressure at her throat lessened, though the grip across her chest grew tighter. Without warning, Ethan shunted her towards the table. Unable to see where she was going, she banged her hip painfully on its edge as her ankle gave way.

'Don't even think about trying to get away,' Ethan warned.

'I wasn't,' Cat said quickly. 'It's my ankle. I jarred it. It really hurts.' She lifted her foot off the floor and put a hand down to steady herself.

'You'll manage.'

Ethan started pulling her backward, toward the door. Cat moved with him, using the table to keep her balance. Her fingers moved across the chopping block, the cool smooth flesh of the rabbit carcass slipped under her fingertips and she had to fight the urge to recoil.

Ethan attempted another step backwards but Cat stalled. He tightened his grip.

'Ow! Not so hard. You're pulling me over,' she cried.

As she'd hoped, the pressure eased, just enough.

She snatched up the rabbit by a long limb and swung it at Ethan's head, giving it everything she possessed. At the same time as she launched the carcass, she drove her elbow into his ribs and lunged in the opposite direction. She was aware of Phil and Scarface charging past and turned just in time to see Ethan disappear under the weight of the two men.

Amidst the tussle someone cried out.

For a split second everyone appeared to freeze. Then suddenly the fighting resumed, the three men disappearing in a confusion of arms and legs. Cat watched, wide-eyed, as an arm began to emerge from amidst the wrestling bodies, a knife clutched in its hand. Before the arm could work itself loose of whatever was restraining it, Alexander rushed at it and stamped violently onto the wrist A sickening cracking sound rang out followed by the clattering of the blade as it fell to the tiled floor. Cat snatched the weapon up, being careful to steer clear of the flailing limbs. But all of the energy had gone out of the fight. Phil extracted himself first, then offered a helping hand to Scarface, enabling the Cypriot detective to hold the American in an immobilising arm lock while reciting his rights.

Twenty-Nine

In the relative quiet that followed, Cat heard Phil heave a sigh. She looked over and noticed his torn t-shirt. There was blood on his chin. He wiped a bloodied lip with the back of his hand.

He looked over at Cat.

'How's your neck?' he asked.

She glanced down and was relieved to see only a trickle of darkening red liquid marring the collar of her t-shirt. Tentatively she touched her throat and carefully probed the skin, focussing on the area that felt tacky to the touch. A little sore, that was all. She found a stack of clean tea-towels folded on a shelf nearby and ran a couple under the cold-water tap. She passed one to Phil and started to wipe away the drying crust of blood on her neck with the other.

Ethan sat slumped in a chair, nursing his broken arm, looking like a broken man. Phil and Scarface exchanged a few hushed words after which Scarface went to leave. At the door he turned and looked at Cat, gesturing to her neck.

'Are you okay? Do you need medical attention?' His voice was gentle, his eyes soft and full of concern.

'I'm fine, thanks.'

He gave a nod and continued out. When Cat turned back, Phil was next to her.

'Are you really alright?' he asked.

'I think so. Does it look okay?' She offered her neck for his appraisal.

'You'll live. You must be very thick skinned is all I can say.'

She was glad he hadn't noticed the shake of her hands, the knowledge that she had twice escaped Ethan's attempts on her life taking its toll. Deserted by his bravado, Ethan had so far avoided her gaze. She noticed fresh blood trickling down his face from an open wound above an eyebrow. She ran a clean tea-towel under the cold tap and approached him. He said nothing as she began to dab at the seeping wound.

'Why did you do it Garrett? Why Kostas?' Phil said from somewhere behind her back. 'Worried he was going to turn you in?'

Cat glanced away from the cut and noticed Ethan's steel blue eyes glint dangerously. She quickly stood up and moved away, back towards the door, to where the chef, who had already been asked to leave once, was standing.

'He not want to pay for the birds,' the chef said, casting angry looks at the American.

Phil looked at the chef.

'My father, he refused to pay back the money to Mr Garrett for the birds that the police take.'

Cat looked at Ethan.

'Money?' She spat the word out. 'You must have made thousands of dollars with your disgusting racket and yet you killed a man for the price of one delivery?'

Ethan looked up at her, a thunderous look on his face.

'We had a deal! Why should I pay for something I wasn't going to get?'

Cat was about to say something else but Phil put his hand out.

'Just leave it,' he said. 'You can't rationalise with people like him.'

'I know but I'm just so bloody angry. To be honest I'm still trying to get my head around everything. Especially you... I didn't see that coming at all. I knew all about the bird trade and the arsonist. I'd sort of figured Ethan wasn't what he seemed, and although I suspected you were up to something, I would never have guessed...' She looked at him and shook her head. 'Interpol?'

'What did you think I was up to?'

'When I saw you skulking around the night Amy died, it was earlier than you said, so I couldn't help but wonder...'

'You thought I killed Amy?'

'I thought it was possible. What do you expect? I saw you slip out of the hotel only to disappear and then reappear next to Amy's lifeless body.'

'But murder? I thought...? Well, we were getting on so well.'

'So you couldn't possibly be the bad guy? If only life was that simple.'

Phil nodded and gave her a warm smile.

'I know. We'd both be out of a job.'

Now it was Cat's turn to look surprised.

'You know?'

'About you being a detective?' Ethan looked up sharply. It was clearly news to him. 'Yes. Andreas told me,' Phil said. 'Not that he was happy about it. He said you wouldn't be able to keep from meddling in the investigation. I guess it's a good thing he was right.'

'Andreas? He's involved as well?'

'Of course. Why else do you think he was here?'

Cat drew her brows together.

'You've lost me. Who are you talking about?'

'Detective Chief Inspector Haralambopulous—Andreas.'

Ahh, Scarface.

'I didn't know his first name was Andreas,' Cat said. 'Anyway, he should have been more open about what he was doing. As far as I could see he didn't even think he had one suspicious death on his hands, let alone two.'

'There was no evidence.'

Cat was sick of hearing that same worn phrase.

'Well I managed to find some,' she said.

He turned his back on Ethan and lowered his voice, 'Not legitimately though, did you?' His eyes caught hers and she couldn't help but wonder just how much he knew. 'We had no choice but to do everything by the book. There was a lot at stake. It's taken three years to figure out how the supplies are getting into US. With the internet, the demand for such specialities just keeps increasing. It's been a real uphill battle. For one thing, the exports only take place twice a year in spring and autumn, following the annual migration of birds. We only got wind of Vostanis's business last summer and the final evidence against our friend Mr Garrett came through literally days ago. We know now the smuggled goods first go to a warehouse rented in his name. He then uses a US delivery firm to transport the legitimate goods on their second leg to Tony's warehouse. The deaths of Tony and Amy threw the whole investigation into a spin. We thought they were related but—'

'No evidence.' She could see the dilemma. She looked at him and cocked her head. 'So, what were you doing the night that Amy was killed?'

'I was following Brian. Until you showed up. I couldn't afford for you to see me, so I turned back. That's when I came across Amy.'

'You thought Brian had something to do with the exports?'

'No. With the arson attacks. We were hoping to get something to lever a deal with him. We thought he might be able to help us find out who's supplying the birds.'

'Oh.'

'I'd followed him a few times and watched him freeing the poor bloody things in the dead of night. It just so happens that every time I managed to do it, there were never any arson attacks on those nights.'

'Apart from the night Amy died,' Cat said.

'Unfortunately, I can't account for what Brian did that night. I was otherwise engaged.'

'Mmm.'

Cat remembered Brian sitting, watching at the side of the beach while everyone was ushered back into the hotel. It was hard to envisage him trotting off to carry out a pre-meditated fire-strike after that.

'Could it be a rival business—a competitor?' she suggested. 'The arson attacks are hitting the suppliers, making a scarce commodity even scarcer, so the remaining suppliers can get away with hiking the prices up. It could even have been Kostas. I overheard him talking to Ethan about supply and demand.'

'It's possible. To be honest if we could stamp the whole bloody thing out, we wouldn't have to worry who the arsonist is, they could go and be a vigilante somewhere else.'

'That's why I don't think it's Brian.' Cat thought back to that eventful night when she held those tiny trembling hearts in her hands before setting them free. 'He wasn't being a vigilante. He was just trying to do what little he could.'

Phil gave a wry smile.

'Well, I hope we manage to put a stop to it soon, it would be nice to go somewhere else for a change. This is my third year here.'

'I thought you seemed much more at home than I would have expected for a first visit.' Cat's stomach fluttered uncomfortably as a range of possibilities occurred to her. 'What other elaborations did you add? I take it Bethany really is your daughter?'

'Of course. My budget doesn't extend as far as hiring children. Besides, I'm surprised you have to ask, she obviously gets her good looks from me.'

'I don't know. She is very pretty. Maybe she takes more after her mother. I take it you and her mother...?'

'Are still divorced, yes. We still have a cat called Oscar and I still live in London.'

'And will you be seeing home any time soon?'

'Soon enough. I'll get to swap the brilliant Cypriot sunshine for the drizzly grey London skyline. Can't wait.'

Cat thought of what waited for her when she returned home. An empty house and an unseasonably cold, wet and windy May, if recent weeks were anything to go by.

'Maybe I could give you a call when I get back?' Phil said.

'I'd like that. You can fill me in on how this all ends up.'

'Well, we can talk about that if you want but I was thinking more of getting to know each other, over a drink or dinner. Now there are no more secrets.

Cat felt her stomach do a little flip. This time it was a good feeling.

'I think we all deserve a celebratory drink after today,' a familiar voice said from the doorway. Scarface walked over and looked down at the bruised and battered American. 'Time to go, Mr Garrett.'

A pair of uniformed officers filed into the small room and hoisted Ethan to his feet.

Scarface turned to Cat.

'Well, Miss McKenzie, I would like to thank you for your help here. It is time for you to go. I have asked Detective Theophanus to meet you at your hotel to collect the contaminated mushroom sample from you. He is waiting for you there.'

Cat was pleased. She had been worried she wouldn't get the chance to see Glafcos before she had to leave.

'No problem. I can also give him directions to a bin where there's a tied bag of rubbish that contains a pot of mushroom pâté, dosed I imagine with a lethal quantity of amanita. It will be a match for the sample I took and should have Mr Garrett's prints all over it.'

Scarface broke into a smile.

'Well, well, it seems that Mr Garrett's luck has finally run out.'

Thirty

Cat climbed out of the hire car. She paused to watch the antics of a small group of sparrows as they fought over a hunk of bread, chattering and chirping animatedly. A hooded crow hopped towards them and the sparrows scattered. It snatched the bread up in its large beak. A couple of beats of its wings and it was gone and the sparrows were back, scrabbling around in the dirt searching for any stray crumbs.

Cat limped towards the hotel. As she approached the reception desk, she spied Tom through the large glass doors. He was waving energetically, gesturing for her to join him. She looked around the empty lobby before making her way out to the terrace.

'Where've you been? You missed all the excitement,' he said as he ushered her to a quiet corner, out of earshot of the few guests that were enjoying a late afternoon tea. 'The police have been. They searched the Americans' rooms. They started with Tony's room. I saw them leave with a box. No idea what was in it though. And then the manager let them into Ethan's room. They brought another box out of there.'

'When did all of this happen?' Cat asked.

'About two.'

Cat was still at lunch with Ethan at two.

Tom regarded her closely.

'You know something.' His eyes lit up. 'You do, don't you?'

'No, I was just... well, it's just like you said, I'm gutted I missed all the excitement. Are the police still here?'

'I don't think so. They were in and out of the rooms faster than a—' Tom stopped himself. 'Well, they were very quick. Come and join me and Rose. We'll give you all the sordid details.'

'Where is Rose?'

'She's down by the kiddies' paddling pool looking after Bethany. Phil said something about needing to nip into Paphos to get something from the pharmacy. Though I don't know why he couldn't just go to the chemist in the village. He'll wish he had now. He would have been back in time to see all the goings on.'

Cat spotted movement from the corner of her eye and looked over. It was Glafcos. He was leaning out of the glass doors. On seeing her look, he gave a wave. She waved back.

'Sorry Tom, I've got to go. Someone wants to talk to me about Amy. I'll come and find you when we're done.'

She left Tom and returned to the lobby. Glafcos embraced her like an old friend.

'Andreas told me what happened: another knife attack! You are okay, yes?' he asked, looking her over.

'Don't worry. I'm fine.'

'And the lunch... the poisoned food. You are sure you didn't eat any?'

'I'm positive. I was expecting him to try something. One of the theories I had was that he'd killed Tony with death cap mushroom, so when he pulled out the mushroom pâté I just knew. He couldn't exactly use an injected solution like he did with Tony. To be on the safe side, I made sure I only ate things that came out of sealed jars or packets. When he offered me the pâté, I made out I was going to eat it and then "accidentally" knocked my glass of champagne over.' She mimed the speech marks with her fingers. 'While Ethan was clearing up the spill, I stuck the pâté in a tissue in my pocket. I even pretended to eat some a second time when he was busy taking a phone call. I figured that would be enough to make him happy. I think you only need to eat a small amount for it to be fatal. Ethan was due to fly back to the States on Tuesday, just when I'd be in bed with a bad case of food poisoning. By the time I dropped dead of organ failure he'd be home, safe and sound.'

'But what made you suspect him?'

'Funnily enough, he was one of the few people who didn't seem to have a motive or any axe to grind. Or at least it looked that way at the beginning. He worked bloody hard to give anyone who'd listen, including me and Amy, a whole host of reasons as to why the others might have wanted Tony out of the way, while all the time he was playing the poor-me card for himself. He seemed to be able to switch his personality—and the facts—depending on who he was talking to. When he talked to me and Amy, he made out he couldn't afford to take over Tony's business. But then later I heard him throwing his weight around with Jaclyn, plus he was still hanging around at Kostas's even though he'd already supposedly said his goodbyes. I overheard a conversation between Ethan and Kostas and, although I didn't understand it at the time, when I later found out that Kostas was hiding jars of the birds in crates headed for California it all started to come together. It dawned on me that Ethan was playing a very clever game. All his talk of not being able to afford to take over the business following Tony's death... it was just an act. He must be rolling in it. Who knows how many years he's been hiding the cost of the ambelopoulia in Tony's order and taking all of the sales income. And yet there seems no end to his greed. After Tony died and Jaclyn made it clear she didn't intend to carry on with the business, Ethan's scam would have had to come to an end. But he didn't give up that easily. He actually persuaded Kostas to tell Jaclyn she'd have to honour Tony's last order at the original price, which would have included the dead birds. Ethan then made Jaclyn an offer at a fraction of the price the order was worth, making out he was doing her a favour taking it off her hands.

Kostas would have got what he was owed and Ethan would have had a complete shipment to sell with Jaclyn paying for the lion's share of it.'

Glafcos looked confused.

'But how did you know it was Mr Garrett who murdered Mr Vostanis and your friend?'

'Just little things I suppose. Once I realised he wasn't the honest broker he was making out I started to notice other things that didn't quite make sense. The turning point was when I saw an advertising card for Kostas' fall out of his pocket. I knew then he was the murderer.'

Glafcos gave her a puzzled look.

'Huh?'

'On the night Amy died, she and Ethan dined at Kostas. The photographer did the rounds and, like he did every night, he gave all the customers a small card that advertised the restaurant. He wrote a number on the back so they could order copies of the photographs if they wanted to. I found the card that Amy had been given under her bed the day after she died. I didn't know what the handwritten number on the back meant so I underlined it twice in blue ink. I showed it to Ethan, which meant he knew I had it. Unfortunately, I dropped the card when I was some place I had no reason to be. He must have found it and realised I was closing in on him. When I saw it in his car on the way to the picnic, I knew he was on to me.'

'That's it? That was enough to make you think he was going to try to murder you?'

'Yes. Based on where I was when I lost it, I knew.'

'But where...?'

Cat gave a subtle shake of her head. She reasoned that, with the amount of evidence the police had on Ethan, no one would ever need to know of the lengths she'd gone to.

Glafcos waved a hand.

'Never mind. Come, let's go and get this sample.'

They started to make their way to her room but Glafcos hadn't quite finished with his questions.

'How did you figure out what killed Mr Vostanis?'

'The theft of Jaclyn's bag just didn't make sense. Who steals a bag worth over a thousand dollars, with a couple of syringes in it, cash, and God knows what else, and only takes the cash. Any opportunist thief would take one look at Jaclyn, see the bling dripping off her and immediately spot the potential. The only way it made sense was if it had been set up so it could be found after a fairly basic search. I asked myself why anyone would want a bag to appear stolen and then let it be found? Because it presented a perfect opportunity for someone to switch Tony's syringe over.'

'But we tested the syringes. They contained what they should have,' Glafcos said.

'You tested them after the switch.'

'But how did you know what had killed him?'

'I prayed to the God of Google.'

'The what?'

'The internet. I did a little bit of digging and found research that showed that an injected solution of death cap causes hypoglycaemia without any gastric inflammation. I also found that death cap mushrooms are relatively easy to distil into a stable solution. Everything just slotted into place.'

'And you just happened upon this research on the effects of death cap mushroom?' Glafcos asked, his cynicism clear, in spite of his thick accent.

Cat remembered how it had come to her, a slow piecing together of facts that just didn't fit. Aside from the theft of the bag, there were the samples in Tony's room. They were all so precisely annotated, apart from a packet marked up as mixed mushrooms. It had niggled her, playing on her subconscious. It

298

didn't fit with the way the others were labelled, plus there was no reference to them in Tony's order book. She was sure now that the intruder she had disturbed had been Ethan, planting a bag of dried mushrooms including death caps as an insurance policy, just in case the post-mortem showed signs of the toxin. All along it had been intended to look like nothing more than an unfortunate accident.

'To be honest, at first I thought he might have eaten some sort of mushroom that could have caused a hypoglycaemic attack. It didn't take very long to find the link between the death cap and hypoglycaemia. Here we are...'

She slipped the key into the card reader and pushed the door wide.

'And your friend, Miss Reynolds?'

She looked around the tidy room. It was as though Amy had never existed.

'Sadly, he took Amy at face value. She'd been bragging about being some ace forensic scientist, trying to impress him. Only she got him worried and he started to believe she was on to something.' She felt her chest tighten. 'I think I made matters worse.' The words caught in her throat.

'How so?'

'I might have mentioned to Amy some of the stuff you told me. I think she told Ethan.'

'But Cat, none of that would have made any difference.'

'We'll never know.'

'And you knew all of this and yet still you went with him?'

'I knew what had happened but I had no proof. Who would listen to me? Certainly not your mate Detective Humper-whatever,' she said, Scarface's disdainful expression that day in the station clearly etched in her memory.

She crossed the small room to the bathroom and returned with an ice bucket.

'Anyway, here it is.' She pulled a plastic food bag out of the bucket. 'The elusive evidence. I don't know whether it needed to be preserved on ice but I thought it wouldn't hurt, given the heat.'

Cat handed it over to Glafcos who checked the seal on the bag before slipping it in his jacket pocket.

'You know we found traces of dried mushroom in Mr Garrett's room? I expect they will test positive for death cap given what you've just told me.'

'Was that when you searched it earlier today?'

'Yes. He must have had to rush to prepare the pâté. He probably didn't have time to dispose of it.'

'Unless he was keeping his options open,' Cat said, shivering at the chilling suggestion.

'Here, before I forget.' Glafcos reached into his inside jacket pocket. 'Your notepad. It was in Mr Garrett's room.'

'Thanks.' Cat flicked through it, her eyes settling on the last of her entries.

'Hey Glafcos, these arson attacks...'

'Yes?'

'How long did you say they've been happening?'

'Four years. Why? You know something about those too?'

'No. I just wondered. Well hopefully you're one step closer to getting it all sorted.'

'I hope so. The island is too beautiful for such ugliness to be allowed to continue.'

'And it's certainly too beautiful to spend my last day cooped up inside. So if you don't need me for anything else right now I'm going to go for a last stroll on the beach.'

'Of course. But remember, keep in touch. The next time you need a holiday, a proper holiday, give me a call.' He walked to the door. 'And Cat?'

'Yes?

'Take care of yourself. I don't think my nerves can take news of another attempt on your life.'

Thirty-one

The sand was just as golden and the sea as turquoise as the first time she'd walked along the beach watching the bee-eaters swoop overhead. Dry eyed, but with a heavy heart, Cat retraced her steps, thinking of Amy, who had seen so little of the island, let alone of life. She cast her mind back to the events in her own life that had caused her to seek solace in the sunshine. Before, they had seemed so significant, so defining. Now with everything that had happened they seemed so small.

She stopped and looked out to sea. Mesmerised, she watched the waves roll as though on a continuum and thought of all of the grains of sand that were caught up in the rushing waters. Who knew where they would land?

The water lapped at her feet. The cold froth caught her by surprise and she shuffled back onto the dry sand. A smooth pebble, wet and shining, caught her eye. She picked it up and gave a sharp flick of the wrist, intending to send the stone skipping across the surface. It sank on the spot.

She glanced at her watch. Five minutes had turned into forty. Time to turn back.

In the distance Sura, the birdwatcher's wife, was walking her way.

'Enjoying a last afternoon stroll?' Cat said, after managing to make eye contact.

'Yes, it is very peaceful. This is your last day too?'

'Yes.'

'It has not been good for you... your friend. I am very sorry,' Sura said quietly.

'No, not good at all, but thank you. Everybody has been very kind. I don't suppose you've heard; they've arrested the young American guy for the murders of Amy and Tony Vostanis.'

The woman's eyes shot wide. 'Young Mr Vostanis?'

'No, not Michael. Ethan, Tony's assistant.'

'Ah, Mr Garrett. But why?'

'I'm not sure. Something to do with pickled birds.'

'Birds?'

Cat was surprised to see the other woman's face was a mask of ignorance.

'Yes, pickled birds.'

Still no hint of recognition.

Cat decided to push a little.

'I thought perhaps your husband might have mentioned it. I helped him the other night.'

'Ahh, that was you?'

'Yes.'

Sura's expression softened a little.

'He was very grateful. There were many, yes?'

'Yes, too many. It was terrible but we managed to free them all.'

'This time.'

Cat nodded.

'I agree, someone needs to put an end to it permanently. I think the police need all the help they can get to force the businesses to stop.'

'Pah! The police do nothing. But the businesses they pay. They all will pay eventually.' She spoke with a passion that resonated with Cat.

'You mean the fires that have been happening?'

Sura tilted her head, itself a birdlike gesture, before letting her gaze drift to the empty horizon.

The silence mounted.

303

'You know they'll make no difference to the bird trade... the arson attacks, I mean.' Cat said. Sura shot her a look of irritation. 'It's true. The fires might make a point but they're nothing more than a temporary inconvenience to the traders. Look at the restaurant that re-opened this week. It was barely closed twelve months. The insurance would have covered the cost of the repairs. From what I heard, the restaurant is more popular than ever. I wouldn't be surprised if pickled birds feature on some secret menu of theirs. What's worse is that the arsonist is taking police resources away from dealing with the illegal trade.'

'I must go,' Sura said, turning sharply.

'Wait. Please...' Cat reached out a hand and laid it gently on Sura's arm. Sura turned back to face her. 'If the attacks don't stop the police *will* find out who the arsonist is.' Sura shot her a piercing look and in reply Cat started to nod. 'Take my word for it. Then the traders will have nothing standing in their way. But if Brian gave the police the information he has on where the nets are sited and worked with them, then the people responsible could be dealt with. If the arson attacks stopped now and Brian worked with them, I promise, the police would never need find out who the arsonist is. You might even get to relax on your holidays.'

Sura looked down, a thoughtful look on her face. She appeared at least to be giving Cat's suggestion some consideration.

'That is very useful advice. I will consider,' she said eventually, before giving a short nod and walking away.

This time Cat made no attempt to stop her, instead she resumed her own walk, back to the hotel.

Down the beach, a man and a little girl were walking hand in hand. A smile blossomed on Cat's face and for a moment the bittersweet reality of the end of her holiday slipped away as the promise of one more night beckoned.

Before you go...

I hope you enjoyed reading Feather and Claw.

As so many readers rely on reviews to help them decide whether to try a new author, it would mean a great deal to me if you could leave a review on Amazon or Goodreads.

If you'd like to know more about me and my work, check out my website www.susanhandley.co.uk, where you can join my exclusive readers' club. By joining, you will be kept in touch with news on up-and-coming publications. It will also enable you to access FREE exclusive offers. To join costs nothing. Simply provide details of your e-mail address (no spam, I promise). That's all there is to it.

Don't forget, you can also follow me on:
Twitter @shandleyauthor or Facebook @SusanHandleyAuthor

Acknowledgements

I would like to thank my good friend, Tony Gooding for his uncomplaining willingness to read and re-read early drafts of Feather and Claw. It's thanks to his early feedback that the book didn't turn out as some sort of romantic travelogue; also, his words of encouragement certainly helped as I embarked upon yet another revision.

Likewise, I'm grateful to my husband, John, who was made to suffer more than a couple of late nights, passing a critical eye over the work in progress. As he has two eyes, both equally critical, it's no wonder he found so many mistakes. Yet I can't thank him enough, as the final outcome is all the better for it.

Julie Platt once again ran her red pen over the draft. Julie deserves specific praise for her patience as well as her editing skills. Thankfully she stuck with me through the summer months while I prevaricated, before finally handing over my baby and letting her cast her magic over it.

My thanks must also go to Erika Lock and Kath Middleton for their comments on the final draft, and for spotting the most tenacious of grammar gremlins. Kath deserves a second mention, as it's thanks to her that Cat shows a softer side, as Kath was the one who once reminded me, detectives have feelings too!

Finally, I'd like to thank members of the Facebook group Crime Fiction Addict and followers of my Facebook page who took the time and trouble to give me their feedback and advice on the cover art.

Printed in Great Britain
by Amazon